'I'm sorry, Beth.' Aiden pressed his lips together in a sorrowful sort of way. His expression said 'I'm really sorry' but his eyes said 'I need to escape'. 'You're a lovely girl and you deserve someone much better than me. And you'll find him. I know you will.'

'But I don't want anyone else,' I said in a voice so high-pitched, only dolphins could hear it, all my playing it cool and grown-up pretence immediately deserting me. 'I just want you.'

'I'm sorry,' he said again, glancing away hurriedly as hot tears filled my eyes. 'I really am. It's probably best if I just go.'

I gripped the door frame as my boyfriend turned and swayed down the path towards the street.

Turn back, I begged silently. *If I ever meant anything to you, turn back and look at me. Tell me you just made a huge mistake.*

Aiden kept on walking.

'Wait!' I screamed as he crossed the road. 'Don't leave! There's something I need to tell you.'

I was out of the front door and sprinting down the pathway, my stockinged feet splashing through puddles, before I had time to think.

'Aiden, wait!' I shouted as I ran into the road. 'Aiden, I love—'

There was a squeal of brakes, and then *oomph*, I landed face first on cold, wet concrete.

Cally Taylor lives in Bristol with her boyfriend and their ridiculously large DVD/book/music collection. She shares her 'study' with the washing machine and ironing board and writes her novels in any spare moments she can squeeze in between the day job and her social network addiction. She started writing fiction in 2005 and her short stories have won several awards and been published by a variety of women's magazines. Her debut novel *Heaven Can Wait* has been translated in 13 languages and was voted 'Debut Novel of the Year' by chicklitreviews.com and chicklitclub. com. *Home for Christmas* is her second novel.

By *Cally Taylor*

Heaven Can Wait
Home for Christmas

Home for Christmas

Cally Taylor

An Orion paperback

First published in Great Britain in 2011
Orion Books Ltd,
Orion House, 5 Upper Saint Martin's Lane,
London, WC2H 9EA

An Hachette UK company

1 3 5 7 9 10 8 6 4 2

A CIP catalogue record for this book
is available from the British Library.

ISBN 978-1-4091-2158-9

Typeset by Deltatype Ltd, Birkenhead, Merseyside

Printed and bound by
CPI Group (UK) Ltd, Croydon, CRO 4YY

The Orion Publishing Group's policy is to use papers
that are natural, renewable and recyclable products and
made from wood grown in sustainable forests. The logging
and manufacturing processes are expected to conform to
the environmental regulations of the country of origin.

www.orionbooks.co.uk

For my brother and sister,
David and Rebecca Taylor.

Chapter One

Beth

I was trying to arrange November's film listing brochures into neat piles on the counter but I could feel him, the most beautiful man in the world, staring at me across the deserted cinema. His steady gaze met mine and I looked away hurriedly, my cheeks burning with embarrassment. He knew what I was thinking about doing. I just knew it.

Do it, Beth, the right side of my brain urged as I sat down at my desk and switched on the computer. *Go over and talk to him. Say what you need to say. It'll help.*

No way! said the left side of my brain. *That's ridiculous. What if someone walks in and sees you?*

No one's going to come in. It's half past ten in the morning and the first film isn't on until eleven. Go and talk to him!

The right side of my brain made a noise that sounded a lot like *SADDO!* but I ignored it, stood up and crossed the foyer until I was a foot away from the tall, dark, gorgeous man standing near the glass front door. The warm smile on his face made my stomach flip over.

'I've got something I need to say,' I said, avoiding his intense gaze and looking at the carpet instead. Once upon a time it was a deep crimson with a thick pile. Now it was worn and tired, like everything else in the Picturebox cinema where I worked.

'The thing is,' I continued nervously, 'I've loved you from the very first moment I set eyes on you.'

I paused. Handsome man said nothing.

Urgh! No wonder. *I've loved you from the very first moment I set eyes on you* – if declarations of love won awards, I'd be handed an Oscar made of Stilton.

'Sorry,' I said, still staring at the carpet. 'That was too cheesy. What I wanted to say … what I've been trying to say for months … is that … I think I've fallen in love with you.'

Handsome man remained silent and my stomach lurched violently.

'Was it really that bad?' I gazed up into the warmest brown eyes I'd ever seen and brushed a cobweb off his cheek (I'd gone slightly overboard with the Halloween decorations). 'If you were Aiden, would you run for the hills? If you could actually run, obviously.'

The George Clooney cut-out in front of me didn't answer.

'Oh God.' I shook my head and walked back to the counter. 'I'm seriously losing it. What kind of idiot woman practises saying I love you to a cardboard man?'

I slumped into my chair and stared despondently at the computer. After ten months together, Aiden still hadn't told me he loved me. I hadn't said it either, but considering Josh's reaction the evening I'd told *him*

I loved him, you couldn't really blame me for being scared.

I looked back at George Clooney. He was still staring at me from across the foyer. His eyes seemed to twinkle with amusement.

'Yeah, yeah, you can grin. You've probably had millions of people tell you they love you, while I've ...'

I rested my head on my hands and sighed. I couldn't even say it out loud. Twenty-four years old and no one had ever told me they loved me. I'd been told other things, things like 'I'm very fond of you', 'I care about you' and 'You mean a lot to me', but no one, not one single man, had ever said those three little words. People all over the world were falling in love with each other and sharing their feelings. What was so wrong with me? Why did 'Would you like to go out for a drink?' inevitably lead to 'It's not you, it's me'? Was I really that unlovable? It was almost worse than being a twenty-four-year-old virgin (which I wasn't, thank God).

I'd lost my virginity to Liam Wilkinson, school heart-throb, on a pile of coats at his seventeenth birthday party. I'd floated around on a cloud of 'wow, I can't believe that really happened' for the rest of the weekend, then returned to earth with a bump when we went back to school on Monday.

'Hi, Liam,' I'd said breathlessly, after I'd plucked up the courage to talk to him in the corridor. 'Just wanted you to know that I had, like, the most amazing time ever at your birthday.'

'Cool.' He'd touched the top of his spiked-

3

within-an-inch-of-its-life hair, his gaze drifting over my head to the group of girls giggling at the other end of the corridor. 'Glad you enjoyed it, Beth. I was so pissed I can't remember anything.'

Two weeks later, he'd declared his love for Jessica Merriot by graffiti-ing her name on the wall of the science block. He was suspended for two weeks but claimed it was worth it.

Every man I'd ever dated had been in love before. I knew because I'd seen the way their eyes went glassy at the mention of their first love or their ex-girlfriend. They'd never fallen in love with me, though. Not one of them. And I had no idea why. I wasn't a psycho. I wasn't high maintenance. I wasn't stupid or cruel or selfish. I was just me, Beth Prince, the 'you're lovely and funny and sweet but I'm still going to dump you' girl. What was I doing wrong? Was I missing the lovable gene?

'What should I do, George?' I said aloud. 'Should I tell him?'

I needed to tell Aiden how I was feeling; not about the fact that no one had never loved me – I didn't want him to realise I was a complete loser – but that I loved him. Okay, so Josh, my ex, had visibly blanched after I'd said 'I love you', but that didn't mean Aiden would. Maybe he was scared. Maybe *his* ex, Magenta, had hurt him so much he couldn't say it any more. Maybe he was waiting for me to say it first. Maybe, maybe, maybe ...

Aiden Dowles was different from the boyfriends I'd had before. He was scarily posh, but also charming, grown up, well travelled and impossibly intelligent. He could talk for hours, and I'd sit and watch him, my mouth wide open, as he told me about the time he'd worked in an orphanage in Nepal, or bungee-jumped in New Zealand. I'd never met anyone like him before. He was like an action-hero version of Ralph Fiennes.

Over the last month, the urge to tell him how I felt had become unbearable. Every time I saw him, it rose up from my chest and sat in my throat, just waiting to come out of my mouth ('A bit like sick after a night out drinking,' as my flatmate Lizzie had charmingly put it). I couldn't put it off any longer. I *had* to do it.

I'd planned the perfect scenario and everything. Aiden had invited me to a friend's Halloween party and I'd spent ages searching the internet for the perfect costume. All of his friends were uber-posh, uber-skinny types who could make a binbag look expensive and stylish, and I knew they'd probably dress up for the party as sexy Morticia Addams clones in tight black dresses, or dead size-zero brides with the blood artfully applied so it didn't spoil their make-up. There was no way I could compete with that kind of perfection – not least because I'd struggle to fit one thigh into a size-zero wedding dress – so I'd decided to go for a comedy angle instead. I'd ordered a massive orange pumpkin costume from eBay. It came with a matching hat – complete with stalk, and elastic for tucking under your chin to keep it on. As soon as I tried it on I burst out laughing. I looked ridiculous – like a big orange blob with a teeny tiny pinhead and wobbly white thighs. Lizzie had popped her head round my bedroom door to find out what was so funny, and had laughed so hard she wet herself. It was her idea, once she'd returned from a speedy trip to the bathroom, to wear the costume with hold-up stocking and high heels.

'You have to!' she'd insisted, looking me up and down with a grin on her face. 'The costume's brilliant but you need a little bit of sauciness too, Beth. And some kind of sexy black corset or body underneath. Imagine Aiden's face at bedtime when you whip off your pumpkin to reveal your inner vixen. His eyes will pop out of his head!'

I wasn't sure I had an inner vixen, but I loved Lizzie's idea of surprising my boyfriend with a bedtime transformation. Maybe he'd leap off the bed, sweep me off my feet and ravish me. Afterwards, when I was lying in his arms, I'd look up at him, meet his tender gaze and …

'I love you so much,' I said, sitting up straight in my chair and squeezing my face into a smile so the words came out brightly. No, that sounded too twee – like something a five-year-old American girl would say to her granny. Rubbish. I stared at my screen, determined to get some deep meaning into the phrase.

'I loooove you,' I said with gusto.

Great! If I wanted to sound like an Italian gigolo.

I picked up the film script of *When Harry Met Sally* that was lying open, as always, on the edge of my desk. (It's my favourite film, ever. Nora Ephron is a genius.) How did they say it to each other? How did they make it sound so bloody perfect and romantic? I flicked through the pages, my eyes flying over the words I knew so well, then slapped the script closed.

I couldn't copy a film. I had to find my own way of saying how I felt.

'I LOVE you,' I said with feeling. Then, louder, and with more passion, 'I love you, I love you, I love you.'

'Thanks,' said a deep voice from across the cinema. 'You're not so bad yourself.'

I stared at George Clooney in shock. His lips weren't moving. The man standing beside him, however, was grinning at me in amusement.

'Fuck!'

My first thought, as I slid down in my chair and crouched under my desk, was *Quick, hide!* My second, as the bin pressed into my hip and the side of my face squished up against the filing cabinet, was *What the hell did you do that for?*

'Hello? You okay?'

Oh God, his voice was getting louder. He was coming over to the desk. No! Why couldn't he act like a normal person, recognise that I was suffering an acute attack of cringeitis and just leave me to die quietly?

'It's okay to love me,' the amused voice continued. 'My colleague's daughter is convinced she's going to marry me when she grows up. She is only two, though … Hello?' The voice was even closer, like he was leaning over the counter. 'Are you okay down there? Should I call 999?'

Yeah, great. Call the police and add to my embarrassment, why don't you?

'I'm fine, really,' I mumbled as I crawled backwards from under the desk, my hair covering my face. 'I just dropped my … er … paper clip.'

'Paper clip. Okay. Vital bits of office equipment, paper clips. You wouldn't want to lose one.'

I gripped the edge of the desk, still on my knees, and peered over the counter. The man standing on the other side was about thirty. His dark brown hair was wavy in a ridiculously sexy just-got-out-of-bed way. His lips were wide and generous and his eyes were the most beautiful shade of hazel I'd ever seen. I ran a hand through my hair and felt myself blush furiously.

'Can I help you?' I slid back into my chair and sat up straight. Come on, Beth, at least try to appear professional!

The customer smiled and slipped his hands into the pockets of his dark jeans. 'Is Mrs Blackstock in?'

'Edna? You want to speak to her?'

Oh God. Why did he want to speak to my boss? Was he going to report me for professing my undying love to the shop fixtures?

'Yes.' He nodded, then held out a hand. 'I'm Matt Jones.'

I shook it. 'Beth Prince. Are you after a job, Matt?'

He looked too old to be a student after a few part-time hours, but all sorts of people came in, so it wasn't beyond the realms of possibility.

'Kind of,' Matt said, the left side of his mouth lifting into a lopsided smile. 'Is she in?'

'No.' I wondered if I should explain that I hadn't actually seen Edna Blackstock in over a month. She was about a hundred years old – well, definitely seventy-something – and the Picturebox had been in her family for years. When I'd first started, she'd been in several times a week, making all kinds of wacky suggestions (my favourite was that we should introduce a new line of Marmite-based sandwiches, starting with Marmite and Spam), but after her husband died three years ago, her visits became less and less frequent. Now we hardly ever saw her. 'Maybe I could help you? Have you ever worked in a cinema before?'

'Yep.' Matt pushed his shoulders back proudly. Wow, pretty confident for someone who'd just strolled off the street after a job. 'A few.'

I bit the top off a felt-tip pen and scribbled his name on a piece of paper. 'Any I might have heard of?'

'Apollo.'

'Poor you.' I raised my eyebrows. Apollo was a horrible, soulless multinational cinema chain that showed big-action no-plot movies and made its money out of overpriced tickets and stale popcorn. It was the complete opposite to the lovely, cosy cinema where I worked. We screened a mixture of popular classics and independent films, and our customers could buy Fairtrade coffee, home-made cakes and doorstep-sized sandwiches from the café upstairs and take them in with them. Yes, the cinema was a bit run-down, but that gave it character. 'Which one?'

'A few.' He sounded amused. 'Would you like me to list them for you?'

'If you like.'

There was a pause, and I looked up.

'I'm sorry.' Matt was grinning from ear to ear. 'I'm not being fair. I'm the south-east manager for Apollo and we're expanding our business in Brighton.'

9

'Really?' I looked at him in surprise. 'Aren't there enough Apollo cinemas here already?'

'Not in this part of town.'

'What?' We were the *only* cinema in the north of Brighton.

Matt pulled a face. 'I take it Mrs Blackstock didn't tell you she's thinking of selling the Picturebox to us?'

'No.' I could hardly breathe. 'No, she didn't.'

'Oh God. I imagined she'd have told all the staff already. Er …' Matt glanced towards the front of the cinema, then froze and turned sharply back to me. His eyes were wide, his face suddenly pale. 'Is there another way out?'

'Um, yeah.' I pointed towards the screening room. 'Go through there and take the door on the right. There's a code – 2243. That'll get you out onto the street. Make sure you slam it shut behind you. If anyone sneaks in to the next film, I'm holding you accountable.'

'Thanks.' He glanced back at the front door, then skidded towards the screening room.

I looked in the direction of the street and shook my head, confused. It didn't look any different to normal – just people milling past with bags of shopping in their hands. What had he seen that had scared him so much?

'By the way,' came Matt's voice again, his head poking round the screening room door. 'I preferred your last "I love you". It sounded the most sincere.'

And then he was gone.

Chapter Two

Matt

No man ever sets out to become a dick.

Honestly.

You need to believe me on that one.

We don't sit around in bike parks when we're little kids, our BMXs piled up at our feet, and discuss how much we'd like to be a dick when we grow up. Most of us, anyway, and definitely not me. So how had I managed to go from 'nice bloke' to 'total dick'? That was the question I was discussing with my best mate Neil in the Pull and Pump, our favourite Brighton pub.

I'd been to the Picturebox to discuss the acquisition with Mrs Blackstock, totally put my foot in it with the girl who worked there, and then had to run away because I'd seen Alice, my psycho ex, peering through the glass doors at me. So not only was I a dick when it came to relationships, I'd turned into a professional penis too.

'I don't want to be a dick.' I leaned towards Neil, my voice low. A vampire with pink hair and bleeding eyes was staring at us from the next table. It was only 7 p.m., but the pub was already packed. Instead of the normal crowd of scruffy post-work drinkers, we were surrounded by ghosts, ghouls and zombies eyeing up the tables for somewhere to sit. We were pretty much the only two people not in fancy dress, and I could definitely sense a 'not impressed' vibe from our glowering local vampire.

'All I did was split up with Alice,' I continued, ignoring her. 'I didn't cheat on her, I didn't flirt with her mates and I didn't treat her badly. I even finished with her face to face instead of taking the coward's way out and texting or emailing, but she's ...' I paused. 'Well, she's stalking me.'

Neil raised an eyebrow. 'Has someone been watching too many late-night episodes of *Murder, She Wrote*?'

'I'm not kidding,' I whispered. 'I can't go anywhere without her following me. Like this morning,' I reached for my pint and wet my throat, 'I went to visit a cinema that we're trying to buy, and she followed me there.'

Neil grinned. 'There's drugs the doctor can give you for paranoia, mate.'

'I'm not paranoid.' I sat back in my seat. 'I split up with her three weeks ago, and since then she's showed up at my flat or my office every ... single ... day. She posts notes through my letter box and rings me constantly. She even emailed me some photos of her so that I'd know,' I made quotation marks in the air with my index fingers, 'what I was missing.'

Neil looked intrigued. 'Naked photos?'

'It's not funny.'

'Then call the police, or,' he reached for his pint and smirked, 'send the photos to Readers' Wives. They pay quite well ... apparently.'

'I can't call the police,' I said, ignoring the Readers' Wives comment. 'It's not like she's threatened me or anything, and anyway, if I walk into a police station and say, "I'd like to file a complaint because a beautiful blonde has threatened to shag me stupid," they'd just laugh me right out of the door.'

'Hmm.' Neil looked thoughtful. 'I see your point.'

'So? What do I do?'

'Take her up on the sexual favours, then dump her again?'

I stared into my pint and shook my head. 'I don't know why I thought talking to you about this was a good idea. I'd get more helpful advice from the back of a pack of Tampax.'

A hissing sound made me look up. Neil was sitting bolt upright, his eyes fixed on the pub doorway behind me.

'Don't look round, Matt,' he said, 'but your ex-girlfriend just walked into the bar.'

I slumped down in my seat, waiting for the punch-line.

'And,' he breathed, 'she's staring right at you.'

'Talk to me,' I hissed. 'Make it look serious, like we can't be interrupted. Pretend your dog died or something.'

'Um …' My best mate stared wildly around the pub, as though searching for inspiration.

'Quick!' I urged, as the sound of stiletto heels on wooden flooring grew louder.

'I can't!' He pulled a face. It was the face of a truly crap mate. 'My mind's gone blank.'

'Say something! Anything!'

'Ummm … I was gutted when Man U lost the other day.' He reached across the table and gripped my arm. 'Mate, I actually shed a tear.'

'Nice try,' I sighed, 'but not quite what I was after. I was hoping for more of a—'

'Hello, Matthew.'

You wouldn't have thought that two words could make me feel quite so terrified. But they did.

'Hi, Alice.'

My ex-girlfriend was swaying precariously beside our table. Normally a pocket-sized five foot two and a bit, she'd elevated herself a good six inches by strapping on a pair of the most ridiculously high heels I'd ever seen. Her long blonde hair was straightened within an inch of its life, her make-up was perfect, her beige trench coat skimmed the top of her thighs, and … she was absolutely trollied.

'Aren't you going to invite me to sit down?' she asked, shoving me along the bench and plonking herself down beside me before I had a chance to reply.

'Actually,' I started, 'Neil was just about to tell me about—'

'He won't mind.' Alice flashed a smile across the table at my best mate. 'You don't, do you? I can give the female perspective on whatever it was you were going to tell Matt. I'm good at advice.'

Neil stared at me, his expression frozen into a rictus grin. His eyes flashed a desperate *What do I say to that?*

'Alice.' I twisted to face her. 'What are you doing here?'

She shifted slightly, looked me up and down and then crossed her legs. As she hooked one thigh over the other, her trench coat rode up, revealing a flash of suspender belt. She made no effort to yank it back down. I glanced away hastily, but her eyes met mine and she smirked.

'It's Halloween and I didn't have any plans,' she said lightly, 'so I thought I'd come to the pub.'

'To my local?'

She looked at me steadily, no hint of shame or embarrassment in her bloodshot blue eyes. 'A pub's a pub. I had no idea you'd be here.'

'Really?'

'Really, Matt. I've had a tiring day,' she yawned dramatically and threw her arms back as though casually stretching, 'and I fancied a drink. What's wrong with that?'

I stared at her in horror. The exaggerated stretch had caused her coat to gape open. All she was wearing underneath was a sheer black bra.

'Jesus!' I said, gripping her lapels and pulling them together as I glanced nervously around.

Neil's chin was practically resting on his chest, and the vampire at the next table was coughing so violently her mate was asking if she needed the Heimlich manoeuvre.

'Alice! What the hell? Forgot to put some clothes on, did you?'

'What?' She flashed me a look of utter innocence, then held her hands over mine and peeped down her front. 'Oops!'

'Oops?' I repeated incredulously. 'What do you mean, oops?'

She glanced at Neil. 'Be a darling and get me a drink, would you?'

My best mate was out of his seat and halfway across the bar like a shot. Traitor! Alice watched him go, then turned, or rather lurched, back towards me. She threw an arm around my shoulders and leaned in close, her breath hot against my ear.

'You should see what I've got on under this coat,' she whispered. 'Or rather what I haven't. Come home with me, Matt. You won't regret it.'

'Alice.' I gripped her gently by the shoulders and held her away from me. She looked stunning, as always, but there was no way I was going home with her. Not after what she'd put me through. 'I don't think that's a good idea.'

'Matt. Darling Matt.' She reached out a hand and stroked my cheek, her voice a soft purr. 'I'm not suggesting we get back together or get all heavy or anything. I just thought we could have a bit of fun, for old times' sake. A bit of escapism. It's Halloween, and everyone's pretending to be someone they're not. You're single, I'm single, what's to lose?'

Possibly the first layer of my epidermis, I thought wryly, remembering the time Alice had lost her shit when I'd come home three hours late one night and thrown a boiling-hot cup of coffee at me.

'It's not happening,' I said more firmly. 'Sorry. We split up for a reason, Alice, and it's time to move on.'

A flash of anger crossed my ex-girlfriend's face, and

she pulled away from me sharply. Like a snake about to strike, I thought nervously.

'Move on?' she repeated, her eyes narrowed. 'Just like that? Move on? Just because you say so? Is that how it works, Matt?'

'Whoa!' I held out my hands. 'I'm not telling you to do anything. I'm just saying – it's been three weeks since we split up, and I think we should both get on with our lives. Separately.'

'You do, do you?' Alice slipped off the bench and wobbled to a standing position. She pulled her coat tightly around her and crossed her arms over her chest. 'Yeah, that would suit you nicely, wouldn't it, Matt? If I just *moved on* quietly. If I just forgot about what we had. If I rolled over and stopped fighting for our relationship. Wouldn't that be nice and simple – for you?' She practically growled the last two words.

'Alice, please,' I begged as I clocked the curious looks of the skeleton and the witch who'd joined the vampire at the next table. 'Keep your voice down. People are starting to look.'

'I don't give a shit,' she roared, staring down a bloke dressed as Freddy Krueger who was gawping at her from a table near the toilets. 'In fact they're welcome to listen. The more people who find out the truth about you, the better.'

'Which is?' I asked, then instantly wished I could stuff the words back into my mouth and swallow them.

'That you're a liar. The worst kind. You told me you loved me, Matt, and then you dumped me, just like that—'

'Not *right after* I told you I loved you,' I interjected. 'It was months after—'

'Tomayto tomato. The timing isn't the point. The point is that when you love someone, you fight for the relationship; you don't leave it the second things get difficult.'

'Difficult?' I repeated incredulously. 'Alice, things were more than difficult in our relationship. Remember when you—'

'When I what? Reacted to you being a dickhead? It's not my fault if you confuse passion with aggression.'

'Really?' I jumped to my feet. 'And since when was throwing a cup of coffee at someone passionate? Or deleting all their female Facebook friends? Or ripping up their favourite T-shirt just because an ex-girlfriend, an ex-girlfriend from *ten years ago*, had bought it? And how about—'

'Yeah, yeah.' She waved a dismissive hand. 'And you did nothing to deserve any of that, did you? I just did it because I'm a complete psycho?'

Well …

'The fact of the matter, Matt,' she continued, her voice so loud I could no longer hear the jukebox, 'is that, unlike you, when I love someone I can't turn it off with the flick of a switch. I still love you, Matt. What's wrong with that?'

I was just about to explain, again, why we'd split up when, to my absolute horror, she started to cry.

'You can't tell someone you love them and then change your mind, Matt,' she shouted at me as tears spilled down her cheeks. 'You just can't.'

'Alice, wait!' I called as she turned on her heel and hurried out of the pub, swaying violently from side to side and knocking into tables as she went.

'Dick,' said the vampire at the next table.

Chapter Three

Beth

Eight and a half hours had passed since Matt Jones had shouted, 'I preferred your last "I love you". It sounded the most sincere,' as he'd sprinted out of the cinema, but I still cringed whenever I thought about it. If it wasn't bad enough that he'd witnessed my public declaration of love for a cardboard cut-out, I'd mistaken him for a student too. Great first impression, Beth! Knowing my luck, he'd get in touch with Mrs Blackstock and tell her he wasn't surprised the Picturebox was failing – she had a total fruit loop running the front of house! Not that my boss took me seriously anyway – why else would she ignore every single marketing or promotional idea I'd ever put to her?

I gazed around the cinema, taking in the crimson carpet, the cream columns intricately decorated with carved panels that stretched up to the arched ceiling, and the dusty chandelier that clung to it for dear life. The fixtures and fittings were faded and sad-looking, but a feeling of magic still hung in the air. I couldn't go into the screening room, with its heavy velvet curtain across the screen and the curved-backed seats arranged in neat rows, without stepping back in time. I'd imagine clipping tickets in the 1940s and watching laughing women with painted-on stockings wiggling their pencil-skirted bottoms into their seats, dashing British soldiers or American GIs at their sides. The cinema would have seemed the height of sophistication and glamour back then. Would those women have lost sleep over a man who hadn't said 'I love you' after ten months? Probably not. They had bigger things to worry about – like whether their sweethearts were even alive.

I sighed, and fanned my hot cheeks with a programme. Maybe I should take what had happened with Matt as a sign that I should keep quiet about how I felt about Aiden. Everyone knows bad things happen in threes, and I'd already clocked up two in a row. I reached for my phone, and was just about to text Lizzie to ask her what I should do when the door to the cinema swung open and a familiar greasy-haired shape strolled across the foyer.

'Morning, Pimp.' Carl planted his elbows on the counter and looked me up and down. 'You're looking a bit rosy today. What's up, acne medication stopped working?'

I tilted my head so my hair swung forward and covered my cheeks. 'I could say the same about your shampoo.'

'Touché!' Carl grinned, revealing his grubby yellow teeth, then leaned over the counter and reached for my phone. 'Not bad, Beth, certainly better than your normal inane drivel.'

I snatched my mobile away. The last time he'd got hold of it, he'd switched the language to Polish and it had taken me for ever to work out how to change it back.

'Grow up,' I muttered as I shoved the phone into my bag and turned back to my computer screen. Keep your temper, Beth, keep your temper.

Carl, or Creepy Carl as Lizzie called him, was the cosmos's idea of a sick joke. We'd met on the first day of primary school and shared the same desk. I'd felt him glancing at me all the way through the lesson, but was too shy to say anything, and concentrating instead on the words I was copying off the board. At the end of the class, he leaned towards me.

'You smell of poo,' he hissed.

I ignored him and hurried to join Lizzie as she filed out of the classroom with a group of girls, hoping I'd never see Carl again. No such luck! Two hours later, he chased me round the playground with a stick covered in dog poo, while the other kids watched. Each time he touched my hair with the stick, he shouted, 'Poo Head Prince!' and they all laughed.

By the time I was eleven and it was time to apply to secondary school, I spent most evenings lying in bed desperately hoping that Carl Coombes would go to Hayworth High, not St Swithens comprehensive, where I was going.

Guess who was the first person I saw on my first day of secondary school?

Yep, Carl Coombes.

So Poo Head Prince was back, for a couple of months

anyway. After that, Carl seemed more interested in playing 'ping the bra strap' than taking the mickey out of me, and I started to relax, believing he'd finally stopped torturing me.

When acne appeared on my cheeks and jawline during the summer holidays, the day after my thirteenth birthday, I was horrified. I tried everything – medicated skin scrubs, spot treatments, even toothpaste – to try and get it to disappear, but nothing worked. The only way I could hide my zits was to tip my head forward so that my hair covered my cheeks.

Carl noticed my spotty skin on the first day back at school.

'Jesus!' he shouted, pointing at me across the classroom. 'What happened to your face?'

My cheeks burned even redder as thirty pairs of eyes swivelled in my direction. 'They're … they're just pimples,' I stuttered, repeating the least offensive word Mum had used to describe my disfigurement.

'Pimples?' Carl had laughed. 'Looks like you went to the pimple factory and rolled around on the conveyor belt.'

And so I was christened Pimples, shortened to Pimp, a nickname that stuck with me all the way through school. Even when my skin cleared up, I was still one of the quietest kids in the sixth form. I was worried that if I said something or answered a question, it'd spark a new nickname. The only thing that got me through each day was the prospect of creeping into a darkened cinema to watch a film.

Getting a job at the Picturebox after I left school

(with *really* bad A-level results) was a dream come true. Okay, so it was only part-time, and all I had to do was check tickets at the door and sweep up popcorn and cake crumbs at the end of the film, but the customers were lovely and, even better, I got to watch films for free. Sometimes I'd sit in on a showing even if I'd seen the film dozens of times before. I'd settle into a seat on the back row as the projector whirred in the booth up above me and gaze at the audience as they stared, transfixed, at the screen. I'd daydream about owning my own cinema. I'd make it a magical experience, just like it was in the Picturebox's glory days.

Eighteen months after I'd started, one of the front-desk staff left, and Mrs Blackstock asked me if I'd like the job. We were 'a family', she said, so I'd still have to take tickets on the doors and sweep up, but it was mine if I wanted it. Did I? I was over the moon! Well, until Carl Coombes strolled through the door, announcing that he'd dropped out of university and would be working with me while he decided what he wanted to do with his life. I'll be honest, I wanted to quit there and then, but there was no way he was going to part me from the one thing in my life that made me happy. I hoped that if I just ignored him, he'd get bored and go away. That was three years ago, and he didn't look like he was going anywhere fast. Well, unless what Matt Jones had said about Mrs Blackstock selling the cinema was true, in which case we both were.

Please don't let it be true, I prayed silently, as I grabbed my coat and bag, sidestepped a smirking Carl and crossed the foyer. *Not when my life is going so well.*

Matt's visit and Carl's sarky comments disappeared from my head the second I reached my front door. Aiden was due round at eight o'clock so I had less than an hour to have a shower, do my make-up, sort out my hair and get changed.

'Lizzie?' I called as I pushed the front door open and stepped into the hallway. 'Liz, are you in?'

Lizzie's my flatmate. Actually, since her dad owns the two-bedroomed terraced house we live in, I'm technically *her* flatmate. Her dad's business really took off when we were ten, so instead of going to St Swithens like me, she got packed off to a posh boarding school in Dorset. The next time I next saw her, she knew how to play lacrosse (I didn't even know what that was) and sounded like the Queen. It didn't matter, though, and we continued to be friends all the way through secondary school, writing to each other during term time and hanging out in the holidays. We were still best friends when we took our A levels, even though Lizzie was posh and confident and I ... wasn't.

'Lizzie?' I shouted again. 'Are you in?'

I poked my head around the living room door, half expecting to see Lizzy's clothes, together with those of some unknown bloke, strewn all over the sofa. I'd lost count of the number of times I'd woken up in the morning to find some guy I'd never seen before strolling out of the shower with Lizzie's towel round his waist. We're different like that, me and Liz. She finds it hilarious that I cry at romantic films like *The Notebook* (and know all the words), and thinks the concept of soulmates is ridiculous. She can't stand Aiden either, even if she was indirectly responsible for us meeting in the first place.

I was at work at the Picturebox on a Saturday night almost exactly ten months ago when I met him. It was unusually busy – couples, singles and crowds of students had been in and out all night – so I didn't notice when a tall, fair-haired man in chinos and a navy V-neck jumper walked in. Actually, that's a lie. I *always* look up when someone comes in. Call me stupid, and Lizzie frequently does, but I'd always secretly hoped that the love of my life would walk into the cinema and sweep me off my feet. It doesn't matter that I'm ten stone twelve and you'd need a forklift truck to sweep me anywhere; that didn't stop me dreaming. I'd always been a dreamer. When I was nine and my parents were screaming at each other, I'd wriggle under the duvet with a torch and a copy of *Cinderella* or *Sleeping Beauty*. I never stopped believing in happy endings, even when Mum and Dad got divorced a couple of months later.

Anyway, Mr Chinos had just approached my booth when the phone rang. I snatched it up.

'Hello, Picturebox. How can I help you?'

The voice on the other end of the line said something I couldn't make out.

'Could you say that again?' I asked. 'It's a bad line.'

'It's Lizzie,' the voice hissed. 'I need your help.'

'Liz,' I whispered back. 'You know you shouldn't ring me at work.'

'I wouldn't have to if you'd just turn your bloody mobile on.'

'Well I can't get anything done when you're con-
tinually texting me about your latest date from hell.'
I sighed. 'You're on a date from hell now, aren't you?'

'Sort of.'

'What do you mean, sort of?'

'I'm half on a date, half not.'

'Huh?'

'I'm stuck in the window of the Gladstone pub.'

'What?' I said loudly. Mr Chinos stared at me. So
did the couple standing behind him. I lowered my
voice. 'How did that happen?'

'My sanny towel with wings tried to fly away so I
chased after it. Why do you think I'm stuck in the
window? I'm trying to escape. Mr Fabulous turned out
to be Mr Flatulence. And he won't shut up. I swear,
he only pauses to fart. They're silent, but I can tell he's
doing it; he leans to his left and raises his eyebrows for
a split second, then keeps on talking. Hello, I've got
eyes! And a nose, too! He's vile, Beth. Absolutely vile.
Anyway, I excused myself to go to the loo, because I
couldn't breathe, and then I had a fabulous idea. Well,
not so fabulous as it turns out, because I'm fucking
stuck in—'

'Hang on, Liz,' I said, as Mr Chinos coughed softly.
'Don't go anywhere.'

'Very funny,' she hissed.

I smiled up at Mr Chinos as he ran a hand through
the straight fair hair that flopped into his eyes. 'Can I
help you?'

'I'd like a ticket to see …' he started, holding up the
programme in his hand.

27

'Help!' said my phone.

I mouthed *sorry* at Mr Chinos and clamped my mobile to my ear. 'Lizzie, are you okay?'

'No I'm bloody not. A seagull just shat on my head *and* it's starting to rain.'

'Well at least it'll wash the poo out of your hair.'

'Aren't you the comedienne today?'

'Yes.' I smiled at Mr Chinos, who was still waiting patiently. He was a lot more refined-looking than the kind of guy I normally went for, with his perfectly straight nose, high cheekbones and strong jawline, like the sort of posh hero Jane Austen's characters swooned over.

'I'm sorry,' he said. 'But if you could just let me have a ticket for—'

'BETH!'

'What?'

'There's a bunch of teenagers in the street filming me with their mobile phones, and I refuse to end up on You-bloody-Tube hanging out of a pub bog with seagull shit on my cheek. Come and rescue me, or I swear our friendship is over!'

'I will … I'm just … the cinema's busy. It's not a very good time to leave.'

Mr Chinos mouthed something at me I couldn't make out. I tilted my head so the phone was wedged between my shoulder and my cheek, and covered the mouthpiece with my hand.

'Sorry, my best friend's stuck in a toilet.'

He raised an eyebrow.

'Not actually *in* the toilet,' I corrected. 'She's stuck in the window of the toilet. She was on a date.'

'Classy date!' He grinned ruefully.

'No, no. The date was in the pub. She's in the toilet because she was trying to escape. And she wants me to rescue her but there's a massive queue behind you now and I can't leave because if I do my boss will probably fire me but if I don't go and help Lizzie she'll probably kick me out of the flat so it's a choice between losing my job and losing my home and—'

'Whoa.' He put a hand on mine. I hadn't even realised I was drumming my fingers on the counter until he held them still. 'It's okay.'

I looked down at his hand, then back up at his face. His blue eyes seemed to bore into mine. I didn't move my hand away.

'Go and rescue your friend,' he said. 'I'll take over behind the booth. Just run through what I have to do and I'll pick it up. I used to work in HMV when I was younger. How hard can it be?'

I stared at him in astonishment. 'You'd do that? For me?'

'Yes.'

It was ridiculous really. There I was, standing in the cinema where I'd spent six years of my life waiting for my knight in shining armour to walk through the door, and here he was. I was in distress – well, Lizzie was really – and a complete stranger had just offered to make everything right. Things like that didn't just happen randomly. It *had* to be a sign that Aiden was the man for me.

What happened in the cinema that day we first met became a bit of a running joke between me and Aiden. Whenever one of us was down or grumpy, the other just had to say, 'It could be worse, you could be stuck in a toilet!' and then we'd both laugh. Well, *I* always laughed. Aiden didn't seem to find it quite so amusing after the hundredth time I said it.

In a way, it was weird that we'd ended up together. Our taste in films was about as diverse as it could be. I liked romantic comedies, while he adored Japanese art-house films. I was a chocoholic; he was allergic to dairy. He had a degree in journalism. I'd never been to uni. But despite our differences, I found him endlessly fascinating and could sit for hours listening to him tell me about his job as a reporter for the local paper, and his massive family. He talked, I listened. That was us. We fitted together perfectly, just like couples did in romantic comedies. Well, sort of. I don't think Harry would have grabbed Sally's hand on their first date, leaned across the table and said, 'Darling, I'm so glad we met. You've saved me a fortune on internet dating.'

So now, on Halloween, almost exactly ten months later, I was going to tell him just how much he meant to me.

What could possibly go wrong?

Chapter Four

Matt

'Shot?' Neil asked, handing me a small glass of something green and vile-smelling.

We were standing at the bar, a cold breeze blowing in from the door, which was still wide open after Alice's sudden exit. To my right, a group of zombies had their heads together, whispering and occasionally nodding in my direction.

I reached for the shot, raised it to my mouth, then paused. That was what a dick would do, wasn't it? He'd ignore the fact that his ex-girlfriend had just run out of the pub in tears and get pissed with his best mate instead.

I set the shot glass back on the bar. 'I can't.'

Neil looked at me as though I'd just told him I liked to dress up in nappies and a bib in my free time.

'What?'

'I need to check Alice is okay.'

'Right.' He reached for his pint and took a sip. 'So what you're basically telling me is that you're going to ditch your best mate so you can go and comfort the girl who's stalking you? Is it just me, or does that sound a bit ...' he paused for effect, 'fucking mental?'

'Probably.' I shrugged. 'Anyway, I'm not going to comfort her. I'm just going to talk to her. She's pissed out of her head and, I dunno, maybe all this ... embarrassing herself in public is the end of it and she'll realise that enough is enough and leave me alone.'

'Yeah, and Dita Von Teese has just joined a nunnery.'

'Could happen.'

He looked incredulous. 'No way, Dita Von Teese would never—'

'No, you twat, Alice finally moving on.'

Neil shrugged and reached for his pint. 'On your head be it, mate. On your head.'

It didn't take me long to catch up with my ex-girlfriend. She was sitting on a doorstep further down the street, a stockinged foot in a puddle, a broken stiletto in her hand and an expression of pure misery on her face. It was tipping down with rain and she was soaked to the bone.

'You!' she said accusingly as I splashed down the street towards her. 'Come to laugh, have you?'

'No.' I crouched down beside her. 'I wanted to check if you were okay.'

'Why?' Her eyes narrowed accusingly.

'I dunno. You seemed upset.'

'No shit.' She pushed her wet hair back from her face and looked me up and down. I'd seen that look before. It was the 'there's hell to pay' Alice special. I braced myself for the onslaught, but none came. Instead she put her hand on my arm and smiled sweetly. 'It was lovely of you to come after me, Mattie. I appreciate it.'

'Really?'

'Of course.' She paused. 'Could I just ask you one thing? Would you mind helping me home? My shoe's broken.' She cradled it to her chest and looked at it sorrowfully, like it was a dead cat or something. 'I can't walk.'

'Okay.' I stood up purposefully. 'I'll call you a cab.'

'Come with me,' she said, reaching out a hand. 'Please, Matt. I think I've twisted my ankle.'

'I can't tell you how pleased I am that you came back,' Alice said, hopping across her living room carpet, a glass of beer in each hand. She handed one to me, then plopped on to the sofa beside me. The sofa was a three-seater, with plenty of room for us both to sit comfortably without touching, but my ex-girlfriend had positioned herself so close to me that her damp forearm was pressed again mine.

She gazed at me adoringly. 'I always knew you would.'

I swallowed nervously. As much as I didn't want to admit it, Neil had been right. Going after Alice had been a *huge* mistake. Huge.

'Sorry?' I said feebly, hoping desperately that she didn't mean what I thought she meant. 'I'm not sure what you're talking about.'

Alice laughed lightly and flicked back her hair. Oh God. She was flirting with me. 'What do you think I'm talking about, Matt?'

I shifted as far to my right as I could, which was only about half an inch, and took a big gulp of beer. Our arms unpeeled with a wet squelch.

'Mattie?' Her voice had taken on a distinctly shrill tone. 'What did you think I was talking about?'

I stared straight ahead, my eyes fixed on the bay window across the room, and tried to work out whether it was locked. If it wasn't, I might be able to cross the room, open it and jump out before Alice could reach for a sharp implement, but if it was—

'Matt?'

Her eyes were boring into the side of my skull. Shit. I was trapped. If I told her the truth – that I thought she was implying that by going back to her house I'd somehow agreed to us getting back together – she'd either freak out and scream at me for assuming that was what she'd meant, or she'd be really pleased and hug and kiss me. Neither of which I wanted to happen. I glared at the TV and stereo. They were both silent. Switch yourselves on! I commanded mentally, Uri Geller-style. Please just magically turn yourselves on and break this horrible, torturous silence. Subject me to a never-ending playlist of cheesy ballads on Heart FM or an eternity of Gok Wan's *How to Look Good in Your Granny's Girdle and a Pair of Support Tights*; just please, please put me out of my misery.

I shook my head. Enough! Pull yourself together, Matt, and stop talking to the fixtures and fittings. Who do you think you are – that weird girl from the Picturebox? Don't tell Alice the truth. Say something else. Anything!

'You're pleased that I helped you get home,' I mumbled nervously.

I snuck a quick glance at my ex-girlfriend. She looked confused.

'Oh,' she said. 'Of course. That's … great.'

I glugged my beer. If I could just neck what was left, I could make my excuses and we could both pretend this had never happened and …

Oh shit. Alice's hand was on my thigh.

'Darling Mattie,' she purred, leaning in so close I could feel her breath on my neck. It smelt a hundred per cent proof. 'We had fun together, didn't we? A lot of *naughty* fun.'

Her fingers inched towards my groin.

'Loo!' I said, leaping to my feet and sprinting out of the living room before she had a chance to reply.

I sat down heavily on the closed loo seat and clamped my hands to my head. She obviously thought that me accompanying her home meant … Shit, shit, shit. Matt, you utter dick! Right. I sat up sharply. Time to grow some balls. Leave the bathroom. Go into the living room. Thank Alice for the beer and tell her it's time for you to go. And then leave. End of problem.

I reached for the handle of the bathroom door and yanked it open. Go into the living room, I repeated to myself, and then thank—

'Alice!'

My ex was standing directly outside the bathroom, blocking my exit. Her hands were on her hips, her head was tipped coquettishly to one side – and she'd discarded her coat.

'Oh God.' I took a step back.

Alice pushed out her bottom lip in what I think was supposed to be a sexy pout and took a step towards me. 'You weren't thinking about leaving, were you, Matt?'

'Well, actually …'

'It's just that my ankle's still hurting,' she said in a slightly creepy little-girl-lost voice, 'and I think a lie-down might help, so if you could just carry me up the stairs to the bedroom, I'd be ever so grateful.'

'Well the thing is, I've got to—'

I didn't get to finish the sentence. Before I knew what was happening, Alice had launched herself across the bathroom, thrown her arms around my neck and was clinging to me like an intoxicated limpet.

'No!' she squealed, pressing her face against my chest. 'No, don't leave me again, Matt.'

The force of the unexpected death-hug sent me reeling backwards across the bathroom, Alice still firmly attached, until I came to a sudden halt as the back of my thighs hit the sink. There was a thud, then an even louder crash as a glass toothbrush holder toppled off the side and smashed on the ceramic tiles.

I stared in surprise at the shards around my feet.

'Sod the glass!' Alice ordered. She'd extricated herself from around my neck and turned her attention to my belt buckle instead. Her fingers fumbled with the fastening.

'Whoa!' I put my hands on her shoulders and gently pushed her away. 'What are you doing?'

'What do you mean, whoa?' She shot me a sulky

look. 'Time to drop the virginal little soldier act, Matt. Let's just get on with it.'

'Get on with it?' I frowned. 'Alice, I'm not sleeping with you.'

'Oh really?' She put her hands on her hips and flicked back her hair. 'Why else did you come back here?'

'Because,' I scooted a shoe across the bathroom floor, sweeping the remains of the toothbrush holder towards the bin, 'I was worried about you. You turn up at the pub, pissed out of your head, in your underwear ...'

'And a coat. Don't make out like I'm some kind of slut.'

'I'm not. I was just ... Oh never mind. I just wanted to make sure you got home safely.'

'So why not just put me in a cab and go back to Neil?' She crossed her arms angrily.

'Because you said your ankle was hurting and you needed me to ...' I ran my hands through my hair. 'Oh for God's sake, Alice. If I'd stuck you in a cab and gone back to the pub, you'd have called me a dick. Instead I helped you home and now I'm some kind of tease. I can't win, can I?'

Alice glared at me and sat down heavily on the edge of the bath. 'You can spin it however you want, but no one forced you to come back here, Matt. The truth, whether you're willing to accept it or not, is that you regret us splitting up and want to get back together.'

My jaw fell open. 'No. Alice, I'm sorry, but that's not true. Look.' I perched on the bath beside her. She looked cold, sitting in the bathroom in her underwear, rubbing her arms, and even though the backs of my thighs were throbbing violently, I couldn't help but feel sorry for her. I could still remember why I'd fallen for her in the first place – she was so vibrant and full of life. She was the most spontaneous, unpredictable woman I'd ever met, but that quality came with a price – her moods were as changeable as the wind. I never knew from day to day which Alice I was going out with – scary, jealous Alice or fun, carefree Alice.

'Look,' I began again, pressing my hands between my knees, 'I'm sorry things didn't work out between us, really I am, and I could launch into all kinds of platitudes about how it's not you, it's me, but the fact is we just weren't right for each other. We're too different. It was never going to work.'

'Really?' Alice reached for a towel and wrapped it around her shoulders. 'If we're so different, how come we had such great sex?'

'It's not about the sex.' I shook my head. 'You can't be in a relationship with someone unless you feel totally comfortable with them, and the fact is, you were just a little bit ...well ... scary.'

My ex looked at me steadily. 'I prefer the word passionate.'

'Call it what you want; the fact is you were too *passionate* for me. Alice, you flew off the handle about every little thing. I didn't cheat on you, not once, but you were so suspicious. I lost count of the number of times I found you going through my phone. And you checked up on me all the time. I'd be with my grandad and you'd ring up and moan that I spent more time with him than you. If I had to stay late at work for a meeting, you'd blow a blue fit and accuse me of being with another woman. I just couldn't take it, Alice. I had to keep you constantly updated about what I was doing, where I was going, who with and for how long. I felt like I had a boyfriend ASBO or something, and I hadn't done anything wrong.'

'Maybe if you'd spent more time with me, I wouldn't have had to do that.'

I shook my head. 'We spent lots of time together, Alice. I hardly saw Neil the whole time we were together, and I neglected loads of my other mates too. I don't regret that, because I wanted to spend time with you, but we just stopped making each other happy. And I'm sorry about that. I'm sorry it didn't work out. I really am. But we need to move on, both of us.'

'Move on? *You* want to move on, you mean! Just admit it, Matt. You've met someone else.' She sprang to her feet, her injured ankle miraculously healed, and glared down at me. 'Who is she? Someone you were screwing while we were together? All that shit about late meetings at work – I always knew you were lying.'

'Oh my God.' I shook my head in despair. 'Alice, I *promise* you. I didn't cheat on you when we were together, and I haven't met anyone since. To be honest, a girlfriend is the last thing I need at the moment. I've got more than enough on my plate with Grandad and the Picturebox deal and—'

'Liar!' She lurched around me, her fingers reaching for my jeans back pocket. 'I bet your phone tells a different story.'

'Enough!' I stood up, both hands held out in front of

me. 'Alice, that's enough. I came back tonight because I wanted to make sure you were okay. And you are, and that's great, but I can't deal with this. I really can't.'

I eased my way past my ex-girlfriend and strode down the hall towards the front door.

'Matt!' she called as I unlatched it and stepped out on to the street. 'Matt! Don't you dare walk out on me! Matt!'

Chapter Five

Beth

I perched on the edge of the sofa, the diaphanous pumpkin costume splayed out around me, and glanced at my watch: 9.09 p.m. Aiden was exactly one hour and nine minutes late.

And he wasn't answering his mobile.

Not that I'd heard from him all day. There was no text saying good morning when I'd woken up, no phone call to talk about the party, nothing.

It's fine, I told myself as I stood up and wandered over to the window. He probably thought I'd said ten o'clock. Eight o'clock and ten o'clock do sound a bit similar when you mumble. Which I do – frequently – according to Aiden.

Yes, that was definitely what had happened. He'd misheard me. He'd turn up dressed like a dashing but evil Victorian gentleman (Jack the Ripper, or possibly someone a bit less scary) and whisk me away to the party, where we'd get drunk, have a brilliant time, then grab a taxi home and tumble into bed. After being thoroughly ravished, I'd say, 'Aiden Dowles, I love you' – without sounding like a love-struck teenager – and he'd say, 'Beth Prince, I love you too,' and everything would be amazing. Or maybe he wouldn't say 'I love you too' straight away. Maybe he'd say 'Ditto', like Demi Moore and Patrick Swayze in *Ghost*. Or maybe he'd just smile, or look shocked in a pleased kind of way, and stroke the hair out of my eyes and lean in for a kiss. Then, in the morning, when I was cooking breakfast, he'd sneak up behind me in the kitchen, wrap his arms around my waist and whisper, 'I love you' into my ear. Or maybe ...

Urgh! I clutched my heart. It was beating wildly. Stop it, Beth. You're making yourself more nervous. Chill out and think about something else. Like, um, how you look.

I wandered back into my bedroom and stared at my reflection in the full-length mirror next to the bed.

Make-up free from eye bogeys?

Check.

Ridiculous pumpkin costume?

Check.

Hold-up stockings?

Bugger! One sheer black stocking had concertinaed around my ankle.

I moved to yank it back up again, then paused. I couldn't even *see* my ankle, never mind bend over – my enormous pumpkin body was in the way. I wriggled my way out of it, grabbed hold of the stocking and attempted to pull it up my leg. Easier said than done. Getting my thigh into it was like squeezing a pillow into a condom. 'One size fits all' my arse.

Stocking back in place, sort of, I pulled the pumpkin

costume back over my head and glanced at my reflection again.

'I hope Aiden appreciates this,' I said aloud.

My reflection said nothing. In fact my reflection looked a teeny tiny bit worried. I glanced at my watch, for the hundredth time: 9.27 p.m.

The brrr brrr of my landline phone made me jump out of my heels. 'Aiden!'

I sprinted out of the bedroom, my stilettos clacking on the laminate flooring, threw myself on to the sofa, stomach first, and grabbed the phone.

'Aiden,' I gasped, as my pumpkin costume rode up and banged me on the back of the head.

'Beth?' said a female voice.

My heart immediately slowed to its normal rhythm. 'Oh. Hi, Mum.'

'Delighted to talk to you too!'

'Sorry. I'm expecting Aiden and I'm a bit nervous because I'm planning on telling him that ... ' I caught myself. Mum didn't believe in gushy outbursts of emotion. She didn't believe in a lot of things – things like marriage, displays of affection, or men being honest, trustworthy members of the human race. Especially not that last one. 'Anyway, are you okay?'

'Marvellous. Listen, Beth, I just wanted to let you know that I've booked a ticket to Australia for you.'

'What?'

Mum owned a really successful recruitment business in the UK. So successful, in fact, that she was planning on opening a new branch in Australia and then emigrating out there. She'd been trying for three months to convince me to go with her.

'Australia. The flight's on the twenty-fourth of December,' she said steadily. 'Think how exciting it'll be, darling – winging our way to a new life over Christmas.'

'Mum.' I sighed heavily. 'I've told you before. I don't want to move to Australia. I love Brighton and I've got some great friends here, not to mention Aiden. And a good job.'

Mum snorted.

'What?'

'Printing out tickets and putting money in a till isn't my definition of a good job, darling. I know you'd make me a fantastic PA if you just gave it a go.'

'But I don't want to be a—'

'There's nothing wrong with being a PA, young lady. I started off as a secretary back in 1971, and look at me now, I'm—'

'The director of a highly successful recruitment company,' I finished. 'I know there's nothing wrong with being a PA, but it's not what I want to do. I'm happy in the film industry.'

'Film industry? Ha! That's like someone who works behind the record counter in Woolworths claiming they're the next Simon Cowell.'

'Woolworths shut down ages ago.'

'See!' she said, as though that proved her point.

'Okay,' I said, trying to keep the exasperation out of my voice. 'Working in a cinema isn't the same as working in the film industry, but it makes me happy, and—'

'What's happiness got to do with anything? I thought I was happy the day I married your dad, and look how that worked out for me. Abandoned and on the scrapheap at forty-four.'

'You weren't abandoned. You left him.'

'Only because he drove me to it! Your dad treated me like part of the furniture. He talked to those bloody parakeets of his more than he did to me. Monosyllabic, that's what he was. I could have sat down to dinner in my birthday suit and he'd still have said, "Lovely grub, Edwina. Pass the salt."'

'Mum! Stop it!'

She let out a long sigh. 'I see. That's how it is, is it? Now you don't want to talk to me either. I can tell who you take after.'

'It's not that. I just don't like you talking about Dad like that. And I really can't chat for long. Aiden's due any minute, and something very special is going to happen tonight. Hopefully.'

'Special!' She snorted down the phone. 'What are you expecting? Some kind of proposal?'

The thought had fleetingly crossed my mind, but I'd dismissed it almost as soon as it had arrived. Okay, that's a lie. I'd allowed myself a little five-minute daydream during a quiet patch at work. In the fantasy, Aiden would turn up at my door, hand me a big white box containing a beautiful designer gown and ask me to put it on.

'Sssh,' he'd say when I'd try and object, 'don't spoil the surprise.'

Once changed he'd usher me into a waiting limousine

and hand me a glass of chilled champagne. A couple of minutes later we'd arrive at the West Pier and he'd take me by the hand and lead me, under a moonlit sky, along the seafront until we reached dozens of pumpkins, carved into heart shapes, burning brightly under the bandstand.

'Beth,' he would say softly, dropping to one knee as I stared around in wonder. 'Will you ...'

'Beth!' Mum's stern tone cut through my thoughts like a blowtorch through ice cream. 'The sooner you realise that life is not a romantic comedy, the better. You're so much like your father in that respect. Always dreaming, always fantasising about what could be instead of facing up to your responsibilities. Your father seemed to think he was that inventor chap from the *Back to the Future* films, not an electrical engineer from East Croydon.'

'Hey! Dad made some great gadgets. Remember that alarm that went off in the kitchen when it was just about to rain? It saved the washing from getting drenched loads of times.'

'And it destroyed my nerves in the process! Look, Beth, I don't know if it's you, or your generation, but you can't have it all. Life isn't a fairy tale. There's no such thing as a perfect man or a dream job. If you forgot all about men and got yourself a proper, sensible career, you'd be much more fulfilled.'

'Like you, you mean?'

'Exactly like me. I just want what's best for ...'

The rest of the sentence was drowned out by the tinkling chime of my doorbell.

'That'll be Aiden,' I said, bouncing off the sofa. I glanced at the mirror above the fireplace, yanked down my pumpkin costume and patted my hair with my free hand. 'Can I ring you back? We're going out, and …'

Mum sighed.

'Bye, Mum!' I said cheerily. 'Speak to you soon.'

'Goodbye, darling. Oh,' she added, 'about the ticket to Australia – should I send it to you, or hang on to it and give it to you at the coach station on the twenty-fourth?'

Hadn't she listened to a word I'd just said?

'I'm not going, Mum. I'm sorry. Hopefully it's not too late for you to get your money back. I'll call you tomorrow, okay? Bye!'

'Coming!' I called as I skipped out of the living room and into the hallway, then turned the front door handle. 'Aiden!'

Standing – well, swaying – outside, with one hand on the door frame and the other in his pocket, was my boyfriend. He peered up at me through bloodshot eyes, his expression grim.

'Hi, Beth,' he said blankly.

I smiled, too relieved to see him to mention the fact that he was obviously drunk. And late. 'You made it!'

He hadn't bothered dressing up for the party, but I didn't care. He looked so handsome in the soft glow of light from my hallway, his hair slicked back from the rain, his wool-mix work suit hanging crumpled from his shoulders. It was like a scene from a film – like he'd walked through a storm to get to me and risked life, limb and a hefty dry-cleaning bill. My heart twisted

47

with excitement and I licked my lips nervously. Sod the plan to make my declaration post-ravishing. This was it. The perfect moment. I had to say it.

'Aiden.' I cleared my throat and rested my hands on my enormous pumpkin stomach. 'There's something I've wanted to tell you for a very long time. What it is … what I'm trying to say, Aiden, is that I lo—'

'Beth.' He held up a hand. 'We need to talk.'

Just like that, one of my hold-up stockings gave up its grip on my thigh and rolled down to my ankle.

And my heart went with it.

'Sorry?' I said, blinking hard to try and wake up from what was obviously a horrible dream. 'Could you say that again?'

Aiden rested one hand on the outside wall of my flat, as though to steady himself, and wiped the other over his rain-drenched brow. A low rumble of thunder filled the air, and a streak of lightning crackled over Brighton.

'I need some space, Beth,' he said steadily.

I stared at him, my brain whirring madly. What? Why would he say that? Things had been going so well. At least I thought they had. I wouldn't have decided to spring an 'I love you' on him if I'd sensed something was up. My gut instinct would have kicked in and warned me not to – wouldn't it? He had to be messing around. He just had to.

'Space?' I repeated, as I stepped backwards into the hall, holding my arms in front of me. 'Look, there's some space. You've got a whole extra metre.'

Aiden didn't laugh.

'Please.' My arms flopped to my sides. 'Just come in. It's tipping down. You said you wanted to talk, and it's much warmer inside. I bought some of that expensive wine you like, and we could—'

'It's not working out, Beth.'

Aiden's face was expressionless. There wasn't the hint of a crinkle at the corners of his eyes or the twitch of a smile on his lips. Normally I could tell exactly what mood he was in before he even opened his mouth, but this time I couldn't read him at all. It was like someone had made a clone of my boyfriend, removed all his emotions and then asked him to knock on my door. And it scared me.

'What's not working?' I asked playfully. Part of me thought that if I kept it light, if I encouraged him to talk, he'd stop being so cold and weird and that horrible empty look in his eyes would go away. 'My outfit? You're not impressed, are you? Oh no. I thought you'd find it funny, but you were hoping I'd wear something sexy. It's fine. I'll get changed. It'll only take a second to grab my little black dress. Honestly. It's not a big deal.'

Aiden looked down at his feet. His Adam's apple bobbed up and down as he swallowed. 'It's not about what you're wearing, Beth.'

'Is it … have you changed your mind about taking me to the party?'

Aiden shook his head. A raindrop trickled from his hairline and curved its way down his cheek. I felt an urge to reach out and wipe it away. Instead, I rubbed my palms down the sides of my pumpkin.

'What is it, then? Is it something I've done? Said?' I asked. The second the words had left my mouth, I regretted saying them. I didn't want to know the answer.

'It's …' Aiden plunged his hands into his pockets and looked up at me. 'It's not you, Beth. It's got nothing to do with you. It's—'

'Don't say it,' I begged, holding out my hands. 'Please, please, please don't say it.'

'It's me,' he finished lamely.

And there it was – that horrible relationship-get-out clause that had been used on me so many times before. But I wasn't going to go down without a fight. Not this time. And I definitely wasn't going to cry.

'Um,' I said, swallowing down the lump in my throat. 'Okay. You've had a few drinks, it's Halloween and there's probably a full moon or something. Everyone acts a bit strangely when there's a full moon. Particularly werewolves. They sit in the middle of fields and howl. Not that I'm comparing you to a werewolf. God, no. I don't care what Lizzie says, I think you've got lovely eyebrows, and they don't meet in the middle. They're a little bit bushy, maybe, but nothing that a trip to the—'

'Beth.' Aiden pressed his fingers against his temples, as though the sound of my voice was giving him a headache. 'Please don't make this any more difficult than it already is.'

'But it doesn't have to be difficult. You're just having one of those men-withdraw-to-their-cave moments I've read about in *Men Are from Mars, Women Are from Venus*. And I'm cool with that. Honestly. Go back to your cave and build a fire or, um, draw some pictures of stampeding buffalo on the wall or whatever, and I'll wait until you're ready to come out again. You want some space, and that's cool. I love space.' I threw my arms wide open. 'Space is good. I need space too, I just didn't tell you I did. I can, um, I can use the space to do some ...' I glanced desperately around for inspiration, '... some decorating. I've been meaning to paint the hallway for ages, and a bit of space would give me the perfect opportunity to—'

'I'm sorry, Beth.' Aiden pressed his lips together in a sorrowful sort of way. His expression said 'I'm really sorry' but his eyes said 'I need to escape'. 'You're a lovely girl and you deserve someone much better than me. And you'll find him. I know you will.'

'But I don't want anyone else,' I said in a voice so high-pitched, only dolphins could hear it, all my playing it cool and grown-up pretence immediately deserting me. 'I just want you.'

'I'm sorry,' he said again, glancing away hurriedly as hot tears filled my eyes. 'I really am. It's probably best if I just go.'

I gripped the door frame as my boyfriend turned and swayed down the path towards the street.

Turn back, I begged silently. *If I ever meant anything to you, turn back and look at me. Tell me you just made a huge mistake.*

Aiden kept on walking.

'Wait!' I screamed as he crossed the road. 'Don't leave! There's something I need to tell you.'

I was out of the front door and sprinting down the

pathway, splashing through puddles, before I had time to think.

'Aiden, wait!' I shouted as I ran into the road. 'Aiden, I love—'

There was a squeal of brakes, and then *oomph*, I landed face first on cold, wet concrete.

I don't know who was more upset – me or the woman who'd narrowly avoided running me over.

'Oh my God,' she squealed, jumping out of her car and sprinting over to me. The front of her Audi had clipped my hip as I'd run into the street after Aiden. She'd been driving slowly, but the impact was enough to send me spinning towards the pavement. One of my treacherous heels caught in the gutter, and I fell through the air, arms waving wildly, then landed with a thud. I stared up at her, too shocked to move.

'Are you okay?' she asked as she leaned over me, a concerned look on her face. 'Can you talk?'

I tentatively moved my limbs. They didn't feel broken.

'I think so,' I groaned, as I shifted into a sitting position.

'You mustn't move!' the woman ordered, shoving my shoulder so I slumped back on to the pavement. 'You might have a broken back or something.'

'No ... really.' I peeled my face out of a puddle and sat back up. 'I'm fine. Honest—'

Doof! I was back in the puddle again, a firm hand on my shoulder.

'You really must stay where you are. The paramedics

will tell you if it's okay for you to move.' She patted the pockets of her jeans, then glanced back at her car. A young boy was hanging out of the back window, staring at us curiously. 'I'm going to ring for an ambulance. Stay here, I'll be back in a second.'

I watched as she crossed the street and ducked into her Audi. I didn't need an ambulance. I just needed … I sat up and gazed down the street. Where was Aiden? Surely he must have heard the commotion when the car hit me. Why hadn't he come back?

'Rupert!' I heard the woman call. 'Have you been going through Mummy's handbag again? How many times have I told you not to do that? Mummy needs her phone. Where is it?'

I shook my head. The only thing I needed to help heal my bruised hip, and ego, was a stiff drink. I reached for the railings, hauled myself up and limped back towards my house.

'I'll be fine,' I called to the woman in the car. She was leaning over the back seat, wrestling with her son. 'Really. Please don't worry.'

I shut the front door with a click before she had a chance to object, then hobbled into the living room, grabbed the phone from its stand on top of the TV and tapped out a number.

The phone rang and rang for ages, until finally, 'Hello?' said the voice on the other end of the line.

'Lizzie,' I croaked, then promptly dissolved into tears. 'Lizzie, is that you?'

'Beth!' my flatmate said, her voice strangely muffled. 'Are you okay?'

'No,' I croaked. 'I was just hit by a car.'

'What! Are you hurt?'

'No ... yeah ... Aiden left me.'

'Before or after he ran you over?'

'Lizzie!'

'What? I wouldn't put it past him. The man's been treating you like a doormat for ages. Running you over is just the next ste—'

'He didn't run me over.' I wiped the back of my hand across my face, and sniffed miserably. 'Where are you? Can you come back?'

'Of course, darling. I'll be there in a jiffy. Actually ...' There was a pause, a rustling noise and the sound of bedsprings squeaking. 'I'm a bit tied up. Literally. Nathan said he was off to get some strawberries and cream, but that was two hours ago. You didn't learn how to untie knots in the Brownies, did you?'

'You deserve someone much better than me,' Aiden had said.

Why did men always say that? Why did they break your heart and then try and convince you they were doing it for your own good? As the taxi sped towards the address Lizzie had given me on the phone, I stared out of the window at Brighton's bright lights glowing in the darkness, and tried to make sense of what had just happened. Why would Aiden dump me when things were going so well? Why would he ask for space when we only saw each other a couple of times a week? The more I thought about it, the more convinced I became that the reason he'd left me wasn't because things weren't working out between us, but because he'd met someone else.

It wasn't like he was the first bloke to cheat on me.

My first proper relationship had been with a guy called Dominic Holloway. I was eighteen, and met him in the Gloucester nightclub in Brighton one Saturday night. I'd spotted him the second I'd walked in. He wasn't particularly tall, but he had a cheeky grin, a T-shirt with a Manga design on the front, a pair of very cool skater trainers, and he sauntered around the club like he didn't have a care in the world. Everyone was staring at him, including me. He seemed to radiate cool. I was waiting at the bar, getting more and more frustrated as people pushed in front of me and got served first, when Dom appeared at my side, glanced across at me and said, 'Want a drink?' Simple as that. For a second I thought he'd asked me for a dare, and scanned the room behind him, looking for sniggering friends. But no, he really was interested in me. We chatted for a few hours in one of the dark booths in the corner of the club. Dom told me all about his obsession with skateboarding and BMX, and I listened, utterly enthralled. When he asked what I was into, I said, 'Films.' Dom nodded and said, 'Cool, but everyone's into films. What else are you into?' There wasn't anything else, so I didn't talk to him about how I thought *Casablanca* was one of the greatest films of all time, and how I couldn't watch the scene where everyone in the bar stands up to sing the Marseillaise without crying. And I didn't mention how the dance-like choreography of the fight scenes in *The Matrix* influenced loads of films that came after it, like *X-Men* and *Daredevil*.

Instead I said, 'Nothing really. Tell me more about you.'

As we sat in the dim gloom of the sticky-floored nightclub and I listened to Dom talk, only pausing to kiss me passionately, I thought he was the most fascinating man I'd ever met in my life.

Over the next two months, Dom shared his life with me – he took me to the skate park, let me borrow his spare BMX so we could go for bike rides along the seafront, and lent me a couple of books about famous graffiti artists. And then, the day before my nineteenth birthday he rang me up and told me that he'd met someone else. He never told me her name. 'It's nothing you did wrong, Beth,' he explained lamely. 'It's me. I'm just a bit crap.'

My second relationship – ouch. While I'd lusted after Liam Wilkinson and hero-worshipped Dom Holloway I really, really loved Josh Bagley. Josh was a barman-cum-performance-poet. We met in the library one Monday afternoon. I was twenty-two. I was wandering up and down the aisles, running my fingers across the spines of the books, trying to decide whether to choose a short-story collection by Annie Proulx (I'd just seen *Brokeback Mountain* and was blown away by it) or a Graham Greene novel (*The End of the Affair* is one of my all-time favourite doomed-love-affair films), when I noticed a tall, slim man with dreadlocks that reached to his waist standing at the end of the aisle, looking at me with a half-smile on his face.

'Have you thought about trying some poetry?' he said. 'I know a collection that will blow you away.'

To be honest, I thought the San Franciscan beat poetry he recommended wasn't all that amazing, but Josh had the warmest eyes and the gentlest smile I'd ever seen in my life, so when he invited me to see him perform some of his own poetry, I leapt at the chance. I went along to the Sanctuary Café in Hove, a little underground Mecca for unsigned musicians and performance poets, to see him. The venue was about the size of a postage stamp, but I managed to find a seat at a table with a middle-aged lesbian couple called Den and Bern. Josh spotted me the second he stepped up to the microphone, and as he performed his piece about modern warfare and traditional values – he rhymed 'fucking bombs' with 'granny's scones' – his eyes didn't leave mine.

After what had happened with Dom a few years earlier, I told myself that I *would not* let myself fall for Josh, with his kind face and his melodic voice, and I managed to keep control of my emotions for five whole dates. I didn't snatch up the phone the second it rang, I didn't text him non-stop, and I didn't ask him where I stood. Josh listened to me, and when I built up the courage to tell him about my dream of owning my own cinema, he didn't laugh. Gradually my defences started to drop. When he told me he thought I'd look beautiful in a tie-dye skirt, I went out and bought one, and when he commented that his favourite smell in the world was patchouli, I bought some joss sticks and had them burning the next time he came round to the house (Lizzie said they made the place smell like a hippy's armpit). I even plaited my hair and put little beads at the end. When Josh told me I looked like a cross between a brunette Bo Derek and a Rastafarian princess, I thought my heart might explode with happiness.

We'd been together for five months when I told him I loved him. We'd spent the evening lying on my bed, reading poetry to each other by candlelight, and had just had sex. Josh was lying on his back with his eyes closed. His hands were folded behind his head, his dreadlocks spread over my pillows like coils of rope. He looked so beautiful I couldn't stop myself from blurting out how I felt.

'I love you,' I said, running my hand over his naked chest. 'I can't quite believe that you're mine.'

Josh's eyes flew open.

'Oh,' he said.

Oh? I'd just confessed my love for him and all he could say was oh?

'Beth.' He turned his head to look at me. 'People don't possess each other. You do realise that, don't you?'

'Of course!' Relief flooded through me. Thank God. He was just worried that I'd said he was mine, not that I loved him. 'I don't own you and you don't own me. We just enjoy spending time together.'

'Good.' He smiled, then turned his head and looked up at the ceiling. 'For a second there I thought you were going to tell me to dump Crystal and Dog.'

Who the hell were Crystal and Dog? I waited for

Josh to put me out of my misery, but he didn't say a word.

'Who are Crystal and Dog?' I asked finally.

'Friends,' he said breezily. 'Like you.'

'What? Josh, we're not friends. We've been seeing each other for five months and we've been sleeping together for four.'

He shrugged. 'If you're going to get all semantic on me, Beth, I'll choose another word. How about … lovers.'

'Lovers!'

Josh was still for a second, then he inhaled slowly and deeply through his nose and exhaled through his mouth.

'Beth.' He sat up. 'I'm not a monogamous creature. I thought I'd made that clear from the start.'

I clutched the duvet to my chest, suddenly uncomfortable with being naked. 'When did you tell me that?'

'In my poem – "You cannot chain me to your punani".'

'I thought that was about underpaid factory workers in India!'

'No.' He frowned. 'It's about the way women use their sexuality to emasculate men. You said you found it touching.'

'That doesn't mean I understood it!'

'Ah.' Josh swung his legs over the bed and reached for his jeans. I watched, too stunned to speak, as he slipped into them and pulled his hemp shirt over his head.

'I'm sorry, Beth,' he said as he reached my bedroom

door. 'I don't think this is going to work out. You're lovely, so you really mustn't blame yourself. It's not you, it's—'

'Don't say it,' I warned. 'Don't you dare say it.'

'Me.'

The phrase was still buzzing through my head long after the front door clicked shut and I burst into tears. When I finally stopped crying, about fifteen million years later, I promised myself that I'd never tell another man that I loved him until he said it first. Never, ever, ever ...

I was still thinking about Josh when the taxi pulled up outside a house on Cromwell Street in Hove, and the driver looked at me expectantly.

'This is number fifty-five, love.'

I handed him some cash and made my way down the steps to Nathan's basement flat. The key was exactly where Lizzie had told me it was – under the doormat – and I nervously let myself in.

'Lizzie?' I called as I walked down the dark hallway. 'Liz, where are you?'

'In the bedroom, next to the kitchen,' called a voice from the other end of the flat. 'And, er, Beth, you might want to close your eyes when you come in!'

Chapter Six

Matt

Ten hours had passed since Alice had launched herself at me in her bathroom, then screamed something about making me pay as I made my escape. I'd be lying if I said I wasn't worried (particularly as she still had the spare key to my flat), but I had more urgent things to worry about. I walked into the office at 8.45 a.m. to find Sheila, my PA, looking concerned.

'Ballbreaker is waiting for you,' she mouthed, pointing towards my office. 'And she doesn't look happy.'

I groaned. Ballbreaker, or, to give her her proper name, Isabel Wallbaker, is the national manager for Apollo Corporation. Otherwise known as my boss.

'Thanks, Sheila. You couldn't grab me a strong coffee, could you? I'm going to need it.'

'No problem. Good luck,' she added as I made my way into my office.

Isabel was sitting behind my desk, her back to me as she casually rifled through some of my unfiled paperwork.

'Morning boss,' I said, forcing a smile and taking the seat opposite her. 'What do I owe the pleasure?'

'The Picturebox,' she said, swivelling round, her blood-red nails hitting my desk like ten bloody claws. 'What's the progress on the acquisition?'

'I spoke to Mrs Blackstock on the phone, and she's considering the offer.'

'Considering?' She raised an overplucked eyebrow.

I nodded uncomfortably. 'That's what she said.'

'And you don't think you should be putting the pressure on so she does a little more than just consider it?'

I didn't, no. Putting pressure on slimy businessmen or money-grasping industrial-estate owners was one thing, but Mrs Blackstock was a pensioner. She was the same age as my grandad, for God's sake! The Picturebox was knackered, admittedly, and needed a full refurb to get rid of the hideous fading wallpaper and the weird damp charity-shop smell that hit you when you walked through the door, but I wasn't about to put the hard sell on its little old lady owner. Even if I did think she was mad not to snap up the frankly ludicrous sum we were offering.

'I don't think pressure would help in this situation,' I said calmly. 'Mrs Blackstock is elderly and I don't think she'd respond well to the hard sell.'

'Is that so?' Isabel narrowed her eyes and tapped her fingernails slowly and rhythmically on my desk. It sounded like a death march. 'And your bonus, Matt? How would you *respond* if that wasn't forthcoming?'

'Sorry?'

'You do realise that your bonus is dependent not only on the annual sales figures for the existing cinemas, but also on you meeting targets set by head office?'

I nodded.

'And this year's target is the acquisition of the Picturebox. No Picturebox, no bonus. You're a salesman, Matt, not a campaigner for Help the Aged. Seal the deal today, or you get nothing.'

I opened my mouth to reply, but my throat tightened and the words dried up on my tongue. She'd got me. Either I turned the screws on Mrs Blackstock to get her to sign, or my grandad would lose his home. Nice.

Isabel smiled tightly at me. 'I look forward to hearing from you later.'

Edna Blackstock's house was bigger than I'd imagined – an enormous five- or six-bedroom Victorian affair in Hove with a sprawling garden and a private driveway. I half expected to be met at the door by a butler or a maid; instead, I was greeted by a tiny grey-haired woman in a flowery apron. Her back was so curved she was almost bent double.

She peered up at me, her pale blue eyes watery beneath her enormous bifocal glasses. 'Ah, you must be the nice gentleman from the cinema chain. Come in, come in.

'Do excuse the mess,' she added as she led me into the kitchen and swiped at a wooden chair with a tea towel. 'I've been making fruit cake. Please, sit down.'

I eyed the chair – it looked as ancient as Mrs Blackstock herself – and perched nervously on the edge.

'Okay,' I said, hauling my briefcase on to my lap and clicking it open. 'As I mentioned on the phone the other day, we're prepared to offer you a substantial sum for—'

'Cup of tea? Cake?' My host slid a loaded plate across the table towards me. My stomach rumbled angrily as the smell of warm, rich cake filled my nostrils. God, it looked good – moist, light and jammed with sultanas, nuts and cherries. I pushed the plate away and shook my head. Accepting anything from her would be unprofessional.

'No thank you.' I flicked through a pile of papers and pulled out the contract. The sooner I got this over and done with, the sooner I could leave. 'So, about the contract …'

'Are you sure you won't have a slice?' Mrs Blackstock peered at me from across the table. There was a smudge of flour on the end of her nose. 'I don't really have anyone to bake for these days, and I do hate waste.'

'Fine,' I said, reaching for the plate. If eating cake would help seal the deal, then screw professionalism. I just wanted to grab her signature and get out of there. 'I'll just have a little bit.'

I picked up the slice and took a bite. Brandy-soaked fruit, warm cinnamon and crunchy walnuts tickled my taste buds. It was delicious.

'The cinema has been in my family for a long time,' Mrs Blackstock said as I continued to chew. 'When Bert and I, that's my late husband, inherited it, we had so many plans for it. We'd run it together and then pass it on to our children. Well, *child* – I so wanted a son and a daughter, but we only had Charles. Did I mention my son to you on the phone?'

I shook my head, my mouth still full of cake.

'Charles lives up in Edinburgh. He's a chef – must have inherited his love of food from me – and he has no interest in films. He says his life has quite enough drama as it is without watching someone else's. And he's awfully busy. Chefs work incredibly long hours, you know. Anyway,' she gestured for me to help myself to another slice, but I shook my head, 'he isn't interested in taking on the cinema. He thinks I should just sell it and be done with it.'

I swallowed down the last of my mouthful. 'I see.'

'Even my accountant has started making noises about me selling up, so what can I do? It would break my heart to lose the darling place, but if your company is as passionate about films as you tell me, I'm happy to pass it on to someone who'll take good care of it and restore it to its former glory. You will take good care of it, won't you, Mr Jones?'

I eyed the cake and the huge slice Mrs Blackstock had carved out of it. Maybe if I grabbed it and stuffed it into my mouth, I wouldn't have to answer.

'Of course,' I lied, forcing myself to make eye contact with her.

'Excellent.' She smiled. 'And the staff?'

I frowned. 'What about them?'

'You'll take care of them too?'

'Well,' I coughed into my hand, 'there will be a restructure, obviously.'

Mrs Blackstock looked horrified. 'The staff will lose their jobs?'

'Well … um … there will be, as I mentioned, some

unavoidable restructuring and, due to a bit of a reshuffle at some of our other Brighton branches, the majority of the staff will be recruited internally. However, there will be one position – that of manager – that Picturebox staff who've worked for you for more than two years will be able to apply for. We'll be holding an interview weekend in Wales in December.'

'December?' She looked surprised. 'So soon?'

I nodded. 'If the Picturebox relaunch is going to take place in the new year, we need everything to happen sharpish. Including getting the contract signed.'

'Just one job.' Mrs Blackstock pressed her floury hands to her cheeks. 'That is unfortunate.'

'Unavoidable, I'm afraid,' I said, pushing the contract across the table towards her. 'In this current economic climate, redundancies are largely unavoidable.'

Why did I keep saying the word 'unavoidable'? It was like I'd developed a form of corporate Tourette's.

Mrs Blackstock prodded the contract nervously with a finger, like it was a flour-covered bomb.

'So,' I handed her a biro, 'if I could just get your autograph on pages—'

'One second, dear.' She placed a wrinkled hand over mine. 'I'd like to break the news to my staff before I make it all official. It's going to come as a terrible shock.'

Not as much of a shock as you imagine, I thought, remembering my encounter with Beth Prince the day before.

'As I mentioned earlier,' I said, carefully releasing my hand from her surprisingly strong grip, Ballbreaker's warning about my bonus still ringing in my ears, 'time is of the essence. We can only guarantee the purchase price for a limited time, so it's of the utmost importance that you sign to—'

'Mr Jones.' Mrs Blackstock fixed me with a surprisingly steely look. 'I may look like a doddery old lady, but the Picturebox has been in my family for decades, and I've fought – and won – plenty of battles over the way it's run. I'm not about to roll over now I'm selling it, and I won't let a young whippersnapper like you strong-arm me into doing something before I'm ready.'

'I'm so sorry,' I said, aghast. 'I really didn't mean to …'

She stood up and straightened her apron, her expression still steely. 'I'll be in touch, Mr Jones.'

I looked at the contract, still unsigned, in the middle of the table. Ballbreaker would kill me if I walked out without …

'Here.' Mrs Blackstock had rounded the table and was pressing a Tupperware box full of fruit cake into my hands. Her face had softened and her blue eyes were shining again. 'Take this. I insist. If you don't want it, give it to someone you love.'

I smiled for the first time in twenty minutes. I knew exactly who I'd give it to.

'Well?' Ballbreaker barked down my mobile. I'd only just set foot outside Mrs Blackstock's house and she was already on my case. 'Did she sign it?'

I clutched my empty briefcase a little bit tighter.

The unsigned contract was still on Mrs Blackstock's floury kitchen table. 'Not yet.'

A whistling sound travelled down the phone line, possibly steam coming out of Ballbreaker's ears. 'What?'

'She wanted to tell the staff first.'

'She wanted to WHAT? Why couldn't she tell the bloody staff AFTER she'd signed the contract? Is she totally cuckoo or what?'

'Actually, she's really nice. I thought she—'

'I don't care if she's Mother Bloody Theresa. I want that contract, Matt.'

'I'll get it.'

'When?'

'After she's told the staff.'

'And when will that be?'

'Soon?' I ventured.

'Find out!' Ballbreaker barked. 'And quickly.'

'Okay, okay. I will. Honestly. I've got it all under control.'

'It doesn't sound like it.' My boss sighed. There was no point her going into full bollocking mode yet – there was still over a month until the recruitment weekend in Wales, and the builders were on standby to start the refurb on 27 December. 'So go on,' she said wearily. 'Did Blackstock mention the refurbishments?'

'No, but she did ask for my word that we wouldn't mess around with the fixtures and fittings.'

'And what did you say?'

'That she had ...' I cleared my throat, 'nothing to worry about.'

Ballbreaker laughed. It was a strange sound – half

seagull squawk, half hyena cackle. 'Excellent! I'm proud of you.'

At least one of us was.

'Right.' Her voice cut through my thoughts like a power saw through butter. 'Get that little baby signed and in the post as soon as possible. Is the recruitment weekend in Wales all arranged?'

'About that …' I started.

Ballbreaker sighed. 'What?'

'Do we really have to go all the way to Wales just to recruit a manager? We're really busy, and a whole weekend of leadership tasks is a bit extreme, isn't it? Can't we just, I dunno, hold the interviews in my office or something?'

'A bit extreme? A bit extreme!' Ballbreaker snorted as though I'd just told the funniest joke in the world. 'Do you know how much money Apollo makes each year, Matt?'

'I've got the south-east figures back in the office if that's what you're—'

'Screw the south-east, Matt. I'm on about world-wide.'

'I dunno. Maybe—'

'Billions, Matt! Billions. And do you know why? Because every branch, every tiny little arse-end-of-nowhere cinema follows, to the letter, the protocol established by head office in Washington. Protocol that has made Apollo world leader in the entertainment field. *World* leader.'

'Yeah but—'

'Tell you what, Matt.' In a millisecond, Ballbreaker's

tone had switched from amused to pissed off. 'If you're such a bloody know-it-all, how about you ring up the CEO in Washington to tell him that you think his recruitment policy is a bunch of shit? I can look up his number if you'd like?'

I took a deep breath. I was *not* going to lose my cool. 'You don't need to do that, Isabel, it's fine.'

'What's fine, Matthew?'

'The recruitment weekend in Wales,' I said steadily. 'It's not a problem.'

'Good. Get it sorted,' she barked, then cut me off.

I shook my head, shoved my phone deep into my pocket and headed towards Lewes Road. There was someone I needed to see.

Chapter Seven

Beth

Hearing about your best friend's sex life is one thing. Seeing it is another. I'd spent over an hour updating the Picturebox website, but I couldn't get the image of Lizzie trussed up like a Christmas turkey out of my head. It was burned on the back of my retinas. Lizzie, on the other hand, wasn't the slightest bit bothered that I'd seen her naked. She was just relieved to be set free. Relieved, and then absolutely furious at Nathan.

'I'm going to kill him,' she'd fumed as she wriggled back into her little black dress. 'So not funny. I could have died of hypothermia.'

I touched the radiator. 'I doubt it, Liz. The heating's on. And he did leave your mobile on the pillow so you could reach it.'

'With what?' She pulled on her heels. 'Have you got any idea how hard it is to make a phone call with your nose?'

I laughed.

'Yeah, yeah, you can laugh.' She cracked a smile and stood up. 'Ah, sod him.' She looped her arm through mine. 'Let's go home and get pissed. Tell Auntie Lizzie what happened with Aiden.'

And I did. More than once. The more wine I drank, the more upset I became about what had happened. So then I had to have some more wine, and then I got even more upset. It was the vicious circle of the newly dumped, and it only ended when my best friend convinced me it was time to go to bed.

'It'll be okay, Beth,' she said as she tucked me up and stroked my hair back from my face. 'I promise you. We'll talk more tomorrow, okay?'

I'd passed out almost immediately, then woke up what felt like five minutes later when my alarm went off. My head was throbbing and my eyes had turned into a couple of hard-boiled eggs. I tried putting on extra make-up, but it just made them look like hard-boiled eggs smeared with eyeliner.

I dragged myself into work, hoping it would help distract me from what had happened the night before, but it was one of the quietest mornings I could remember. We had five customers in to see *L'Appartement* at 11 a.m., and a dozen mothers with accompanying grizzling babies for the 'Sob Showing' (a session just for mums and babies so no one could object to the screaming and crying). Still, the fewer people that saw my puffy face, the better.

I was just checking my reflection in my pocket mirror for the hundredth time when the door to the cinema swung open. I didn't recognise who it was at first, it had been so long since I'd seen her, but as she shuffled her way towards the counter, her back bent double, her oversized tweed coat hanging off her narrow shoulders and her curly white hair topped with a green felt hat, I soon remembered.

'Mrs Blackstock,' I gabbled, hastily shoving my make-up bag off the table. 'How nice to see you.'

'Hello, Beth.' My boss pulled her coat tightly around her and rubbed her arms vigorously. There were wet marks on her shoulders and the top of her hat. 'Absolutely pouring down outside. It feels like it's never going to stop raining.'

'Terrible, isn't it?' I shrugged in agreement. 'Are you here for yesterday's takings? They're in the safe in the back. I could get them if you like.' I stood up so quickly I hit my head on the shelf above me. A dozen programmes tumbled to the floor.

Mrs Blackstock held up a thin, wrinkled hand and waggled it in my direction. 'Sit down, please, Beth. There's something I'd like to discuss with you.'

'Discuss?' I slumped back into my seat and gripped hold of the counter. 'Is this about the man who came in the other day? Matt something? I didn't mean to be rude to him. Honestly. I thought he was a student after a job. If I'd known he was from Apollo, I'd have made him a coffee and—'

'No, no.' My boss shook her head. 'It's not that.'

She gazed in wonder at the pumpkin sculpture I'd created in the middle of the foyer, then wandered over to the wall of legends and ran a finger across a framed photo of James Dean. She frowned and flicked a huge pile of dust to the floor. We hadn't been able to afford cleaners for months. The staff did their best to keep

73

the cinema clean, but there was only so much we could do.

'Beth.' She turned back to me, her expression grim. 'The Picturebox hasn't been performing as well as expected over the last year, and—'

'I know,' I said desperately. 'But we can turn things round again. I've had some really good ideas. Sensible ones. I've kept them all in a file ...' I reached down for my bag. 'I could show them to you now if you like.'

Mrs Blackstock shook her head. 'No thank you, dear.'

'But they'd work. I know they would. We could run a loyalty scheme, like they do in the supermarkets. Watch five films and see the sixth free.'

'Model our cinema on the supermarkets?' She looked aghast. 'Oh no, dear. No, that wouldn't do at all.'

'But it's been proven to establish customer loyalty and increase sales in line with ...' I tailed off. She really didn't look convinced. 'Okay, not loyalty cards. So how about ...' I flicked through my folder, 'themed nights based around popular culture? We could show the Eurovision Song Contest. It's hugely popular in Brighton, and if we gave people the opportunity to watch it here, they could get dressed up and enjoy it with their friends and other fans. I just know it would generate loads of—'

'A song competition for Europeans? Sounds dreadful. Imagine what the Germans would come up with!'

'It's not dreadful. It's a cult programme that has been around since ... Never mind ...' I turned the pages desperately. 'How about this. We do late-night reduced-rate viewings for students. Maybe on a Monday or Tuesday night, when it's not very busy and—'

'No.' Mrs Blackstock shook her head once more. 'I'm sorry, Beth, but all these ideas are far too modern for the Picturebox.'

'They're not! Honestly, they'd fit right in. And they'd work, I know they would. Could I just tell you my idea for a 1940s/50s themed weekend of romantic films and—'

'I'm sorry, Beth.' My boss fixed me with a steely look. 'I am selling the cinema. I've given it lots of thought, and I've made my decision.'

'Not to Apollo!' I said, utterly aghast. 'You can't do that! They'll rip everything out and turn it into a soulless hole.'

'Oh Beth.' She shook her head like I was a toddler throwing a tantrum. 'I do think you're overreacting slightly. Of course they're not going to rip everything out. Matthew Jones himself promised me that they'll respect the Picturebox's history.'

'And you believe that? They're lying to you, Mrs B! They don't care about our history, they only care about making money.'

'I'm sorry, Beth, but I've got no choice. My son doesn't want the responsibility and my accountant tells me the Picturebox is haemorrhaging money. My hands are tied, I'm afraid.'

'But …' The words tailed away. Mrs Blackstock looked so crushed, I had to hold my breath to stop myself from crying. She'd totally given up. On the cinema. On our little team. On me.

In twenty-four hours I'd lost my boyfriend, narrowly escaped being run over, and now I was about to lose my job. What next? Would I lose my home too? Lizzie's dad had told her he didn't want any 'dole scum' living with her.

'That's it?' I said. 'There's nothing we can do? You're selling the cinema and we're all out of a job?'

Mrs Blackstock took a step towards the counter and placed a wizened hand over mine. 'There is still hope, Beth. For one person at least. Mr Jones mentioned that a management position will be made available. It's open to Apollo employees and anyone who has worked for the Picturebox for at least two years.'

'I'll do it!' I jumped up excitedly and hit my head on the shelf. Again. 'I've worked here for six years,' I said as I scrabbled around on my knees and picked up the programmes that had fallen to the floor. 'Could you tell him I'd like the job?'

'I'm afraid I don't have any say in the matter,' she shrugged sympathetically, 'but I'm sure Mr Jones will welcome any questions you might have. I expect he'll be in touch soon. If you could circulate the news to the other staff, that would be wonderful.'

She shuffled off across the foyer. When she reached the front door, she turned back and looked at me steadily.

'Thank you, Beth,' she said, so softly I could barely make out the words, 'for everything you've done.'

I couldn't tell if it was her age, or the way the light was streaming through the glass front door, but I could have sworn there were tears in her eyes.

The rest of my day went completely to pot. I short-changed a customer, knocked a full cup of coffee all over my computer keyboard and offered a man who came in with his five-year-old son the latest horror flick when he'd requested a family-friendly film. Then, to top it all, Carl walked into the cinema, took off his coat and sauntered up to the booth.

'Hi, Beth,' he said, resting his elbows on the counter. 'I was just wondering – did you ever run away from home when you were a kid?'

'No,' I replied, surprised he wasn't greeting me with an insult like he normally did. 'Why?'

'Didn't your parents ever ask you to?'

'Here.' I rolled my eyes and passed him a piece of paper. I'd typed up everything Mrs Blackstock had told me earlier and written a letter to all the staff. 'You might want to read this.'

Carl scanned the page, then shoved it back across the counter. 'And? This place is knackered. It needs new life blowing into it.'

I stared at him in horror. I couldn't believe that after three years, he didn't have the slightest bit of loyalty to the gorgeous old cinema where we both worked.

'What?' He raised an eyebrow. 'Old Blackstock couldn't organise a game of tag in a playground. It's her own fault the Picturebox has gone to the dogs.'

'But you're going to lose your job!'

'Am I?' He prodded the piece of paper with his index finger. 'Says right here there's a job with my name on it.'

'A manager's job.'

'Ah!' Carl laughed. 'I get it. You think you've got it in the bag just because you've worked here longer than the rest of us. I've been shagging since I was fourteen, doesn't make me a porn star.'

'It's not about how long I've worked here. It's about the experience I've …' I shook my head. There was no point arguing with him. He'd just wind me up.

'Anyway,' I stood up and reached for my coat, 'I'm off. I'm meeting Lizzie in town.'

'Not Aiden?'

I sighed heavily. If it wasn't bad enough that I had to work with the little slime bag, he knew my boyfriend – ex-boyfriend – too. Back in October, Carl had joined a wine-tasting society in Hove, the very same one Aiden was a member of. The next day he'd bounded into work with the smuggest grin I'd ever seen. I couldn't shut him up. He went on and on about his new best friend, making out that Aiden had told him loads of secrets about me.

'What?' Carl's eyes flicked over my face as he tried to read my expression. 'Things not working out with lover man?'

My expression must have changed, because he suddenly looked jubilant.

'Oooh! They're not, are they?' He peered at me. 'He didn't dump you, did he, Pimp?'

'None of your business!' I turned away sharply and stalked out of the booth.

'Do *not* cry in front of Carl,' I muttered under my

breath as I hurried across the foyer. 'Do not, do not, do …'

'Knew he'd see sense eventually,' he called after me. 'This is you we're talking about, Pimp. I'd say you were destined to die alone, surrounded by cats, though even they won't love you!'

'So?' Lizzie said as I walked up to the counter of Wai Kika Moo Kau, the busy café in the heart of the North Laines where she occasionally worked. 'Have you heard from Aiden?'

'No, not for …' I started, then instantly burst into tears. I swiped at my eyes with the back of my hand. Damn it! I'd held it together all the way here from the Picturebox as well.

'Oh sweetheart.' Lizzie pulled at the strings of her white apron, yanked it off and, ignoring the disapproving glance from her co-worker, rounded the counter to hug me.

'Let's get you something to drink,' she said as she angled me towards an empty table at the back of the café. 'Unfortunately we don't do wine. Cappuccino do?'

I nodded miserably.

'Two cappuccinos, please, Ben,' she shouted across the café. 'Extra chocolate sprinkles!'

Her colleague shot her an exasperated look, then turned back to the customer he'd been serving.

Lizzie shuffled her chair closer to mine and put her hand on my arm. 'What is it, hon?'

'I just want him back,' I said miserably. 'It's been less

than twenty-four hours since I last saw him, and I miss him so much.'

'Really?' She looked incredulous. 'Surely you could just open the local newspaper if you wanted another dose of his pretentious drivel.'

I laughed, then immediately felt disloyal. Aiden wasn't pretentious. He was just a bit opinionated sometimes.

I dabbed my damp cheeks with a napkin. 'What should I do, Liz?'

'Honestly?' She squeezed my hand. 'Forget him.'

'But I don't want to.'

'I thought you might say that.' She beamed at her colleague as he placed two cappuccinos on the table in front of us. 'Thanks, gorgeous! Owe you one.'

Ben rolled his eyes, then stalked back to the counter. It seemed like she owed him more than that.

'Lizzie …' I sat up straighter and smoothed down my jumper. 'What's wrong with me?'

'Nothing!' She looked at me like I was mad. 'You're perfect just the way you are.'

'Aiden obviously didn't think so.'

'That's because he's a tosser and his breath smells of pickled onions.'

'Lizzie!'

'Well he is, and it does.' She reached for her cappuccino, took a sip, then wiped her mouth with the back of her hand. 'You deserve loads better than him.'

I sighed. 'That's pretty much what he said.'

'Then maybe he isn't quite as much of a wank stain as I thought. Anyway, you're well rid of him.'

'But I don't want to be rid of him. I want him back! Please, Lizzie. Help me.'

She frowned. 'How exactly?'

'Tell me honestly – what can I do to look … I dunno … hotter? I know you think I look fine as I am, but I need you to be brutal. Imagine you're some makeover person from the TV whose job it is to turn me into a total fox. What would you do?'

My best friend shuffled her chair away from me as though to get a better view, and tipped her head to the left. She frowned, then tipped it to the right. It felt hideous being scrutinised so obviously, but I didn't say a word. Whatever she said would be worth it – as long as it helped me get Aiden back.

'Well …' she said finally, wrinkling her nose. 'I guess you are a bit pale.'

'Okay.' I nodded. 'So I need some fake tan, then.'

'Yup. And …' She cast her eyes over my hair. 'Mousy is fine, it's almost anti-cool retro … or something … but I think you'd look better, more va-va-voom, if you got a few highlights or something. And learned how to blow-dry it properly. Your bob does look a bit helmet-like sometimes.'

'Lizzie!'

'Sorry! Sorry!' She pulled a face. 'Too much?'

'No, no, carry on,' I said, the tiniest bit terrified about what she'd come out with next.

'This,' she said, plucking at my black jumper like it was infected. 'I know it's your favourite top, but honestly, Beth, it looks like it's a hand-me-down from your Great-Auntie Marge. Your morbidly obese Great-Auntie Marge. It's huge!'

'It's not, it's baggy,' I objected, pulling the sleeves down over my hands. 'And it's comfortable.'

'You could be seven months pregnant under that thing! You've got a great figure, Beth. Not that anyone would know.'

'Really?' Wow, okay, Lizzie thought I had a good figure. Maybe this makeover thing wasn't quite so hideous after all. 'So what should I wear?'

'Something that shows your shape off. Obviously. Oh yeah, and you need to buy some decent heels instead of those vile …' She paused and clocked my expression as I stared at my feet, 'Those sensible boots you insist on wearing with everything.'

'The boots have to go too?'

'I'm afraid so. Look, Beth,' she pushed my cappuccino across the table towards me, 'you don't have to do this, you know. It's not right – changing the way you look for Aiden.'

'I'm not! I'm doing it for … me,' I finished lamely.

'Really?'

'Well … yes and no.' I took a sip of my drink. It was cold. 'If Aiden hadn't dumped me, I probably wouldn't have decided to change my image, but it can't hurt, can it? I've been wearing the same sort of clothes – jumper, jeans, boots – since school, and I can't remember the last time I had a different hairstyle. Maybe this is just the kick I need to be a new me.'

Lizzie narrowed her eyes. 'I know who I'd rather kick. Tosser!'

'Honestly!' I looked her in the eye. 'I really want to do this, Liz. Why don't we go clothes shopping together? I can get some new outfits and you can give me your … opinion. Then we can pop into Boots and get some fake tan and hair dye and stuff.'

'Hmmm …' From the expression on her face, I could tell Lizzie still wasn't convinced. 'Don't you think it's a bit soon? You've only been split up for a day.'

'Please,' I begged. 'I really need your help.'

She looked at me for the longest time.

'Okay,' she said finally, 'but only if you abide by the two-week rule first. '

'Fine. I agree!' I paused. 'What's the two-week rule?'

'I'll tell you but you're not going to like it, Beth.' She squeezed my hand. 'Not one little bit.'

Chapter Eight

Matt

There's only one person in this world who, no matter what he says or does, helps me get my life in perspective. He's old, he's wise, he's got a face like a walnut and he likes a nice cup of cocoa with a shot of brandy in it before he goes to bed.

'Hi, Grandad,' I said, as the door to number 75 Mafeking Road creaked open and a pair of familiar eyes peered out at me through the crack.

'Matt!' Grandad's face lit up like the pier on a dark night. 'If it isn't my least favourite grandson.'

That's Grandad's favourite line. He uses it every time he sees me, and it always makes him laugh. Not least because I'm his *only* grandson.

I waited on the doorstep, a grin on my face, for his second line.

'I thought you'd forgotten all about me,' he said on cue.

'Fat chance.' That was my line.

I'd visited Grandad at least once a week for as long as I could remember. In fact I'd been his only visitor since Gran died three years ago. My mum, whose dad he is, disappeared from both our lives when I was nine years old. She fell in love with the guy who ran the yoga class in town, and went to a retreat in Spain with him and some of the other women in the group. All the other women came back; Mum didn't.

For a couple of weeks Dad kept up the pretence that Mum was still on holiday, but eventually he got sick of me asking when she'd be back, and sat me down and explained that, while she didn't love him any more, she still loved me.

'Then why did she leave me?' I asked.

He didn't know how to answer that.

After a few months Mum tried to convince Dad to send me over to join her. He wasn't keen, and when he discovered that El Santuario de Santa was more of a cult than a yoga retreat, he went to court to get custody of me. And won. At first, Mum came back to the UK to see me a couple of times a year, but gradually her phone calls, letters and birthday presents tailed off. The last time I saw her was when I turned eighteen.

'You're a man now,' she'd said over dinner at Pinocchio's restaurant in Brighton, 'and you can decide for yourself where you want to live. You're always welcome to come and stay with me and Carlos.'

I never took her up on the offer. It probably sounds a bit weird, or cold, but she's not really Mum to me any more; just a woman who looks a bit like me.

Dad remarried a few years after they got divorced, to a lovely but vacant South African girl called Estelle from the admin office at his work. He's still with her. After I left school and got my own place, they moved to Cape Town, and if Dad's monthly phone calls are anything to go by, he's revelling in sunny, semi-retired bliss. He enquires about Grandad from time to time, but, like Mum, he's pretty much forgotten about him.

'So are you going to come in, or are you just going to stand there looking gormless?' Grandad said, opening the door wide.

'Oh go on then.' I handed him the Tupperware container that Mrs Blackstock had given me and followed him into the kitchen, where a teapot in a knitted cosy that was older than I was took pride of place in the centre of the table.

'What's this?' Grandad asked, tipping his head towards the Tupperware box as he poured thick, overbrewed tea into a chipped china cup and pushed it across the table towards me.

I took a sip. 'Fruit cake, made by a customer of mine. Hey,' I grinned at him, 'she's about the same age as you *and* she's single. Want me to set you up?'

'A woman who can cook?' He snapped off the lid, sniffed the cake and nodded approvingly. 'I'd marry her tomorrow!'

'She'll be rich soon, too,' I said as he lifted out a generous slice. 'With any luck. Anyway, how have you been?'

He looked at me. 'A bit chilly, but not bad. It could be worse. I could be dead.'

I grinned as he threw his head back, his gummy jaws slapping together as he laughed.

'And how's Paul? Done anything interesting lately?'

Grandad is obsessed with daytime TV, especially

Paul O'Grady. He once told me, 'I don't care if he dances on the other side of the ballroom. If yer funny, yer funny, plain as.'

'Paul?' he said, shoving the cake into his mouth and chewing enthusiastically. 'He's only gone and started bringing his other dog in. She's nice enough, but no match for Buster.' He crossed himself. 'Bless his soul. A man needs a proper dog, not something small enough to put in a handbag.'

'I could get you a dog if you want. Just say the word. We could go to the rescue place in Shoreham, or I could buy you one.'

'Oh no.' He shook his head vigorously. 'You don't want to be doing that. Them dogs at the home need a nice family to look after them, not an old git like me.'

Grandad's a proud man. He worked for the electricity board for over fifty years and only had two weeks off the entire time (and that was when he fell off a ladder when he was cleaning the windows at home and broke his arm). He and Gran were always careful with money, but lost all their savings when their pension fund went under in the early eighties. I didn't realise quite how skint he was until two years ago, when I found a letter from Mr Harris, his landlord, stuffed down the side of the faded armchair in his living room. He'd bought the house from the previous landlord the year before and put the rent up significantly but Grandad had continued to pay the normal amount. As a result there was a shortfall of nearly three grand and he was threatening to evict him if he didn't pay up. I tried talking to Grandad about contacting the Citizens

Advice Bureau to get him some housing benefit or something, but he wouldn't have it.

'I don't take charity from no one,' he'd said. 'I worked all me life and I'm not about to start sponging off the government now. I get me state pension like I'm entitled to, but that's all I'm taking, thank you very much. And if that's not good enough for Mr Harris he can turf me out himself.'

He wouldn't budge, so I did the only thing I could do – I stole the letter and contacted Mr Harris. He didn't care who paid the rent just so long as he got it, so I set up a direct debit to cover the difference and that was that. No more danger of Grandad losing his house and having to go into a home.

'Being put in a home is a fate worse than marriage,' he used to joke to me, but I could see the fear in his eyes.

It's not been easy paying nearly two lots of rent every month. In fact I *have* to get my bonus each year or we'd both be screwed, but what can I do? He's my grandad and I'm all he's got. Actually, he's all I've got too.

'Cat got your tongue?' Grandad asked as I stared into space. 'That was your cue to tell me I'm not an old git.'

'Sorry, sorry. You're not—'

'Bugger that.' He smiled a gummy smile. 'How are you, lad? How's that blondie you were courting, the one that could cause a row in an empty room?'

I shook my head. 'You don't want to know.'

'Yes I do.' Grandad patted my hand with his heavy

paw. '*EastEnders* ain't nearly as entertaining as your life.'

I felt almost upbeat as I strolled home an hour later. After Grandad had asked about Alice, we'd wandered into his living room and I'd settled myself into what had been Gran's armchair and spilled my guts. At first he had listened attentively, nodding his head in all the right places, but by the time I'd got to Alice's sudden appearance in the pub, he was snoring gently. It didn't matter, him nodding off; it had been good to get it all off my chest. Well, nearly all of it. I hadn't told him the truth about Mrs Blackstock and the unsigned Picturebox contract. If I didn't get it sorted, and quickly, Ballbreaker would kick my arse – hard. And the less I thought about that, the better.

Chapter Nine

Beth

Hello, you've reached Beth Prince's voicemail. Please leave a message – and your name and number if I don't know who you are – after the beep.

Beeeeeeeeep!

I hung up the work phone, then reached for my mobile and deleted the missed call on the screen. It was working, then. No doubt about that.

I put my elbows on the counter, propped my chin on my hands and sighed. It was 15 November – more than two weeks since Aiden had dumped me and I'd heard NOTHING from him.

Absolutely nothing! Not a text, call or email. It was like he'd dropped off the face of the planet.

The night he'd dumped me, Lizzie had confiscated my phone, claiming I was driving her mad by snatching it up and checking it whenever the sofa creaked or the pipes clanged. When she gave it back to me the next morning, I dived on it, utterly convinced there'd be a text waiting from Aiden. I even knew what it would say – that he'd sobered up and realised what a terrible mistake he'd made by dumping me. But no, no text.

And nothing since. I'd been tempted to call or SMS him a million times, but Lizzie had absolutely forbidden me.

'Men respond to distance, not words,' she'd told me in Wai Kika Moo Kau as she'd whipped my phone out of my hands again and dropped it down the front of her T-shirt. 'If you're to have a hope in hell of getting him back, you need to give him time to realise he's made a mistake. Sending him multiple texts telling him how much you miss him will scare him off. What you need to do is maintain an air of mystery. Let's face it, you've been a bit of an open book so far.'

I had to admit that running into the road screaming his name after he'd dumped me on my own doorstep wasn't the most enigmatic thing I'd ever done.

'So,' she'd continued, 'what we need is to implement the two-week rule which means you do absolutely nothing—'

'Nothing?'

'Yes, *nothing*, for two weeks. You are forbidden from contacting him. No, don't look at me like that – it's for your own good. At first he'll be relieved that you're not bombarding him with texts and calls begging him to give you another chance, and then, as more time passes, he'll start to get curious. He'll wonder what you're up to and why you haven't been in touch. You're going to be Little Miss Aloof, Beth. No one will ever have played post-dumping as cool as you, and that'll intrigue him.'

'Really?' I was sceptical.

'Really. I read about it. Anyway, when the two weeks

are up, I'll give you the makeover you keep badgering me about, and then we'll accidentally arrange for you to bump into Aiden and blow his stinky smelly socks off!'

'Lizzie!'

'Sorry, couldn't help it. But you need to trust me on this, Beth. If anything's going to get him back, this is it.'

I hoped so. I really, really did. It had killed me not to text or call Aiden for two weeks.

I turned back to my computer and clicked on the spreadsheet I'd been working on. A split second later the front door opened and Matt Jones walked in. I hadn't seen him for about a fortnight either.

Ha! He looks knackered, I thought as he rubbed a hand over his face and strolled across the foyer towards my desk. Good. I hope he's having sleepless nights. It's the least he deserves for buying up lovely cinemas, then ripping them apart.

'Hi, Beth.' He leaned heavily on the counter and gazed at me through the divide.

'Matt.'

He ran a hand through his hair and glanced at the spreadsheet on the monitor. 'How's business?'

'Good,' I said, Alt-Tabbing away so he couldn't see the figures I'd entered. Hmmm. Was 'good' the right answer? Maybe if I admitted business was shit and custom was down, he'd withdraw his offer to buy the business and we'd all get to keep our jobs.

'Actually, it's not great,' I said. 'I think people might be moving away from this area to other bits of Brighton. It's been really quiet.'

'Really?' He glanced back at the shop window as an enormous crowd of people shuffled down the street and a group of students walked into the cinema and studied the poster by the door. 'Looks busy to me.'

'Appearances can be deceptive.'

'Uh-huh.' He looked back at me and grinned. His eyes twinkled as he smiled, and I couldn't help but notice how gorgeous they were. Like Josh Hartnett or Johnny Depp or ... I looked back at the monitor and pressed a button on the keyboard. Get a grip, Beth. No one's eyes are as lovely as Aiden's, and anyway, this is the man who's going to put you out of a job. He probably kicks puppies on his days off.

'Anything I can help you with?' I asked curtly.

He handed me a sheet of A4 paper. 'I wanted to give you this.'

I glanced at it. 'What is it?'

'The schedule for the interviews. They'll be taking place on Saturday the sixth of December; that's about three weeks' time. I'd appreciate it if you could give all the staff a copy.'

'Right.' I read the first couple of lines. 'Where's the Brecon Beacons?'

'Wales.'

'Wales?'

He nodded. 'The interviews will take place over the weekend, after a series of personality profiles, question-naires and leadership tasks.'

'Leadership tasks ...' My heart sank. Oh God. It was like my worst kind of nightmare. We'd be sitting around tables making bridges out of straws or doing stupid role-playing exercises.

'It's not that bad,' Matt said, as though he'd read my thoughts. 'I know it sounds full on, but we have to recruit ...' he put on an American accent and made quotation marks in the air with his index fingers, 'A-grade managers. It's company policy. Sorry.'

I wrinkled my nose. 'So if I only sit the interview, I won't get the job?'

'Nope. We need to be able to evaluate your communication skills, your ability to make good decisions and your leadership style. You have to take part in all the activities, I'm afraid.'

He turned to go, and was halfway to the front door when he paused and glanced back. 'Oh, and Beth ...'

'Yeah?'

He looked me straight in the eye. 'Do I strike you as the kind of man who's a bit of a dick?'

'No,' I lied.

'Hmmm,' he said, and turned to leave.

I waited until the door clicked shut, then looked back at the piece of paper he'd given me.

Uh-oh.

There wasn't just going to be a leadership task; there was also a one-on-one interview. And we had to present a business plan for the future of the Picturebox.

My folder was still sticking out of my bag. I wasn't short on ideas on how to make the cinema more profitable, but a business plan? I didn't have the first idea what one of those even looked like!

I glanced at my phone again. There was only one

person I could ask. The dial tone sounded three times, and then, 'Hello, darling!'

'Hi, Mum.'

' Well …' she said, pausing for effect.

'Well what?'

'Oh.' She sounded taken aback. 'I thought you were ringing to tell me you'd changed your mind about Australia.'

I shook my head. 'No, sorry. But I do need your help.'

'Really?' she said incredulously.

'Yes.' I could count the number of times I'd asked for Mum's help since I'd turned eighteen on, er, no fingers. 'Do you know anything about business plans?'

'Do I?' She snorted so loudly, I had to hold the phone away from my ear. 'Beth, you do realise you're talking to South-East Businesswoman of the Year here, don't you? There's nothing I don't know about business plans. Why are you interested all of a sudden?'

'Er …' Oh dear, now for the tricky bit. 'Well, the thing is … the Picturebox is being sold to Apollo, and there's only one position available and it's as the manager, and—'

'You've lost your job!'

'Well, no, not yet. But I need your help, Mum. I really do.'

There was silence on the other end of the line.

'Mum?' I said. 'You will help me, won't you?'

The sound of my mother inhaling deeply filled my left ear.

'What?'

'Beth.' She sounded terse. 'I'm not one to believe in signs and superstitions, but do you not think that this … this situation … might just be the wake-up call you need to stop wasting your time at that bloody cinema and come to Australia with me to start a proper career?'

Now it was my turn to fall silent. The last thing I wanted was another discussion like the one we'd had on Halloween.

'Please,' I said calmly. 'Let's not argue about this. I really want this job, Mum, and I know I can get it. I've got the experience – not officially, obviously, but I've pretty much managed this place single-handedly for the last few years – and I've got tons of ideas. And it would be the start of a proper career – a career in management. You'd be proud of me then, wouldn't you, if I was a manager?'

Mum sniffed dismissively.

'Look,' I continued, 'I'll do you a deal. If I don't land this job, I'll go to Australia with you. That's how much I believe I can get it, if you help me.'

'Hmmm.' I could almost hear the cogs whirring in Mum's brain.

'Please, Mum. Just let me try.'

'Okay,' she said finally, after what seemed an age. 'I'll help you. But you need to do exactly what I say.'

'Anything! You're the boss. On this occasion anyway.'

'Okay, Beth.' She laughed lightly. 'I've got to go. Someone has just come into my office. I'll pop round yours tonight.'

'Wait!' I said desperately. 'You can't come round

tonight. Lizzie is doing a makeover on m—' but it was too late.

The phone had already gone dead.

I clamped my hand to my forehead and shut my eyes. Oh God. If there were two people in the world who rubbed each other up the wrong way just by breathing, it was Mum and Liz.

Chapter Ten

Matt

I walked out of the Picturebox in a daze. I'd hardly slept the night before, and it wasn't because Alice had texted me at least five times a day for the last two weeks (I hadn't replied to any of them). Nor was it because Mrs Blackstock's signed contract had been in my briefcase for over a week and I still hadn't posted it to Ballbreaker. It was the shock of bumping into an ex-girlfriend the day before. A girlfriend I hadn't thought about for a very long time.

I was on my way to meet Neil, hands deep in my pockets, the pub in my sights, when, 'Hello, stranger!'

I gawped at the tall, willowy brunette who had just stepped out in front of me.

'Jules! My God! I haven't seen you in ...'

'Years!' My ex-ex-girlfriend smiled broadly, her cheeks dimpling. 'Anyone would think you'd been avoiding me!'

'I haven't ... didn't ...' I stuttered as she burst out laughing.

'Chill out, Matt!' She waved her left hand in front of my face. A fat diamond glittered on her wedding finger. 'I'm not going to give you shit. I just wanted to say hello.'

'It's, God … wow, it's been ages. It's good to see you.' I nodded towards the ring. 'Congratulations. When did that happen?'

'Six months ago.' Her brown eyes sparkled as she looked up at me. I'd never seen her so happy. 'His name's Simon. We've been together three years now.'

'Three years.' I frowned as I did the maths. 'That means you met him …'

'A couple of months after we split up, yeah.' She nodded, then smiled mischievously. 'I always told you that someone else would snap me up if you didn't.'

She had, too, and I could still remember the exact moment. We were sitting in my living room, almost eighteen months to the day since we'd first met at a friend's party. We were curled up on the sofa, watching a film, when Jules had made a comment about how lovely it would be if we could do this every night. I'd murmured a non-committal 'hmm' in response, but she didn't let it go. She'd paused the film, shuffled away from me and said the one sentence every man fears: 'We need to talk.'

Three minutes later, and Jules had laid it all out on the table. Where were we going? What did she mean to me? Why hadn't I asked her to move in? Why weren't we engaged? She stared at me, waiting for answers.

I stared back and swallowed nervously. I didn't have any. To be honest, I was a bit shell-shocked by her sudden outburst. I needed some time to think about what she'd just said, but she didn't react very well to my silence.

'I've just spilled my guts to you, Matt,' she said, her eyes flicking over my face as she searched for a reaction, 'and you've said nothing. Not one word.'

I stared at her desperately as she gathered her legs up to her chest and hugged her knees. It felt like we were splitting up, and I didn't want that to happen, but what could I say? I knew I liked her, and I wanted to keep on seeing her, but the things she'd asked me – they were huge. I didn't want to make any promises without thinking things through first. If I did, I might hurt her. But my silence seemed to be hurting her too. I just wanted the whole horrible, uncomfortable situation to stop and for us to cuddle up on the sofa again and pretend it had never happened.

'I don't know what to say,' I said finally, weakly.

'Apathy. Great.' She shook her head in despair. 'Way to go to make a girl feel special, Matt.'

'You *are* special.'

'Yeah.' She sighed, then stood up and yanked her coat off the back of the sofa. 'Then why aren't you fighting harder to keep me?'

'Jules! Wait!'

My girlfriend paused, one arm in her jacket, the other dangling by her side, and turned to look at me. 'What?'

'I just … I need … could you give me some time to think?'

'No.' She shook her head, plunged her other arm into her coat, buttoned it up and wrapped her scarf around her neck. 'No more time. You've had eighteen months. If you don't know what you want by now, you never will.'

I watched, frozen with indecision and fear, as she crossed the living room and headed for the door. *Do something!* my brain screamed. *Stop her! Tell her not to go!* But I couldn't speak. I couldn't move. It felt like a scene out of a film – like it wasn't really happening. Like she wasn't really leaving me.

She turned back when she reached the door, and my heart leapt. It was okay. She wasn't going. She was …

'The thing is, Matt,' she said, her expression a mixture of frustration and sadness, 'you shouldn't need to think about whether or not I'm the girl you want to spend the rest of your life with. You should just know. And I wish more than anything in the world that I was that girl, but I'm not. I don't think I ever could be. This hurts, I'm not even going to pretend it doesn't, but out there somewhere is the guy who thinks I am that girl. And when he meets me,' she half smiled, 'he's going to snap me up and never let me go.'

'Jules, don't,' I said, my heart in my throat. 'Please don't go.'

'Matt, don't make it harder than it already is.' She raised a hand in a half-hearted wave. 'It's for the best. Bye!'

A second later, the front door clicked shut and she was gone.

'Matt? Matt! Oh God. Don't tell me you're pissed off that I met Simon right after we split up?'

The sound of Jules's voice brought me back into the present.

'What? God, no.' I reached for her hand and gave it a squeeze. 'I'm really pleased for you. Honestly.'

'Are you?' Her eyes searched mine, and she smiled. 'Good, because us splitting up was the best thing that ever happened to me!'

'Cheers!'

'So?' She punched me lightly on the shoulder. 'How about you?' Her gaze fell to my left hand. 'Ah. So you haven't been snapped up yet, I see?'

I shrugged. 'Nope.'

'Girlfriend?'

'We split up a few weeks ago.'

'Really?' Jules raised an eyebrow.

'What's that look supposed to mean?'

'Let me guess …' She took a step backwards and looked me up and down thoughtfully. 'She wanted commitment and you didn't?'

'Well, no. Not exactly. She was just a bit … intense.'

'Uh-huh. And you ran away?'

'I didn't run anywhere.' I frowned. 'We just split up.'

'Quite.'

'Quite what?'

'The first sign of trouble in a relationship and you shut down, Matt. Emotionally, I mean. That's how you run away.'

'No.' I shook my head. 'I don't. I—'

'Oh come on.' Jules laughed. 'This is me you're talking to. I know you, remember. You've spent your whole life running away from your problems.'

'Hey, that's not—'

'Hello, darling!' I watched, open-mouthed, as my ex-ex broke off our conversation to answer her mobile. 'Yep. Just on my way to the caterers now. I'll be there in five. Okay? See you in a bit. Love you!'

She shoved her mobile back into her bag, then turned to face me.

'It's been lovely seeing you again.' She hugged me tightly, air-kissed the side of my face, then pressed a hand to my cheek. 'You take care now. And no more running away. Time to grow up, eh, Matt.'

She hurried away, her heels clip-clopping on the pavement. I stared after her, long after she'd turned right at the end of the street and disappeared.

A day later, I still felt like I'd been punched in the guts. It was what Jules had said about me running away from my problems that I couldn't shake off. That was what Mum had done, and I'd never been able to forgive her for it. There was no way I was like her.

Was there?

I started to walk faster, speeding up towards Lewes Road. There was only one person I could ask.

'If it isn't my least favourite grandson,' Grandad said, opening the door wide. He looked me up and down, then glanced at the old Omega wristwatch he'd bought back in 1960-something and had faithfully wound every single day since. 'Bit early for a visit, isn't it?'

'I know.' I squeezed past him and stepped into the hallway. It still smelt of pipe smoke, even though

Grandad hadn't smoked in over ten years. 'I just needed to talk to you.'

He frowned, and put his paw-like hand on my shoulder. 'You all right, son?'

'I will be.' I forced a smile. 'Did you just say something about a cup of tea?'

'So,' Grandad said, as he lifted the lid off the teapot and stabbed at the teabags with a dessert spoon. 'What's new?'

I gazed at his lined, smiling face and wondered whether coming over was such a good idea. I could count on the fingers of one hand the number of times he'd talked about Mum over the years. It wasn't that he didn't think about her, or love her – quite the opposite; I'd seen how his expression changed from delight to sorrow when he glanced at her gilt-framed photo on the bookshelf in the front room.

'Do you …' I started, then paused to wet my throat with a sip of tea. 'Do you think I'm like my mum, Grandad?'

He looked steadily at me, then slowly put the teapot back on the table. 'Why'd you ask, lad?'

'I just … I dunno … Something someone said to me yesterday.'

'What did they say?'

I shook my head. I couldn't repeat what Jules had said. Although Grandad had never said as much, I knew he blamed himself for Mum abandoning me. He thought he'd been too soft on her growing up, because she was an only child.

'Nothing specific,' I said. 'It was just a passing comment.'

'Hmmm ...' He cocked his head to one side. 'Well, you do look a bit like her. You've got similar eyes, dimples in your cheeks when you smile, and you look like you combed your hair with a balloon.'

'Mum had nice hair!'

He grinned. 'Just you, then.'

'And personality-wise?'

'Well, you're a stubborn little sod when you want to be. When you were a baby, there was always a right battle between you and your mum when it came to bedtime. You refused to sleep alone.'

'Anything else?'

'You're softer than you look.'

'Hey.' I flexed my biceps. 'I've been working out at the gym.'

He shook his head. 'That's not what I mean.'

'Do you ...' I glanced at the clock on the other side of the kitchen. It was in the shape of a plastic kettle, with *Tetley* printed in blue in the middle. During one visit, a few years ago, Grandad had presented me with a carrier bag full of empty Tetley teabag packets and instructed me to cut out the tokens so he could get his free clock. He'd joked that it would be a family heirloom one day. I looked back at him and cleared my throat. He sipped his tea and eyed me over the top of his cup. 'Do you think the reason I'm thirty and single is because I keep, er, running away from commitment?'

Grandad made a gurgling sound and coughed

violently. I leapt out of my seat and banged him on the back.

'Are you okay?'

'I will be when you stop slapping me,' he gasped.

I slipped back into my chair shot him a concerned look. 'Are you sure you're all right?'

'Course I am.' He dabbed his face with a tea towel. 'I was just a bit taken aback by your question, that's all. In my day, we left the mushy stuff to the womenfolk.'

'Sorry. Forget I said anything.'

'So how's business?' he asked, changing the subject as he hobbled across the kitchen and hung the tea towel next to the sink.

'Same as usual. Still working hard.'

'That's good.' Grandad sat back in his seat and poured himself another cup of tea. 'Nothing like a bit of hard graft to keep a man on the right track.'

'Apollo is opening a new branch on London Road soon. We're buying the Picturebox.'

'Is that so?' He raised his white eyebrows, suddenly interested. 'And what about that nice girl that works there? Is she staying on? Beth, isn't it?'

Weird. I must have told him Alice's name a hundred times, and he still couldn't remember it, but he knew the name of every shopkeeper and stallholder within a mile radius.

'Beth's a lovely, kind girl,' he continued. 'Pretty, too. Don't you think?'

Did I? The first time I'd laid eyes on her, she was professing her love to a cardboard cut-out of George Clooney, but there was definitely something cute about her – like the way she covered her face with her hair when she got nervous and blushed violently when she was embarrassed. She had a lovely smile too, and stunning eyes.

I shook my head, annoyed with myself for even thinking about her. I was sworn off women, and who could blame me when random girls in the pub called me a dick and my ex-ex had pretty much accused me of being an emotional cripple.

'I don't really know her,' I replied non-committally, as Grandad pushed a fresh mug of tea across the table towards me.

'And that blonde one, still keeping you on your toes, is she?'

Alice? Surely I'd told him … Oh yeah, he'd fallen asleep when I'd been relating my ex's recent exploits.

'We split up.'

'Another one?'

I shot him a look. 'What's that supposed to mean? You make it sound like I'm Casanova, when in fact I've only been out with, what, seven or eight women.'

He looked at me steadily. 'I'm not making it sound like anything, son.'

'Then why say "another one"?'

He shrugged. 'I'm not getting any younger, and I'd like to see you happy and settled with a good woman before I go.'

A shiver ran down my spine and I shifted in my seat. I didn't like it when he talked like that – about death. He might be eighty-something, but he was as quick-witted as someone half his age. Okay, so he didn't move as quickly as he used to, but compared to the other pensioners I'd seen shuffling down London Road, he was as strong as an ox. I couldn't bear to think about a life without him in it, and I definitely didn't want to hear him talk about it.

'I'm happy,' I said, meeting his gaze. 'Well, happy enough.'

'You'd be a hell of a lot happier with a good woman in your life.'

'Yeah, and a bullet in my brain.'

Grandad shook his head. 'Your friends might buy that sort of talk, lad, but I know you. You need the love of a good woman.' He paused to sip his tea, then looked back at me. 'The trouble with people of your age is that you're willing to work hard at your jobs but bugger all else. In my day, there was none of this living together business. Once you were married, that was it, for better or for worse. It wasn't done to run away.'

Run away? Was I being paranoid, or was he telling me pretty much the same thing that Jules had – that I baled out of relationships the second they got difficult?

'This blondie,' Grandad continued. 'Alice, is it? She liked you, didn't she?'

I nodded my head.

'Now I don't know why you split up …' I opened my mouth to reply, but he held up a hand to stop me, 'and I don't particularly want to know, but women who love you aren't ten a penny. I should know that.'

His expression sagged. I could tell he was thinking about Gran.

'But …' I began.

'Matt.' He slapped his big grey hand on mine and patted it once. 'My eyesight isn't what it was, but even I can see you're not happy. Why else would you turn up here asking if I think you're like your mum? I'm not good at advice – that was your gran's job – but what say you give this Alice lass a call and take her out for dinner? Who knows, maybe the two of you could sort things out?'

I stared at him, feeling conflicted. It was true, I wasn't particularly happy, but taking Alice out to dinner? How could that possibly be a good idea? We hadn't exactly got on famously the last time we'd been together.

'Son.' Grandad slapped my hand again. 'Give the girl a chance, and prove you're a man with backbone who doesn't run away from his problems. Do it for me, if nothing else.' He grinned mischievously. 'Help the aged and all that!'

'If I do,' I said, a slow smile creeping on to my lips, 'if I take Alice out for dinner, will you promise me you'll stop emotionally blackmailing me?'

'Emotional blackmail?' Grandad pretended to look horrified. 'I don't know what you mean. I'm an innocent old man, me.'

Chapter Eleven

Beth

'Darling, if you could just glance at this chapter ...'

'Beth, for God's sake stand still, or it'll end up streaky!'

'Beth, if you're serious about this new job, you should really read this page about ...'

'See! Told you, mate. Now you've got fake tan in your ear.'

In a move the England rugby team would have been proud of, I swerved away from Lizzie's gloved hands, ducked under Mum's outstretched arm and darted into the hallway. 'Stop! Both of you, stop!'

'Huh?' they said simultaneously, as they stared at me from the confines of the cramped bathroom.

Lizzie stuck out her bottom lip. 'I thought you needed my help.'

'I do!' I held out my hands, then crossed them over my chest, suddenly self-conscious. I didn't make a habit of prancing around the flat in just my underwear, particularly not in front of my mum. 'I need both of you to help me, but I can't cope with the two of you talking to me at once.'

'Honestly, Beth.' Mum clamped her hands on her hips, nearly knocking Lizzie into the bath in the process. 'If you can't multitask, you shouldn't have asked us both to help you on the same night.'

'Actually,' Lizzie commented, ducking out of Mum's way and sitting down heavily on the closed loo seat, 'I think you'll find you gatecrashed, Edwina.'

Mum shot her an irritated look, then glanced back at me. She shook her head disapprovingly. 'Look at you, darling. Preening yourself when you should be preparing for an interview. Anyone would think you weren't serious about this job.'

'I am! But Lizzie's right, Mum. You just assumed it was fine to come round tonight. I was just about to tell you what Liz and I had planned when you put the phone down.'

'Fine,' Mum huffed, tucking her book under her arm and glancing towards the front door. 'I know when I'm not wanted. I'll just go home, shall I?'

'No!' I looked at her imploringly. 'Please stay. I'm sorry, Mum.' I looked from her to Lizzie. 'How about Lizzie does what she needs to do while you read to me from the book? What's it called again?'

'*Visualising Success*,' she sniffed. 'I've mentioned it before, but you weren't interested then.'

I shot her a smile. 'Well I'm interested now.'

Fifteen minutes later, I waddled out of the bathroom, desperately trying not to blink eyelash dye on to my cheeks, and headed for the bedroom. My body was smeared with fake tan, my hair was decorated with tin-foil highlights, my top lip was pink from wax-ing strips, my teeth were encased in plastic bleaching moulds and my feet had been buffed within an inch of their life. There wasn't any part of me that Lizzie hadn't pimped or primed (although I'd drawn the line at a 'whip it all off' Hollywood bikini wax. Mum was relieved about that too).

'I want you back here asap,' Lizzie called after me as I stepped into the bedroom. 'That stuff's fast-acting, and if you don't wash it off in five minutes, you'll be so mahogany you could pass for David Dickinson in drag.'

'No worries,' I said, glancing at the clock on my dressing table: 8.15 p.m. Okay, so that meant I had to be back in the bathroom by 8.20 at the …

'Mum! What the hell are you doing?'

My mother had kicked off her heels and was standing on tiptoes in the middle of my bed, her arms reaching above her head.

'Helping you,' she said, bouncing up and down on the duvet. 'I'm not a *Jackanory* presenter, darling. There's only so much reading I can do. I knew you weren't giving the book your full attention in the bathroom, so I thought I'd make a start in here.'

I crossed the room to the bed and craned my neck upwards. Mum wasn't performing some kind of OAP exercise routine on my mattress. She was trying to fix something to the ceiling.

'What's that?'

'That, darling,' she puffed as she stopped jumping and sat down, her legs tucked neatly under her bum, 'is a positive affirmation.'

I squinted up at the A4 sheet of paper above the bed. Eight words were scrawled on it in my mother's messy handwriting.

I frowned, then looked back at Mum. 'I must have missed the *Changing Rooms* episode about avant-garde minimalist wallpaper. What's that got to do with writing a business plan?'

Mum patted the duvet beside her, but I shook my head. I might never have tried fake tan before, but I was pretty certain it didn't go very well with white cotton.

'Everything,' she said, as I perched on the edge of the rocking chair next to the bed. 'Producing a perfect business plan won't guarantee that you'll get the job, Beth. You need to *believe* you'll get it.'

'I do!'

'Really? One hundred per cent?'

'Well,' I said uncertainly, 'maybe about seventy ... or sixty; perhaps fifty-ish. Apparently the job is open to Apollo staff too, and they might be more experienced than me.'

'Then you need positive affirmations.' She jerked her thumb towards the ceiling. 'Every night before you go to sleep, I want you to read that.'

'Won't that be a bit difficult in the dark?'

'Oh very droll, dear. Are you taking this seriously or not?'

'Sorry.' I fought to suppress my smile. 'I am. Honestly. I really want the job, Mum.'

'Right. So read the affirmation every night, and then again when you get up in the morning. I'd also like you to say it aloud ten times a day.'

'Okaaay.' For the first time in two weeks, I was almost grateful that I was single. Aiden would not have been amused to be woken up by Positive Affirmation Beth every day. A sudden pang of sadness hit me as I thought about his face next to mine on the pillow. I didn't know when I'd get to see that face again, if ever.

'Beth,' Mum said sternly. 'Are you listening to me?'

'Yes!' I snapped myself out of my slump and gave her my full attention.

'Now,' she reached for the ideas folder that I'd left on the end of the bed, 'about this business plan of yours. Pull your chair a bit closer, darling.'

We were still deep in conversation – well, Mum was talking and I was scribbling frantically – when there was a cough from the doorway.

'Beth,' Lizzie said, her hand on her hip, 'have you seen the time?'

Mum shot her a scathing look. 'We're busy, Elizabeth.'

Lizzie's eyebrows nearly shot off the top of her head. 'I'm sorry …'

'Apology accepted.' Mum nodded curtly. 'We haven't got time for interruptions.'

'Whoa!' My flatmate ran her hands through her red hair and stared at Mum like she couldn't believe what she'd just heard. 'Actually, Edwina, I'm not sorry. I came in here to have a word with Beth, not you.'

'Well, Beth's busy.'

'Is she?' Lizzie cast a glance at me. I smiled nervously back. 'I'd say she was looking pretty bored. I think she might have heard the story about your meteoric rise to recruitment power before.'

Now it was Mum's turn to look shocked. She sat up straight, practically puffing out her chest in indignation.

'There's no need for rudeness.'

'Rudeness?' Lizzie's mouth fell open. 'You can talk!'

'And just what is that supposed to mean?'

'You're always rude to Beth. If you're not criticising her job, you're criticising her taste in men or the way she looks. She told me what you said to her when she was a spotty teenager and had hairsprayed her hair forward on to her cheeks. You called her John McCririck. What kind of mother tells her daughter that her hairstyle looks like bushy sideburns?'

'Lizzie!' I said, utterly horrified. 'I told you that in confidence.'

'Yeah, well,' she shrugged, 'she still said it.'

'I may have said that,' Mum was practically bristling beside me, 'but at least I have Beth's best interests at heart. You abandon her to go off gallivanting with any old Tom, Dick or Harry and then expect her to drop everything to rescue you when you get stuck in a public convenience.'

Now it was Lizzie's turn to look aghast. She stared at me and shook her head slowly from side to side. 'Tell me you didn't tell your mother about that, Beth.'

'I ... I ...' I said desperately. Oh God. I felt like a pawn being kicked around a chessboard by two exceedingly pissed-off queens. 'I only told her because she asked how Aiden and me met, and if you hadn't been stuck in the loo, we never would have got together the way we did.'

Lizzie rolled her eyes. 'Fine. I got stuck in a pub toilet, but at least I'm not a bully.'

'Bully!' Mum practically jumped off the bed. 'How dare you say that!'

'Lizzie, stop it!' I said. 'Please don't call my mum a bully. It's not fair.'

'But it's true.' Lizzie's face was nearly as red as her hair. I was seriously worried she was going to burst something. 'You're bullying Beth to go to Australia with you. She doesn't want to go, and I don't want her to go. In fact the only person who wants her to go is you.'

'Ah.' Now Mum was smirking. 'I see. That's what this is all about, isn't it? You don't want Beth to go to Australia. Why's that, Lizzie? Worried that you'll lose the person who picks up the pieces when you mess up?'

'Mum.' I shot her an angry look. 'That's not fair. Don't talk to Liz like that. She's been a great friend to me.'

'Exactly! That's why I'm giving Beth a makeover, because we're great friends and I want her to be happy.'

'And why do you think I'm helping her with her business plan?' Mum shot back. 'I've agreed that she doesn't have to come to Australia with me if she gets the job. If I was such an awful, selfish mother, I'd leave her to it. Whether you believe it or not, the only thing I want for my daughter is her happiness.'

'Well then,' Lizzie huffed, dropping her hands from her hips, 'at least we both agree on something.'

Mum uncrossed her arms. 'Fine.'

'Guys,' I said, frowning at the alarm clock across the room. 'I've got a question.'

My mother and my flatmate looked at me curiously. 'What?'

'What time was I supposed to wash this fake tan off?'

Lizzie's gaze followed mine. When she looked back at me, all the colour had drained from her face.

'Shit,' she breathed.

Chapter Twelve

Matt

Something, possibly a Tic Tac or an Oompa Loompa, was sitting behind the counter at the Picturebox.

'Hi, Matt,' it said as I crossed the foyer. 'How are you?'

'Good.' The more I told myself to stop looking at Beth's satsuma-coloured face, the more I stared. She looked like she'd lost a fight with a tanning booth. Even her dark hair was streaked with orange. In fact, the only white bit of her was her teeth, and they glowed at me with an eerie intensity. 'Are you ... okay?'

She shrugged uncomfortably. 'I've been better.'

She definitely didn't look happy. Hmm, perhaps she hadn't stolen Katie Price's fake tan supply after all. Maybe there was something properly wrong with her. I'd seen a documentary once about a kid who'd turned yellow almost overnight and had to be rushed to hospital. He had really white teeth too.

'Is it your ... um ... liver?' I ventured. It wasn't strictly professional to ask someone about their physical afflictions, but she did look like she might need urgent medical attention.

'Liver?' Beth looked confused.

'Yeah. Is that why you're ... um ... that colour?'

'Oh God!' She clamped her hands to her face. 'I knew it! I knew Lizzie was lying. I *am* orange.'

'So you're not ill?'

She peered at me through her fingers. 'No.'

'Oh.' I shifted from foot to foot, scrabbling for something I could say to make her feel better, but my mind was blank. She looked so self-conscious, I just wanted to give her a hug.

'So,' I said finally, tapping an electronic tape measure against my hand, 'I'm here to measure up. We need to move things along now the contract's been signed.'

'Measure up?' Beth's hands fell from her face and she frowned at me. 'Measure up what exactly?'

'You know.' I sidled away from the desk and shone the tape measure at the wall opposite. The red beam seemed to split it in two. 'Dimensions, ceiling heights, that kind of thing. I'm just getting an idea for costings; these aren't the definitive measurements. We'll get contractors in to do that.'

Beth inhaled sharply. 'Contractors!'

'Yeah.' I checked the figure on the tape measure and scribbled it down in my notebook. I'd costed up fixtures and fittings dozens of times before and I normally welcomed the job as an excuse to get out of the office. Today, for some reason, I couldn't wait to get it done and get out. Sure, the Picturebox was knackered and run-down, but it wasn't a soulless warehouse or a deserted industrial estate; it was a working cinema with years of history. I had as much interior design expertise as Ozzy Osbourne, but even I could see that it had some pretty unusual features. I glanced up at the dusty old chandelier on the ceiling. It would be ripped out in a heartbeat. Probably end up in a skip.

'So that's that, then?' Beth said. 'The contract's signed and sealed?'

'Pretty much.'

What I wasn't about to admit to her was that I still hadn't got round to posting it off to Ballbreaker. Actually, getting round to it wasn't the issue – I passed half a dozen postboxes every day, and there was an out tray on my desk that Sheila regularly emptied; something was stopping me from delivering the Picturebox to Ballbreaker. I wasn't sure if it was pride, defiance or immaturity. Whatever it was, it was pretty stupid, particularly since Grandad's rent depended on the deal going through.

I cast an eye around the foyer and took a few more measurements. It wasn't the biggest of halls, and once the automatic ticket machines were installed, any remaining floor space would be taken up with queuing barriers. The counter would need demolishing too. We'd probably knock through to the staff room behind it and turn that into a booth. But what about the concession stand? We'd have to rip out the coffee and cake area upstairs and …

'So these contractors …' I could feel Beth's eyes burning into my back. 'What will they be doing exactly?'

It was a polite enough question, but there was a definite edge to her voice. Shit. The last thing I wanted to do was upset her, particularly after she'd been so cool about helping me escape when I saw Alice spying on me through the window. Okay, so I'd caught her professing her love to a George Clooney cut-out, and she was the most vivid shade of orange I'd ever seen outside a Fanta factory, but Grandad was right, she was a nice girl. A really nice girl.

'Well, you know,' I said, in what I hoped was a jokey tone, as I turned to grin at her. 'Contracting! Not that the Picturebox needs contracting. I've never seen such a small cinema before. You couldn't swing a baby in here. And if you tried, you'd probably knock it out on the chandelier!'

'What?' Beth's eyebrows, which were strangely dark compared to her hair, almost shot off her forehead, she looked so horrified.

'Not that I'm advocating braining small children on the light fixtures,' I gabbled. 'I wouldn't introduce a kid's head to so much as a light bulb. Could you imagine the mess?'

Her jaw dropped open.

'No,' I added hastily, 'of course you couldn't. Nor could I. It's not the sort of thing I lie in bed at night thinking about – how much damage you could do with a thirty-watt …'

Stop talking, Matt! Stop talking RIGHT NOW!

What the hell was wrong with me? All Beth had done was ask me a simple question about what the contractors were going to do, and I'd turned into a gibbering wreck.

'Um,' I said, my cheeks burning as she shot me a puzzled look. 'I should go. I, er,' I tapped my tape measure against my hand, 'I think I've got all I need. For now, anyway. Right, see you. Bye!'

I don't think I've ever exited anywhere as fast as I left the Picturebox that day. Talk about unprofessional! I'd never done anything so stupid. Why hadn't I just told Beth the truth when she'd asked what the contractors were going to do? Sure, there was every chance she'd have been pissed off if I'd told her exactly what we had planned, but what did I care? If she didn't get the manager's job, I'd probably never see her again.

The truth, I realised as I reached the North Laines and mingled with the hordes slowly browsing Trafalgar Street, was that I did care. I cared a lot. I didn't want Beth to think I was a dick. I didn't want anyone to.

I reached into my back pocket, pulled out my mobile and dialled a number I hadn't called in weeks.

'Alice?' I said. 'Is that you?'

Chapter Thirteen

Beth

I looked like David Dickinson.

With teeny tiny drag-queen eyebrows.

Glow-in-the-dark teeth.

And an orange moustache (waxing my top lip had made it absorb even more tanning lotion than the rest of my body).

My Day-Glo tan hadn't seemed so bad when we'd washed it off – twenty minutes late – the night before, but there was no denying the full orangey horror that stared back at me from the bathroom mirror the next morning.

It was 9 a.m. and Lizzie, the makeover queen, was still snoring loudly in her bedroom. I had no choice but to try and sort the situation out myself. A ten-minute shower with three different kinds of body scrub made no difference at all. Neither did half a tub of moisturiser. Or a scouring pad and washing-up liquid. If anything, I was glowing even more than before.

The only option I had left was to apply a thick layer of Lizzie's foundation and draw on some eyebrows with a stubby black eye pencil I found in the bottom of her make-up bag. It wasn't entirely successful – my tanned neck and chest and pale face made me looked like the demented love child of Katie Price and Edward Cullen. Frustrated, late for work and throbbing from all the scrubbing, I washed it off again, pulled a beanie hat low over my eyes, wrapped a scarf round my mouth and nose and set off for the Picturebox. I got a couple of strange looks as I walked down London Road, but nothing could have prepared me for Matt's reaction. His jaw couldn't have dropped any further if someone had attached a telephone book to his chin.

Still, I thought as I booted up the computer and glanced through my list of things to do, it could be worse. I might look odd, but at least I hadn't started rambling on about swinging small children around the cinema. That was just weird. At first I thought Matt was having a go at our Sob Showing, but no, he was just being strange. He sprinted straight out of the cinema afterwards.

I squinted at my reflection in the dark monitor as the PC slowly whirred and bleeped to life. Was it just the lighting, or was the tan fading a bit? Thank God it was only Matt who'd come in, and not … I glanced from my monitor to my bag. I hadn't checked my mobile for at least an hour. What if there was a text from Aiden? I snatched up my bag and rooted around in it until I found my phone.

Damn. I dropped it on the counter with a sigh. Nothing.

Wasn't he thinking about me at all? For all he knew, I could be lying in a hospital bed, or worse. Surely he must have heard the wheels screeching when the Audi had nearly run me over that night?

'Jesus fucking Christ! What the hell happened to your face?'

I frantically reached for my hat and scarf, but it was too late. Carl was standing at the counter, grinning manically at me.

'Well, well, well,' he said, slowly shaking his head from side to side as though he couldn't believe his luck. 'What *have* we got here?'

'Don't,' I said. 'Don't say a word.'

'I only need one word. And that word is ... Ohhh ...' He smirked and rocked back on his heels. 'Oh, which one should I choose? There are so many that would perfectly describe the sheer horror of you looking so very—'

'Carl!' I snapped. 'What are you doing here? You haven't got a shift today.'

'I know.' His eyes swept the desk as though he was looking for something. 'Aha!'

He lurched forward and grabbed a copy of the Brecon Beacons schedule that I'd printed out for everyone.

'Great,' I said, turning back to my computer. 'Now that you've got what you came for, maybe you could go. I'm very busy.'

'I'll be off in a second.' There was an unusually light tone to Carl's voice, but I didn't really think about it. I was just relieved he hadn't carried on ripping the piss out of my tan. 'I need to get something from the staff room. I think I left my gloves in there yesterday.'

'Fine.' I ignored him as he slipped behind the

counter and disappeared into the staff room. 'Just don't be long.'

Five minutes later and he still hadn't reappeared.

'Hey!' I called. 'What are you doing in there?'

As I twisted round in my seat, my elbow caught a pile of programmes on the counter and sent them skidding on to the floor.

'Bugger.' I slipped off my seat, scrabbled around on the floor to pick them up, then arranged them neatly again. My eyes flicked over the counter, checking that everything was in order.

Strange …

I shuffled piles of paper around on the desk, then knelt down and looked on the floor. I reached for my bag and felt around inside. No, my phone definitely wasn't there.

Oh God. I suddenly felt sick.

No wonder Carl had gone quiet in the staff room. He'd sneaked my mobile off the counter when I wasn't looking. God knows what he was doing with it.

'Carl!' I called, then stopped abruptly. The staff room door had opened and my colleague was standing above me, a bemused look on his face.

'Looking for this?' He held out my phone.

I snatched it out of his hand and scrolled through the functions. It was still in English. Phew. And he hadn't texted or called anyone. Oh God, photos. I flicked through the albums. There wasn't anything incriminating there for him to take the piss out of. And he hadn't taken any new pictures. So what had he …

'You really should take better care of your phone,

you know, Beth,' he said smarmily. 'I found it on the floor in the staff room. You should be thankful I was the one to discover it. I'm not naming names, but some of the staff here aren't the most honest people in the world.'

I glared up at him. 'I didn't leave my phone in the staff room. It was on the counter and you know it.'

'The counter?' His expression was one of pure innocence. 'No, no. You're obviously confused. I found it under the bench in the staff room. Don't I at least get a thank-you?'

'No.' I shoved the phone back into my bag and hugged it to my chest as I sat back down on my chair. 'Didn't you say something about having to be somewhere?'

'Did I?' He raised an eyebrow. 'I don't think I did. Though now you mention it, I am going somewhere pretty special on Saturday night.'

'Is that so?'

'Yep. And I think you'll be very interested when I tell you where.'

'Oh really?'

I didn't care where Carl went. As long as he was as far away from me as possible.

'Uh-huh. Especially when I tell you that Aiden will be there.'

'Aiden!' My voice went up an octave, and Carl smirked with delight. I was interested now, and he knew it. What would he be doing that Aiden would be doing too? Wine club was on a Monday, so it couldn't be that, and they never socialised together outside it.

'Yes, but, you know, if you're busy, maybe I should just leave you to it. You don't want to hear my news.' Carl turned to go.

'Wait!'

I hated myself for playing right into his hands, but I couldn't help it. Ever since Aiden and I had split up I'd tortured myself, imagining what he was up to now. This was my only chance to get a glimpse into his Beth-free life.

Carl looked back at me, the interview schedule clutched to his chest. 'Say please, Carl, tell me what you're doing on Saturday night.'

'Just tell me!'

'Not if you can't say it.' He turned to go again.

'Please, Carl,' I muttered through gritted teeth. 'I want to hear what you're doing on Saturday night.'

'Very well.' He shot me what I think was supposed to be a dazzling smile. 'I'll tell you. At eight p.m. I will be going to the Grand Hotel to attend ...'

Just say it, I willed. Just bloody say it!

'... Aiden's engagement party.'

The foyer swam before my eyes as I tried to process what he'd just said. What?

WHAT!

'Lovely girl, Fi,' Carl continued as I gripped the edge of the desk. I felt like I was hurtling through the air at a hundred miles an hour. My vision was blurry and I could barely breathe. 'I bumped into her and Aiden in the Western Front the other evening. Blonde, pretty, the most massive rock I've ever seen. Massive rack, too.' He laughed to himself. 'Can't see what Aiden sees in her! Everyone who's anyone is going. Well, you're not, obviously. Anyone, that is. Or going. Oh.' He looked me up and down. 'You're looking a bit peaky there, Beth. Is there such a thing as a peaky carrot? Anyway, no time for word play. I really must go. I've got an engagement present to buy. Toodle pip!'

I opened my mouth to call after him as he sauntered through the doors, but the only sound that came out was a strange strangulated squeak.

Chapter Fourteen

Matt

Agreeing to go along with Grandad's 'prove you're a man with backbone' challenge, I realised as I sat in a busy restaurant on a Saturday night in the Lanes and rearranged my cutlery for the fifth time in ten minutes, was possibly the scariest thing I'd ever done in my entire life (and believe me, I've done some *really* scary things).

Grandad hadn't said as much, but he'd basically agreed with Jules that I was an emotional retard when it came to relationships. And, whether I liked it or not, I *was* like my mum. I ran away whenever relationships got tough. Unlike Mum, I didn't run away to be with someone else. Instead I simply gave up, shut down my feelings and went. Nothing and no one had ever been worth fighting for – much better to leave and not risk getting hurt.

Hmmm. Maybe it *was* time to man up and confront my problems. Let's face it, I hadn't exactly been myself recently. First there was that weird shit with Beth in the cinema – where I'd turned into a total gibbering idiot – and then there was the fact that I was avoiding posting the Picturebox contract to Ballbreaker and running out of excuses, fast. Sheila had refused to stop screening her calls and I knew it was only a matter of time until Isabel paid me another impromptu – and probably highly unpleasant – visit. Why would I do that? Withhold the contract when I knew how dire the consequences would be? Was I deliberately trying to screw up my life? I didn't want to admit it to anyone, particularly not myself, but perhaps Alice and I did have some unfinished business, and maybe it needed sorting out once and for all.

I fished my mobile out of my back pocket and checked the time: 9.15.

My ex-girlfriend was fifteen minutes late. Hmmm … maybe she'd changed her mind about meeting up. Her reaction had been distinctly frosty when I'd called, but she'd quickly thawed when I'd asked if she'd like to go out for a meal.

'Fine,' she'd said after a long pause. 'As long as we go to La Dolce Vita.'

My mouth immediately dried – La Dolce Vita was Brighton's most exclusive (and expensive) Italian restaurant – but I agreed enthusiastically. If I'd done the wrong thing by baling on her, I wanted to try my best to put things right.

I jiggled my cutlery around again. There were a lot of sharp objects on the table. What if Alice … No, no … I immediately dismissed the thought. Okay, it was true that she had thrown that mug of hot coffee at me when I was late home, but that was more of a blunt object than a pointy once, and it was a long time ago. Well, six months …

I reached for my mobile. Perhaps I should send her a quick text, just to check she was still coming?

'Hello, Matt,' said a voice from across the restaurant.

Alice, dressed in a long black coat and high heels, was sashaying through the diners. I thrust my mobile back into my jeans pocket and stood up.

'You're here,' she said as she drew closer, a cloud of exotic-smelling perfume filling the air. She put her hand on my arm and turned her face up towards me.

I pecked her on the cheek. 'I'm glad you could come.'

She tipped her head to one side and looked at me curiously. 'Why wouldn't I?'

I nodded, but my stomach was churning. I could think of a hundred ways I'd rather spend my evening – like pulling out my fingernails with pliers, or playing slam the penis with my front door – but it was time to man up. Alice wasn't *scary* (okay, maybe a tiny bit), and I'd loved her once. Maybe Grandad and Jules were right. Maybe I'd given up on our relationship too quickly.

I stepped behind her and put my hands on her shoulders. 'Can I take that for you?'

She glanced back at me, bemused, but let me slide the coat off her shoulders. I couldn't help but raise an eyebrow at the outfit she was wearing. It was the most ridiculously low-cut dress I'd ever seen. Her boobs swelled over the top like a couple of inflatable beach balls.

'Why don't you sit down,' I said, handing her coat to a passing waiter. I waited for her to do so, then rounded the table, sat down myself and reached for my menu, trying desperately to ignore the fact that she was staring at me expectantly.

'Right.' I flipped it open. 'I've already ordered a nice bottle of red. What would you like to eat? I quite fancy the steak.'

'Pork belly main and oysters to start,' Alice said, barely glancing at the menu. 'To share.'

I pulled a face. Why anyone would profess to enjoy gritty lumps of gristle in a shell was beyond me.

'I'd rather not,' I said. 'I'm not a big fan of seafood.'

'Matt.' She cast me a steely look. 'It would be romantic.'

Romantic? Wasn't that jumping the gun a bit? We hadn't even talked about getting back together. Hell, we hadn't actually had a conversation yet. And then there was the not-so-small Mussels Food Poisoning episode in my mid-twenties, when I'd spent forty-eight hours surgically attached to the toilet bowl. I hadn't touched seafood since. Just the thought made me gag violently.

'I can't. I really … Ah, here's the wine,' I said hurriedly, as Alice glared at me. I reached for my glass and held it towards the waiter who'd appeared at my side. He poured out a thimbleful of Rioja. I took a sip and nodded my head. He filled my glass, then looked at Alice. She pushed her glass a millimetre towards him. The waiter tipped the bottle again, then placed it in the middle of the table and wandered away.

'Are you ignoring me?' Alice's sharp tones snapped me back to the present. 'Perhaps there is somewhere, or *someone*, you'd rather be with?'

I shook my head. 'Of course not. I was just thinking about … never mind. What are you having?'

'I told you. I'm having the pork belly main and *we're*,' she raised her eyebrows to emphasise the word, 'having oysters to start.'

Twenty excruciating minutes later, during which Alice listed all my faults – one after another – while I cringed and said nothing, the waiter returned with our starter.

'Oysters to share,' he said, placing the large white plate covered with phlegm in shells between us.

I wrinkled my nose. They looked disgusting.

'Mmm,' murmured Alice as she reached for a shell. I watched, horrified, as she tipped her head back and slid an oyster into her mouth. She swallowed it whole and looked at me. 'What?'

'Nothing,' I said, forcing a smile. 'Just contemplating the exquisite gastronomic treat I'm about to sample.'

'Go on then,' she ordered, gesturing at the plate between us. 'Your turn!'

I tentatively reached for an oyster.

'Mmm,' I said, raising the shell to my lips and closing my eyes tightly. 'Yum, yum.' I gave my mouth strict instructions to open, and tipped my head back like Alice had done. The oyster flopped out of the shell and landed on my tongue. I grimaced. It was like licking the sea bed and finding a bogey.

I jerked my head further back, aware that Alice was still staring at me, and prayed that gravity would force the bugger down. My throat had other ideas, and closed the second the oyster hit it.

'Ack.' I made a noise like a demented seagull. 'Ack, ack, ack!'

My face started to get very hot and my stomach churned violently.

'For God's sake swallow it,' Alice hissed.

I shook my head. My throat was sealed closed. There was no way on earth the oyster was going anywhere. I reached for my napkin.

'For fuck's sake!' Alice exclaimed. 'People are starting to look.'

I'm not entirely sure what happened next. Maybe the tone of her voice made me jump, maybe the oyster tickled the back of my throat and made me cough, or maybe I just retched. Either way, I lurched forward, mouth open. To my relief, and then horror, the oyster dislodged itself from my throat, rolled down my tongue, bounced over my teeth and shot out of my open mouth like a bullet from a gun. It curved through the air as if in slow motion, arched over the wine bottle, skimmed the flickering candle in the middle of the table and landed with a wet *thwapp* on Alice's heaving cleavage.

Time stood still as I looked from the oyster to my ex-girlfriend's face and back again.

Alice blinked, then looked down at her chest. Her eyes grew wide with horror, her mouth dropped open and she let out an ear-piercing shriek.

'Aaaggh!' she yelled, her eyes fixed on the mucousy blob between her boobs. 'Aaaggggh!'

I could feel dozens of pairs of eyes on me, but I couldn't move. I couldn't even speak. It felt like the whole restaurant had gone quiet.

'Madam,' said a deep male voice. 'If you please.'

Like the shopkeeper in *Mr Benn*, the waiter had reappeared at our table. He swiped up Alice's napkin, dusted it across her chest and the oyster disappeared in a flash of white table linen. I looked desperately around the restaurant, too scared to meet my ex-girlfriend's eyes. What should I do? I caught the eye of a middle-aged woman at the table behind Alice. She must have seen the desperation in my eyes because she smiled kindly.

'Say something,' she mouthed as the waiter picked up the tray of oysters, turned on his heel and disappeared towards the kitchen.

'Thanks,' I called after him.

'Not to the waiter!' The woman chuckled. 'To your girlfriend!'

I stared at my ex-girlfriend, feeling as though all the blood had drained from my head and puddled around my feet. 'Sorry, Alice.'

She stared back at me with an expression I knew only too well. Disgust.

'I'm really, really, really sorry,' I said desperately. 'I think it was an allergic reaction. In fact,' I pointed at my throat, 'it may have been anaphylactic shock.'

She narrowed her eyes. 'Give me one reason why I shouldn't walk out of the room right now.'

I was having pretty much the same thought myself.

'Because I invited you here to talk,' I said weakly. 'About us.'

Alice's expression softened momentarily, then swiftly changed to suspicion. 'Really?'

'Honestly. I wanted to make an effort. Why do you think I agreed to try oysters when I can't stand seafood?'

She reached for her wine and eyed me over the top of the glass as she took a sip. 'Was spitting them on to my décolletage part of some kind of idiotic seduction scenario?'

'God, no. No, that was just a terrible mistake.'

'Well …' She lowered her empty glass. She still didn't look convinced. 'Okay then. But anything like that again and I swear I won't be responsible for my actions.'

'I'll be on my best behaviour, I promise,' I said as I reached for the wine bottle. It was a rich, blackcurranty red that cost more than I made in a week, but I knew it was Alice's favourite. 'More wine?'

She nodded, and pushed her glass across the table towards me. I smiled in what I hoped was a reassuring manner and topped it up. As I slid it back towards her, I noticed that the middle-aged woman behind her was trying to catch my eye.

'Phew!' she mouthed, miming wiping sweat from her brow before giving me the thumbs-up. 'Crisis averted.'

I nodded in response and smiled half-heartedly. She obviously meant well, but I really didn't need reminding that I'd just made a total dick of myself in a public place. What I needed to do was get things back on track, have a civilised conversation with Alice about what had gone wrong in our relationship, work out whether it was worth giving it another shot and—

'Who are you looking at, Matt?'

'What?'

Alice was glaring at me from across the table, her glass dangling from her fingers, red wine sloshing around inside as she circled her wrist round and round.

'You're talking to someone at another table.'

'I wasn't talking to anyone!' I said desperately. 'Well, not no one exactly. The middle-aged lady back there was a bit concerned about my coughing fit, I think.'

She twisted around in her seat to have a look. When she turned back, her cheeks were puce. 'Middle-aged woman, eh?'

'Yeah, she ...' I caught my breath. Middle-aged woman's seat was empty. I craned my neck to peer over Alice's shoulder. The only other person at the table was a stunning brunette in her late teens or early twenties – middle-aged woman's daughter, probably. From the way she was fiddling with her mobile, I guessed she was waiting for her mum to come back from the toilet or wherever she'd disappeared to.

'Oh no,' I said, meeting Alice's furious gaze. 'Oh no, no, no. You've got it all wrong.'

She raised an eyebrow. 'Is that so?'

'Yes!' I held out my hands. 'I swear. She was right there – shoulder-length brown perm, glasses, white blouse. Just give it a few minutes and she'll be back.'

Please, I prayed silently to the gods of the restaurant loos. Please don't let her have an upset stomach.

Alice narrowed her eyes. 'You've got an answer for everything, haven't you, Matt?'

'No! I swear!'

'You really are a vile excuse for a human being.' Her wrist rotations had increased, and the red wine swirled dangerously in the glass as she glared at me from across the table. 'You invite me out for a meal and then you make goo-goo eyes at another woman. Do you have any idea how disrespectful that is?'

'Yes. No! I wasn't goo-gooing anyone. I told you. A middle—'

'I know what you told me.' She leaned forward, her elbows on the tablecloth, her eyes fixed on mine. 'You've told me a lot of things over the last year or so, and none of them were true. The late nights at work, your grandad's hospital appointments, the women on Facebook you claimed were just friends—'

'They are friends! Well, they were until you deleted them.'

'It's all bullshit, Matt. All of it! God ...' she shook her head violently, 'and to think I believed you when you said you wanted to talk things through. I can't believe I fell for it.'

'You didn't fall for anything. Alice!' I stared up at her in horror as she stood up abruptly. 'Sit down. Please.'

'Why?' She glanced from left to right, staring down anyone who dared to meet her eye. 'Causing a scene, am I? Worried that your new friend back there will hear the truth about you? Well screw you, Matt. I'm not hanging around here to be humiliated.'

I watched, aghast, as she grabbed her bag off the back of her chair and turned towards the door, her wine glass still in her hand.

'Oh,' she said, spinning back and shooting a smile in my direction. 'I drank all that lovely wine and I didn't give you anything for it, did I? Well, have this!'

A couple of minutes later, my middle-aged friend sauntered across the restaurant and pulled back her chair,
stopping short as she caught sight of me.

'Oh dear,' she said, looking me up and down as I
dabbed at the red wine dribbling down my cheeks.
'And it was all going so well.'

Chapter Fifteen

Beth

Lizzie didn't look happy. In fact, she looked distinctly worried.

'Beth,' she said, as she perched on the edge of my bed and looked me up and down, 'are you sure this is a good idea?'

I reached behind my back and zipped up my new dress. 'Yep.'

'But …' she twisted her hands together, 'what makes you think you'll even get in?'

I shrugged. 'Lax security?'

'And then what are you going to do?'

'I'm not exactly sure.'

'So,' she leaned back on my bed, propping herself up on her elbows, 'let me get this right. You're going to gatecrash Aiden's party – his *engagement* party – and you haven't planned how you're going to get in or what you're going to do then?'

'Pretty much.' I turned to look at my reflection in the mirror, smoothing my dress over my hips. I'd really taken Lizzie's advice to heart about replacing my wardrobe with figure-hugging clothes. I could barely breathe, never mind move.

'But why? Why not just accept that the bloke is an utter fuckwit and move on with your life?'

'Would you?' I turned to face her. 'Move on with your life, I mean, if you'd just found out that your ex had got engaged to someone else a couple of weeks after you'd split up?'

'Probably not. I'd want to chop his balls off.'

'Well then.'

'So should I bring the Kitchen Devil set with us?' She smiled mischievously.

'No.' I shook my head. 'I'm not going to do anything to him. I'm not even sure what I'll say when I see him, but I can't let him get away with this. Too many men have treated me like crap and I've done nothing.'

'Yeah! Beth's finally standing up for herself!' Lizzie shifted forward on the bed and raised a hand in my direction. 'High five!'

I slapped my hand against hers and forced a smile. To be honest, I was shaking with nerves. After Carl's revelation in the Picturebox, it was all I could do to stay in my seat and finish my shift. I'd felt every emotion – from rage to hurt and back again – but after having a bit of a cry in the staff room, I'd resolved that I wasn't just going to sit back and pretend that I was fine with the way Aiden had treated me. After all the months we'd spent together and all the cool things we'd done, the least he owed me was a phone call to tell me that he'd met someone else. But he hadn't just 'met someone else', had he? He'd obviously been seeing her for a while and – the thought made me feel sick – it must have started while he'd been going out with me. I'd been cheated on, again. Waiting for Saturday to finally roll around had felt like an eternity.

'Beth?' Lizzie said softly. 'You sure you're okay?'

I nodded, then reached for the half-empty wine glass on my dressing table and knocked it back in one. I wasn't going to be 'roll-over Beth' any more. I was going to confront Aiden and see what he had to say for himself. If his fiancée was by his side, maybe she'd like to hear his explanation too. So why was I shaking so much?

I looked back at my reflection and tugged at the hem of my dress. It was shorter than anything I'd ever worn before, but it didn't break the 'don't show boobs and legs at the same time' rule that Gok Wan went on about on TV. The front was a high halterneck that disguised my lack of boobs, while the back dipped low, showing off my shoulders and the curve of my spine. The whole thing was covered in tiny silver and black sequins that shimmered when I moved – well, wiggled. I caught Lizzie's eye as she watched. 'So, what do you think?'

She tipped her head to one side and squinted as though she was trying to choose the right words.

'You look like Shirley Bassey. In a good way,' she added hurriedly.

I stared at her in horror. 'In what way is looking like a seventy-year-old Welsh granny good?'

'No, no, nooooo.' She held up her hands. 'I'm not saying you look like her. It's the sequins. They make you look sparkly and different and … you know…' The enthusiasm in her voice floundered. 'Stuff.'

'Stuff? I want Aiden to see me and think, "Shit, I can't believe I let her get away," not "Who let Beth leave the house looking like a sequinned sausage?"'

'You don't look like a sausage!' Lizzie rolled her eyes. 'You look lovely. At least you can see your figure, for a change.'

I looked at my reflection in the mirror. The dress wasn't awful. Was it? Okay, so it was a tiny bit tight – all right, a lot tight – but at least you could tell I had a waist. And legs. And a little pot belly. And …

I turned away from the mirror.

'I'm going to have another glass of wine,' I said as I tottered to the kitchen, clinging on desperately to the tiny bit of self-confidence that hadn't completely disappeared. 'Maybe two. And then we're going out.'

'You okay, Beth?' Lizzie asked as I wobbled along the seafront towards the Grand Hotel, shivering in the freezing late-November wind.

To be honest, I felt a million miles away from okay. I'd only meant to have a couple of glasses of wine to knock the edge off my nerves, but I'd ended up finishing off the best part of two bottles before we left the house. My head was a mess, and not just because of the booze.

I leaned back against a wall and stared out at the sea. The wind was whipping it up into a fury, the waves rising and crashing against the pebbles. How had I managed to get my life so wrong? Here I was, twenty-four years old, working in a dead-end job, living my life through romantic comedies, dreaming about finding a man who'd love me for me, and chasing guys who used me as a stopgap before they settled down with someone else. It wasn't just laughable, it was ridiculous. *I* was ridiculous. And it had to stop.

'I'm fine,' I said, meeting Lizzie's concerned gaze with a determined stare. 'I'm tired of being sweet, understanding Beth. I'm going to go to that party and I'm going to tell Aiden exactly what I think of him.'

The entrance to the Grand was bustling with people. Two uniformed porters stood on either side of the huge glass revolving door, their eyes flicking over the crowd that passed in and out.

'Sure you're okay?' Lizzie whispered as we swung through the entrance and passed into the main hall.

'Fine,' I lied. To be honest, I was having a hard time standing up straight. I was also seeing double. There were two piano players tickling the ivories in the bar to my left, and two sweeping wrought-iron staircases in front of us.

'Excushe me,' I slurred to the two identical porters standing on my right. Which was the real one? 'I'm looking for the Dowles celebrashon.'

The porter's eyes flicked from my heels to the top of my head and his left eyebrow twitched. 'Of course, madam,' he said. 'You need the Albert Suite.'

He gave me perfunctory directions, then turned to smile at a silver-haired woman in a peach and teal Jaeger suit with a string of real-looking pearls around her neck. 'Welcome, madam. How can I help?'

It didn't take us long to find the right room. Several of Aiden's mates were hanging around the door, chatting animatedly, glasses of champagne in their hands. One of them, Pete, glanced at us but didn't seem to recognise me. Beyond them was a beautiful room, decorated in cream and gold, with a sparkling chandelier hanging from the ceiling and an enormous window dominating one wall.

'Come on,' I said, glancing back at Lizzie as I charged into the room. 'Letsh find him.'

She grinned back at me, but even in my drunken state, I could tell she was regretting letting me gatecrash the party. I didn't care. I pushed through the crowd, pausing just long enough to grab a glass of champagne from a silver tray a waiter was holding, and scanned the room for my ex-boyfriend.

'Beth,' Lizzie hissed. 'What are you going to do now?'

I looked back over my shoulder. 'Don't you worry 'bout that. I know what I'm doin'.'

'Course you do.' She looked like she didn't believe me.

'I just want to—'

I was interrupted by the sound of a fork being tapped against a glass.

'Ladies and gentlemen. Some hush, if you please.'

I swung round towards the stage and spotted Aiden straight away. He was dressed in a dark grey suit with a white shirt and maroon tie. There was a microphone in his hand. His hair was neatly styled, he was clean-shaven and he looked impossibly happy. His parents stood on his left, both of them beaming – I recognised them from a photo that he'd kept on the desk in his study. Beside them stood two sandy-haired women who had to be his sisters and a taller, balding man who must be his older brother, Adam. To Aiden's right were an elderly couple I assumed were his grandparents. The woman was wearing a floral tea dress and comfortable grey slip-ons and the man was sporting a brown suit and a walking stick. Everyone was smiling. It was the perfect family scene.

'Ladies and gentlemen,' Aiden said into the microphone. 'I'm absolutely delighted that so many of you could turn up today on this, the happiest of occasions.'

'Hear, hear!' shouted a man next to me.

I fought the urge to thump him.

'As many of you know,' Aiden continued, relishing being the centre of attention, 'this night has been a long time coming and has been shrouded in secrecy, for obvious reasons …'

'No shit,' I whispered to Lizzie, who pulled a face.

'But before we get to the main announcement, there's someone I'd like you all to meet.'

This was it, the moment I'd get to lay eyes on the woman Aiden had left me for.

'Mummy, Daddy, Granny, Gramps, I take great pleasure in introducing you to someone you thought you'd never get to see. Everyone, this is Fi!'

My eyes flicked to the side of the stage as a plain blonde woman climbed the steps, her long silver dress shimmering under the lights. As her eyes met Aiden's and they smiled at each other, I felt as though I'd been punched in the stomach. But instead of doubling over in shock, my feet propelled me forwards.

'Out of my way,' I said as I pushed through the crowd. 'Excushe me. Get out of my way.'

By the time I got to the front of the room, Fi had reached Aiden. I watched, horrified, as he threw his arms around her and hugged her tightly, then I hitched my skirt up to my thighs and half climbed, half rolled on to the stage. Out of the corner of my eye I could see one of Aiden's sisters pointing at me and gasping, a look of horror on her face.

'Excushe me,' I said, pushing Aiden's dad out of the way. 'Please,' I added as he raised his eyebrows. Aiden's arms were wrapped around Fi's back, his face nestled in her glorious blonde hair.

'I'll have that,' I said, grabbing the microphone that was hanging loosely from his hand. I strode to the opposite side of the stage and stood next to Granny.

'I'd like to say a few words if I may,' I bellowed into the microphone. The speakers squealed in protest and several people in the audience put their hands over their ears. Their faces swam in front of me like an enormous multi-headed monster.

'Today is a very happy day,' I continued, only vaguely aware how quiet the room had become. 'A very, very happy day. A day that is so happy that you probably all feel like you live in Happy World … but the truth is …' I punched the air like an evangelical minister preaching to a crowded church. 'The truth is that today is not a happy day at all. No, no. It's a sad day, people. A very sad day, because you have all been lied to.' I caught the eye of a woman in the front row and felt a surge of encouragement, despite the fact that her mouth was hanging open so low her jaw almost touched the string of pearls around her neck. 'And now I, Beth Prince, will tell you the truth.'

'Beth.' Suddenly Aiden was standing beside me, his face pale, his fingers reaching for the microphone. 'Beth, please stop.'

I twisted away from him, swatting at his hand. '*You* stop,' I said into the microphone. 'Stop lying to everyone. Stop pretending you're a nice man.'

'Beth,' Aiden protested. 'I can explain. We're here to—'

'Sssh.' I put a finger to his lips. 'Sssh, sssh, sssh, you.'

Taking advantage of the startled look on his face, I raised the microphone to my lips once again.

'Thish man,' I prodded Aiden in the chest, 'is a cheat and a liar. This man was making love ... no ... shagging me senseless ...' a small child at the front gasped, then dissolved into giggles, 'while all the while he was proclaiming his love to ...' I stalked across the stage and pointed at Fi, '... this woman. And now he's going to get—'

'Beth,' someone hissed. 'BETH! You've made a mistake.'

I looked down into the crowd, the faces blurring into one and then separating again. Lizzie's face slowly came into focus. She was motioning at me, the index finger of her right hand sawing against her throat.

'Why yes, of course I should chop her head off,' I

said, 'and maybe Aiden's too, but I won't. I am many things, but a murderer I am not. Anyway, where was I? Oh yes.' I pointed at Aiden. 'Now this man is going to get married to that woman, and I feel it is my duty to expose him as the liar and cheat he really is. Yesh, ladies and gentlemen, Aiden Dowles is a complete and utter—'

A prod to my shoulder made me pause.

'Yes?' Aiden's grandad was standing beside me, a smile on his wrinkled face.

'Excuse me, young lady.' He beckoned me closer with his finger. 'There's something I need to tell you.'

Convinced that he was about to thank me for revealing the truth about his hateful grandson, I leaned towards him.

'No one's getting married,' he rasped into my ear. 'It would be very wrong if Aiden and Fi were to get hitched.'

'Exactly.' I nodded enthusiastically. 'I'm so glad you agree with me.'

'I think most people would agree with you, my dear.'

'Would they now? Well that does surpr—'

He placed a hand on my shoulder and gazed up at me. 'They're cousins.'

'Urgh!' I snapped away from him. 'Huh?'

He blinked his small watery eyes. 'Aiden's uncle got a lassie pregnant when he was working in Australia in the 1970s and ran back to England before she gave birth. It was all a bit hush-hush in the family, you know? An illegitimate child.'

I nodded, too dumbstruck to speak.

'When our Aiden found out about Fi a couple of years ago, he got curious; you know how he is. He decided to track her down on the interweb and met her for the first time when he went on his travels.'

'Cousins,' I repeated.

Grandad nodded. 'That's right, dear. And Fi has flown over especially for my birthday so that she can meet the whole family for the first time. Unfortunately, Steve, her fiancé, couldn't make it too.'

'Your birthday ...' My eyes flitted over the room, taking in, for the first time, the enormous cake with a big 90 emblazoned on the top, the brightly coloured cards arranged on either side of it, and the unusually large number of grey-haired people present. I twisted round. Aiden's whole family were glaring at me. I looked back at the crowd. They were whispering to each other and pointing at me. Lizzie was slumped against the front of the stage, her head in her hands. As I stared at her in confusion, I suddenly noticed that the person standing next to her was gripping his stomach, doubled over. There was something very familiar about his greasy black hair. And his tatty grey jacket. I was sure I'd seen it before. But where?

My drunken brain was still trying to solve the mystery when the man lurched back to a standing position, tears of laughter streaming down his cheeks as his eyes met mine.

Carl!

'I ...' I said into the microphone as the crowd stared

expectantly back at me. 'I ... Happy birthday, Grandad!' I shouted, then I kicked off my heels and started to run.

Chapter Sixteen

Matt

It was dark, cold and unusually quiet on the seafront. A small group of foreign students were huddled around one of the fish and chip stalls at the entrance to the pier, and a couple were snogging each other's faces off against the railings, but otherwise the streets were empty. Yellow taxis crawled up and down King's Road, their neon signs streaking through the gloom. I considered sticking my hand out, then pulled my jacket tightly around me, crossed my arms over my chest and started to walk down towards the long line of pubs, restaurants and art galleries along the beach.

The evening couldn't have gone more disastrously if I'd tried. So much for sorting things out with Alice. All I'd done was make her hate me.

Ah well, Grandad, I thought as I swerved around a crowd of drinkers outside the Fortune of War pub, you can't say I didn't try.

I kept walking, the crumpled West Pier in my sights. I was about two hundred metres away from it when my eye was caught by a small, huddled figure on a bench facing the sea.

'Beth?' I said as I approached. 'Is that you?'

She was sitting in the middle of the bench, her legs pulled up to her chest, her head buried in her knees. She looked up when she heard my voice and I thought I heard her squeak 'Oh no' before she hid her face again.

'Beth?' I squatted beside her, noticing the goose-bumps on her bare arms, the pair of silver high heels lying discarded on the ground and the champagne bottle on the bench beside her. 'What are you doing down here? You must be freezing!'

The wind caught her hair as she nodded.

'Here.' I slipped off my jacket and draped it around her shoulders. 'Take this.'

We sat side by side for a couple of minutes, Beth still and silent, me staring at her, until finally she pulled the jacket tightly around her and peered up at me. Her eyes looked red, even in the dull glow of the street lamps above us.

'What happened?' I asked. 'Are you okay?'

She shook her head and muttered something I couldn't make out.

'Sorry?'

'You should go, Matt.'

'Why?'

'Because I'm a loser.'

She slurred the word and I tried not to grin at her obvious drunkenness. 'No you're not.'

'I am.'

'Why?'

She hugged her knees closer to her chest. 'Because I

gatecrashed a birthday party for a ninety-year-old man and made a fool of myself.'

I grinned ruefully. It was obviously a good night for people embarrassing themselves in Brighton. 'I'm sure that's not true.'

'Ish true.' She nodded wildly, then her lips turned downwards and a single tear rolled down her face. 'Ish true, Matt.'

'Hey.' I patted her on the shoulder. 'I'm sure it wasn't as bad as you think.'

'It was worse.'

'Oh yeah? Well I bet you didn't accidentally cough an oyster across a restaurant table into someone's cleavage!'

She frowned as though trying to process what I'd said. 'You're just saying that to make me feel better.'

'I wish I was.'

She grinned. 'That's quite a trick. People would pay good money to see that.'

'Apparently they pay in expensive red wine instead.' I pointed to my sodden shirt. 'Look.'

'Hey!' Her eyes lit up. 'You look like Mr Orange from *Reservoir Dogs* dressed like that. Know of any fancy-dress parties tonight?'

'Unfortunately not.' I put an arm around her and gave her a squeeze, relieved that she'd stopped crying.

'Do you know what, Matt?' she said as she leaned in against me.

'Nope.'

'First thing 'morrow, I'm going to hairdressers to get

my hair dyed back to normal, then I'm gonna ess … essfoli … scrub myself violently.'

'You are a bit terracotta.' I grinned. 'I'm surprised Laurence Llewelyn-Bowen hasn't rag-rolled you on to a wall.'

'Rag-rolled me?' She snorted. 'How 1990s are you? I bet you've got starfish stencils in your bathroom.'

'Hey, don't diss the stencils. I used to have dolphins too, but I had to keep picking them out of the tuna nets I've got pinned to the ceiling.'

Beth groaned, but she was grinning from ear to ear. My arm was still around her, but I felt no compulsion to remove it. When she leaned her head on my shoulder, neither of us said anything for a couple of seconds. Above us a seagull squawked, circled a couple of times and then made off for the pier.

'Ever wish you could rewind your life, Matt?' Beth murmured.

'All the time. Particularly tonight.'

'What happened …' she covered her mouth and yawned, 'to you? Why did you spit an oyster on someone?'

'Ah well. Long story short, I went out for dinner with my ex-girlfriend to see if we should give it another go. Only things didn't quite go according to plan. In fact they went so far off plan they pretty much made up their own plan, and before I knew what was happening … Beth?'

Her eyes were closed, her impossibly long eyelashes brushing the tops of her cheeks. She was breathing slowly and deeply, her body relaxed against me.

'You sleep,' I whispered as I laid my cheek against the top of her head and stared out to sea. 'You sleep for a little bit, and then I'll call you a taxi. Sweet dreams, Beth.'

Chapter Seventeen

Beth

All I could remember of the previous night, as Lizzie perched on the end of my bed and handed me a steaming cup of coffee, was:

1) walking through the doors of the Grand;

2) people staring at me as I stood on a stage;

3) the soft feel of Matt's hand in mine as he walked me to my front door.

'Oh God,' I said, sitting bolt upright, the duvet clutched to my chest. 'Tell me I didn't snog my potential new boss last night?'

Lizzie shook her head. 'You were in no state to snog your own hand, never mind him. I've never seen you so drunk.' She raised an eyebrow. 'Nor has the toilet bowl.'

I cringed, my head throbbing so hard I felt like my brain was trying to escape through my ears. 'At least I hit it. I did hit the loo, didn't I?'

'Eventually. After you'd puked in the bath and on the lino. Oh yeah, and before you headed for the bathroom, you threw up in the kitchen sink. You might want to fish yesterday's breakfast bowls out of it before you clean it up.'

A fresh wave of nausea hit me and I grabbed the bin Lizzie had helpfully placed beside the bed.

'Whoa.' She steadied my mug as coffee slopped on to the duvet. 'Are you deliberately trying to trash the whole house? I love having you here, Beth, but please tell me you're not going to make getting trollied a regular habit.'

I wiped my mouth with a scrap of sparkly black clothing I'd found beside the bin, then slumped back on to the bed and covered my face with a pillow.

'I'm never, ever getting that drunk again. I am going to swear off alcohol, join a nunnery and spend the rest of my life never speaking another word.' I paused. An image of an old man's face had just flashed into my mind. I peeled back the pillow and peered at Lizzie. 'What the hell did I do last night?'

'I don't think you want to know.'

I pulled a face. 'That bad?'

'Worse.'

'Go on. Tell me. I can take it.'

'Are you sure?' My flatmate had a sip of her coffee and took a deep breath. 'Well ... we went into the Grand and found where the party was being held. About thirty seconds after we walked in, you clambered up on to the stage, grabbed Aiden's microphone and laid into him in front of all his friends and relatives. I think your exact words were "Thish man is a cheat and a liar", and then you said something about him shagging you senseless.'

'Oh God, no.' I yanked the pillow back over my head and pressed it to my face.

'It was at about that point in your speech,' Lizzie continued, her tone amused, 'that Aiden's grandad decided to have a word. Turns out it was actually his ninetieth birthday party and Fi was Aiden's long-lost cousin, *not* his fiancée.'

'Urrrrggggh,' I moaned from beneath the pillow. 'No.'

'Urgh, yes! And that's when you kicked off your shoes, nicked a bottle of champagne from one of the waiters and sprinted into the night. I went after you, obviously, but you'd just disappeared. I tried all the nearby pubs, but I couldn't find you anywhere. In the end, I went home, in case you'd come straight back, but you weren't here either. I nearly rang the police.'

'Sorry,' I mumbled. 'I was on the seafront.'

'I know. When you finally rolled up in a taxi, you told me you'd gone down to the beach to drown yourself like Virginia Woolf.'

Oh God, I was drunk *and* pretentious.

'Apparently it was too cold for a dramatic death, so you sat on a bench and felt sorry for yourself instead. Then your new boss found you and shoved you in a taxi and brought you home.' She took a deep breath. 'And that's it.'

I pulled the pillow down so I could peer over the top. 'I definitely didn't snog him?'

Lizzie grinned. 'I think you would have told me if you had. You told me pretty much everything else about your life last night. I couldn't shut you up.'

'Sorry.'

'It's okay. I stopped listening and went to make a cup of tea the fifth time you started telling me how you and Aiden met. You were still waffling on about him when I walked back in ten minutes later.'

I sighed. 'Sorry. Again. I'm such a boring drunk. Maybe joining a nunnery isn't such a bad idea after all.'

'That's a bit of an extreme hangover cure, isn't it? Most people have a bacon sandwich and lie on the sofa, moaning.'

'I'm not talking about getting drunk, though obviously I'm never doing that again. I'm talking about men. I'm done with them. For good.'

'Yeah, right!' Lizzie didn't look convinced. 'You're the soppiest person I've ever met. You'll be head over heels about some new guy in no time.'

I shook my head. 'I won't. I honestly won't. I'm sick of meeting someone, getting all excited about them and then being dumped on from a great height. Romance, men who don't cheat, soulmates …' I counted them off on my fingers, 'I don't believe in any of them any more.'

'Good for you!' Lizzie's expression changed from concern to delight. 'I've been telling you for ages not to take relationships so seriously. Men are like night buses, Beth, you never know if you're on the right one. And you're still young. You need to have a bit of fun and play the—'

'When I was a little girl,' I interrupted, twisting on to my side to take another sip of coffee, 'my favourite fairy tales were *Cinderella* and *Sleeping Beauty*. Do you know what I've realised about those stories?'

Lizzie shook her head, bemused.

'That they're both about girls – well, women – who

are really miserable because their lives suck. Lots of fairy tales are. The thing they all have in common is the fact that nothing changes until a prince – a man – turns up and saves them. After that, it's happiness ever after.'

'Bollocks to that! Save your bloody self.'

'I know! I've always known that, even when I was a teenager watching romantic comedies, but the thing is—'

'You still watch romantic comedies!'

'Ssh. I'm getting to the point.' I put my coffee down and propped myself up on my elbow. 'The reason I like romantic comedies is because, unlike fairy tales, they aren't just about the man saving the woman. The woman saves the man too. Remember *Pretty Woman*?'

Lizzie nodded. 'Of course.'

'Then you'll know that, at the end, Julia Roberts tells Richard Gere she's going to save him right back. And in *Jerry Maguire*, Tom Cruise tells Renée Zellweger that she completes him.'

Lizzie opened her mouth to say something, but I waved her away.

'Even the crotchety old weirdo Jack Nicholson plays in *As Good as It Gets* tells Helen Hunt's character that she makes him want to be a better man.'

'But they're films, Beth. Those relationships, they're not real.'

'I know, but stuff like that does happen in real life. Women fall in love with men and men love them back. Or vice versa. You don't have to be all dramatic and save or complete each other, but the feelings should be equal. You need each other, you want each other, you love each other. It happens all the time. But what I don't get ...' I hugged the pillow to my chest as my eyes suddenly filled with tears, 'is why it's never happened to me.'

'Oh, honey.' Lizzie reached forward and squeezed my hand.

I shook my head. 'Don't.'

'It'll happen,' she said softly.

'Will it?' I swiped at my eyes. 'Sometimes I feel like there's something wrong with me. Why else would men take everything I give and then leave me? It's like I'm not good enough or something.'

'Don't you dare say that!' Lizzie looked appalled. 'There's nothing wrong with you, Beth. Nothing at all. You're warm, intelligent, funny and kind. You're gorgeous, and any man that doesn't realise that is a total twat-features. Honestly, honey, you've just been unlucky.'

'Unlucky? Sometimes it feels like the harder I chase after love, the faster it runs away from me, and I'm just so tired of it all, Lizzie. I'm so bloody tired.'

'I know.' She gently rubbed her thumb over the back of my hand. 'I know.'

We both fell quiet, Lizzie gazing at me with concern, me staring at the pattern on the hideously flowery duvet cover Mum had given me for Christmas.

'Do you know what I'm going to do?' I said finally, looking up.

'Hire a hit man to take out all your ex-boyfriends?'

'No, I'm going to concentrate on what I can change.'

'And what's that?'

'Well,' I said, suddenly enthusiastic, 'first of all I'm going to buy those de-tanning cloths you were telling me about so I'm not orange any more. Then I'm going to re-dye my hair. But the main thing I'm going to do is make damned sure that I get the new manager's position at work. The interview weekend in Wales is in two weeks' time, and I'm going to get that job.'

'You'll nail it! No one knows or loves that cinema better than you do,' Lizzie said excitedly. 'Nice one, Beth. You're finally taking charge of your own happy ending.' She raised her coffee cup. 'To Beth Prince and all she conquers!'

I clinked my cup against hers, and forced a smile. 'To me.'

Chapter Eighteen

Matt

My mood was an odd mixture of relaxed and stressed as I strolled to the pub for an early-evening pint with Neil. After I'd dropped Beth at her house, I'd gone straight to bed and slept like a log until my alarm had gone off at 7 a.m. Work was quiet, and I'd kept myself busy arranging the interview weekend in Wales. All in all, life was looking up. Sort of. I'd woken up to find seven texts from Alice on my phone, each one angrier than the next. When I'd replied, apologising for what had happened in the restaurant, she'd called me 'bastard scum' and said she hoped I'd 'rot in hell' for what I did and that 'if karma exists you'll spend the rest of your life unhappy'.

'Jesus,' Neil said as I crossed the pub and approached his table. 'You look like shit.'

Great, more insults.

'Cheers, mate!' I took a swig of my pint, then set it back down. 'Why are you so bloody pleased with yourself anyway?'

He grinned. 'I've only got myself a new job, haven't I?'

'What job?'

Neil was an accounts manager for a computer games company, a somewhat ironic choice of profession considering he'd never played a computer game in his life before he was hired. He still claimed to be the only non-geek in the entire company.

'It's for GameThing,' he said.

I shook my head. 'Never heard of them. Are they based in Hove?'

'Guess again.' He looked smug. 'Try California.'

I felt my jaw drop. 'What?'

'Yep.' He nodded and spread his arms out wide like he was surfing. 'California dude!'

'Wow. When do you go?'

'Next month.'

I stared at him. My best mate in the entire world was leaving the country. Was there anyone in my life who didn't want to bugger off and leave me behind?

'That's great news,' I said, trying to hide how gutted I actually was. 'I'm really pleased for you.'

'No you're not.' He reached for his pint and held it aloft. 'You're as jealous as shit.'

'Maybe a little bit.' As I clinked my glass against his, I noticed a book on the table in front of him. 'What's that?'

'This, mate,' he said, snatching it up and showing me the front cover, 'is the secret behind my new job.'

'*Visualising Success*?' I snorted as I read the title. 'Give me a break! Sounds like new-age mumbo-jumbo.'

'Don't diss it.' Neil looked serious. 'I thought the same as you until I heard the author talking about it on the radio. His business was failing, the bank was sending him threatening letters – he was about to lose his house and everything – but then he started visualising a better future, you know, a more financially lucrative one, and his luck began to change. A massive order arrived, his website started to get loads more hits and the money just rolled in. He's a multimillionaire now.'

'Yeah,' I scoffed, 'probably from gullible idiots like you buying the book!'

'You say that,' he looked me in the eye, not the slightest bit offended, 'but who's the one stuck in Brighton in a job they hate, and who's the one jetting off to the States to land a six-figure salary?'

'Six figures?' I gawped at him. 'You're kidding?'

'Nope.' He shook his head.

'Wow.' I stared at him in amazement. I wasn't convinced that the book was responsible for his good luck, but there was no doubt he'd fallen on his feet.

'Read it.' He pushed it across the table towards me, but I shook my head.

'Nah, man. I'm cool. It's not really my sort of thing. And anyway,' I shot him a look, 'who said I hated my job?'

'Don't you?' He raised an eyebrow.

'Another pint?' I said, reaching for his empty glass.

Neil just grinned. Smug git.

Chapter Nineteen

Beth

I had my eyes closed, mentally repeating the positive affirmation Mum had pinned to my bedroom ceiling, when Jade, a part-time member of staff at the Picture-box, prodded my shoulder.

'Wake up, Beth,' she hissed. 'I think Matt's about to say something.'

It was Saturday 6 December and we were sitting in the bar of the Royal Albert Hotel, somewhere in the Breacon Beacons. It had taken us five hours on the train to get to Abergavenny and then a fifty-minute minibus ride to the hotel, and it was still only 1 p.m. It was also freezing. The weather men on the TV had predicted snow, and I was already regretting my choice of silk blouse (borrowed from Lizzie's wardrobe), cotton-mix pencil skirt and eight-denier tights.

My eyes flew open. 'Thanks, Jade.'

Matt was standing in front of the group in a dark grey suit and pale blue tie with his hands clasped behind his back. He was clean-shaven, and his hair was neatly styled – he couldn't have looked more professional if he'd tried. I couldn't believe he was the same man who'd joined me on a bench on the seafront looking tired and dishevelled.

Matt wasn't the only one who was dressed in a suit. At the end of the row, leaning forward and tilting his head in an effort to catch my eye, was Carl. I'd spotted him, talking to Raj, one of my colleagues, by reception, the moment I'd walked into the hotel. It was exactly a fortnight since I'd humiliated myself at Aiden's non-engagement party, and somehow (through some judicious jiggling of the work rota and a few sharp exits through the back of the Picturebox) I'd managed to avoid Carl and his stupid, smug face for the whole of that time.

'Look who it is!' he'd said, breaking off the conversation to wave at me. 'DJ Prince.' He turned to look back at Raj. 'Did you know Beth's a dab hand with a microphone?'

Raj looked at me in surprise. 'You never told me you spun the decks, Beth!'

'Oh yeah. She's quite the talent. She does everything – weddings, bar mitzvahs, parties for ninety-year-olds – you can't put her near a stage without her jumping up on it.'

Every muscle in my body twitched as I fought the urge to walk across the foyer and slap Carl's stupid smug face. Instead I pressed my lips together, tightened my grip on my suitcase and headed for the ladies' toilets. Once inside, I slumped against the cold tiled wall and tried to get my breathing under control. I was so furious my heart felt like it was trying to beat itself out of my body, but there was no way, NO WAY, I was going to rise to Carl's pathetic comments. Especially not when there was a risk that Matt might appear and see me acting unprofessionally. It was the most important day of my life, and I was going to do everything in my power to get the manager's job. And if that meant pretending that Carl hadn't totally stitched me up at Aiden's party, then so be it.

'Hey,' Jade nudged me, 'are you okay? You look a bit stressed.'

'I'm fine.' I forced a smile and focused my attention on Matt, who was patiently waiting for everyone to stop talking and fidgeting.

'Hi, everyone,' he said, nodding to the room. 'First of all I'd like to thank you for coming …'

'Pleasure,' murmured Carl.

Smarmy git.

'… especially those of you who aren't fans of leadership weekends.' Matt caught my eye and grinned. 'Hopefully it won't be as bad as you think.'

My stomach did a little somersault and I mentally checked myself.

Stop it, Beth.

'I know there's only one management position available,' Matt continued, 'but I hope you all get a lot out of this weekend anyway.'

'Mostly bedbug bites, if my bed's as dirty as it looks,' Jade hissed in my ear.

'As some of you know,' Matt frowned at Jade as she frantically scratched her arms, 'the weekend will be a mixture of leadership tasks and one-on-one interviews. After lunch, we'll jump back in the minibus, which will take us to the first of our leadership exercises – abseiling.'

Jade made a noise like a cat yacking up a hairball, while Raj, who was sitting on the other side of me, punched the air. I stared at Matt, utterly horrified. Abseiling! *Visualising Success* hadn't mentioned anything about throwing yourself off cliff faces. I'd been expecting a conference room and some kind of task that involved blindfolds, obstacles and trust exercises.

'We'll grab a bit of lunch,' Matt continued, shooting me a quizzical look, 'and then you should all go back to your rooms and change into your tracksuits or whatever.'

Tracksuits! What tracksuits? I hadn't packed any trousers. I didn't even have pyjamas to sleep in – just an oversized I ♥ New York T-shirt Mum had brought me back from one of her business trips.

'Jade.' I grabbed my colleague's sleeve as Matt signalled that we should follow him into the dining room. 'You haven't got any spare trousers, have you?'

'I can't wear those,' I said, aghast, as Jade pulled a pair of cropped cotton trousers out of her suitcase. 'They're tiny!'

'No they're not.' She held them up against her impossibly narrow hips. 'They're actually quite baggy.'

'If you're a size six! What are they? Eights?'

She shook her head. 'Ten. You can get into them, Beth. No problem.'

'Only if the hotel does emergency liposuction.' I grabbed a handful of my decidedly generous hips. I was a twelve to fourteen normally – and that was on a good, I-haven't-been-continually-stuffing-my-face-with-chocolate-since-I-got-dumped day.

'Try them on.' Jade thrust the trousers at me. 'You'll be fine.'

Ten minutes later I emerged from her en suite bathroom and waddled towards her.

'See!' she said, clapping her hands together. 'Told you they'd fit. You look great.'

'Mmmm,' I said. The trousers were so tight I could hardly breathe, and my stomach bulged over the waistband like a side of pork. 'You haven't seen them from the back yet.'

'Go on then, turn around.'

I pirouetted slowly.

There was a pause, then a sharp intake of breath.

'What?' I said, twisting back round. 'That bad?'

'Noooo …' Jade assumed an innocent expression. 'Just a bit of VPL. Nothing that taking your knickers off won't sort out.'

'I'm not taking my knickers off!'

'Okay.' She shrugged, her eyes flicking back to my bum. 'Keep them on, then.'

I stared at her. Going commando during the leadership task definitely wasn't part of my visualisation. 'You really think I should take my knickers off?'

'Uh-huh.' She nodded. 'Unless you want to look like you've got six bums.'

Six bums? Lovely.

'Right.' I waddled back towards the bathroom. 'They're coming off.'

'Okay,' said Matt, as he surveyed the six of us, huddled up together at the top of the cliff face, the icy winter wind whipping our hair into our faces. It was so cold I couldn't feel my lips. 'I'm going to split you up into three teams of two.'

'Beth,' he said, 'you'll go with …'

Not Carl, I prayed. Please not Carl. Anyone but Carl. I'd take burping, farting, your-mum's-so-fat-joke-telling Seth over Carl any day. Please not …

'Carl,' Matt finished.

I stared up at the sky. Cheers, God.

'Heads or tails?'

'Sorry?'

'Heads or tails, Beth?' Matt was standing beside me, a ten-pence piece resting on the thumb of his right hand. He smiled. 'I'm tossing to see who goes first.'

'Heads, please.'

I watched as the coin jumped into the air and flipped over several times before Matt grabbed it and slapped it on to the back of his hand. I held my breath as he revealed it.

'Tails. Sorry, Beth.' He turned to look at Carl, who was standing behind him. 'Do you want to go first or second?'

Carl smirked. 'Beth can go first.'

I stared at Matt in alarm.

'It'll be fine.' He rubbed the side of my arm and my whole body tingled. 'Bob, our instructor, will get you kitted out in the harness and tell you what to do. Don't worry. You'll be perfectly safe.' He glanced at his fingers, still on my arm, and looked surprised. His hand fell away.

'Right, guys.' He turned to look at the rest of the group. 'The object of the exercise is to work in teams to collect the flags that are situated at intervals down the cliff face. One member of the team will abseil over the edge ...' I shuddered violently, 'and the other will shout instructions down to them, telling them which way to move to get to the flags as they descend. Everyone got that?'

James, Seth and Raj nodded. Jade looked as horrified as I felt. Carl just grinned.

'I'll be watching from the bottom of the cliff,' Matt continued, turning to go. 'Good luck.'

'I can't do this,' I squeaked as Bob tightened the harness around my waist and thighs and moved my trembling hands into the correct position – one on the rope in front of me and one on the rope behind.

'You'll be fine. Getting over the edge is the worst bit; after that's it's a breeze.'

'It'll be more of a tornado for Pimp,' Carl said, sticking out his tongue and making a revolting farting noise. 'Do you supply gas masks?'

I glared at him. 'We're supposed to be working as a team, Carl.'

He rolled his eyes.

'Okay, Beth,' Bob said, tugging on the rope in front of me. 'We're ready to go. Could you take a couple of steps back for me?'

I took a hesitant step backwards, towards the cliff

edge. My legs were shaking so much I had to concentrate just to get them to move.

'Good,' Bob said. 'Now another one.'

I shuffled backwards another inch.

'And another.'

Jade, her hair piled under a woolly bobble hat, her hands tucked into her armpits, gasped as I took another step back.

'What?' I said, staring at her in horror.

'Nothing.' She shook her head. 'It's just a long way down.'

'Cheers!' I looked back at Bob. He was the only person who wasn't staring at me with alarm or, in Carl's case, delight. 'Now what?'

'One more step and you'll be on the edge. When you reach it, you need to lean back. It'll feel strange, but don't worry, the rope's securely tied. You're in no danger.'

My stomach lurched violently and my legs refused to move.

'You can do it, Beth,' Bob said, his weathered face strangely reassuring. 'One little step and the worst bit will be over.'

I inched backwards and froze when I realised my heels were hanging over the edge of the cliff.

'That's it,' said Bob. 'Now lean back … Back a little more. You need to be almost perpendicular to the cliff face.'

My entire body tensed. I was holding on to the rope so desperately, I could feel the fibres pressing into my palms. As I leaned back, Jade's trousers strained across my bum. Thank God I didn't wear the knickers, I thought as I leaned back a bit further, or Matt would be staring up at the cliff wondering if a girl with twelve arses was suitable manager material.

'That's it,' Bob said delightedly. 'Now don't forget to let out the rope with your left hand so you can move. Let a little bit out now and take a step.'

I did as I was told, and shuffled half a foot down the cliff. The rope was pulled tight, supporting my delicate (cough) frame.

'Okay, Carl,' Matt shouted from below through a megaphone. 'Over to you. Give Beth instructions to collect the flags.'

Carl's greasy face appeared at the top of the cliff. His pointy teeth glinted in the weak December sunshine as he smiled.

'Go down a foot and then move to your left,' he shouted.

I released the rope behind me and moved my feet carefully down a couple of inches.

'You are being timed,' Matt said through the megaphone. 'Sorry, forgot to mention that.'

'Quicker, Pimp,' Carl shouted.

I glared up at him. 'My name's Beth.'

'Whatever.' He shrugged. 'Get a move on! Do you want this job or not?'

Anger, and the fact that I really *did* want the job, motivated me to move faster. I released more rope and took another couple of steps down the cliff.

'Left now,' Carl shouted. 'Left a bit.'

I glanced to my left. A red flag was tied to a metal

ring secured to the wall. I reached out a hand, but my fingers stroked thin air. Damn, too far away.

'The flag isn't going to end up in your hand through telekinesis,' Carl shouted. 'You need to move your fat arse.'

Seth, standing beside him, laughed loudly, and I gritted my teeth. I hoped Matt could hear Carl's 'helpful' comments. I took a step to my left, then another one. Something above me creaked ominously.

'Got it!' I grabbed a flag and stuffed it down the front of my coat.

'Halle-bloody-lujah.' Carl shouted. 'Jesus, Pimp, are we still going to be here at dinner time? I thought you were slow at school, but this is ridiculous.'

'Where's the next one?' I shouted back. He could try and wind me up all he liked, but one of us had to remain professional.

'Down a bit more. Another four feet and then to your right.'

I nodded, let out the rope and took a couple of steps.

'You do realise you're not supposed to waddle your way down the cliff, don't you?' Carl shouted. 'You're meant to jump with both feet.'

'One minute,' Matt announced. 'One minute left.'

I glanced behind me. He was standing about thirty feet below and looking up. I tried to imagine what he could see – my big bum squeezed into too-small trousers and strapped up in a harness. Horrific.

'We're going to lose!' Carl shouted from the top of the cliff. 'What are you doing? Stopping to admire the view?'

'Hey!' I glared at him. 'You try doing this.'

'I couldn't be any worse. Move your fucking arse. Jump down the next few feet.'

'Fine,' I said stubbornly. 'I will.'

I leaned further back, released the rope behind me and pushed myself off the cliff face, dropping several feet and then swinging back. I stuck out my feet, bracing myself for impact as they made contact with the wall, and then ...

Zzzzzzzzzzzzzzzzzzzzzzzzzzzzzzt.

It was the sound of material ripping.

I stared, horrified, at the rope, convinced that I was about to drop to my death, then a sharp, cold gust of wind caught me and I really *did* want to die.

I reached round with one hand and patted my freezing cold bum.

My *naked* bum.

Jade's trousers had split down the seam, and my arse was hanging out, thirty feet above Matt's gawping face.

Aagggggggggggggggggghhhh!

'Move it, lard arse!' Carl shouted from above.

'Let me down!' I screamed.

'Put your hands back on the ropes!' Bob shouted.

'I can't!' I couldn't move the hand from my bum. Not that it was doing much to obscure Matt's view. 'Let me down!'

'Loser!' Carl shouted. 'Once a loser, always a loser.'

'Let me down, Bob,' I squealed. 'Please!'

Matt coughed into his megaphone, then spoke, his voice shaking with what I desperately hoped wasn't laughter. 'Let her down, Bob.'

The next couple of seconds were the longest of my life. Bob slowly lowered me down the cliff face, while Carl screamed abuse at me. When my feet finally touched the ground, I had my eyes shut. Please let Matt be struck down by terrible conjunctivitis, I prayed. Please, please, please …

'Beth.' I kept my eyes tightly shut as a hand touched my shoulder. 'Take this.' I opened my eyes a millimetre. Matt was pushing his suit jacket into my hands. 'Tie it round your waist.'

I grabbed it desperately and wrapped it around me as Matt unclipped the harness and shouted something up at the team. I couldn't look at him. I was staring at the ground, waiting for it to open up and swallow me, and my burning cheeks, whole.

'For fuck's sake, Pimp,' said a voice to my right. 'You are the most useless lump of shit ever to walk the earth. You couldn't manage a threesome in a brothel.'

Carl was standing beside me. He took one look at my bright red face and burst out laughing.

'Jesus, you look like a …'

I didn't hear the rest of his sentence. I was already halfway to the minibus.

Chapter Twenty

Matt

Oh God. I shuffled the pile of CVs in front of me and looked at the next name on the list.

Beth Prince.

I shook my head. Poor girl. Poor, poor girl. It was Sunday, one-on-one interview day, and no one had seen her since the minibus had brought us back to the hotel after James and Seth had completed the final abseil. Not that she'd stuck around to watch anyone else's attempt.

She'd run back to the bus the second I'd turned my back. I found her curled up on the back seat, her hands clamped to her face, my jacket still wrapped around her waist.

She refused to talk to me. Not that I could blame her. I didn't know where to look when her trousers split halfway down the cliff face. I was as mortified as she was, and wanted to get her covered up before any of the other lads clocked what had happened. Particularly Carl. Evil little shit.

The door to the conference hall I was using as my interview room squeaked open, and I looked up.

'Hi, Beth.' I gave her my best warm smile.

'Matt.' She walked up to the desk, her eyes fixed on the carpet the whole way, and sat down.

'Have you got your business plan?'

'Yes.' She nodded shyly and pushed a plastic wallet across the table.

'Excellent.' I opened it and pulled out the document inside. It was ring-bound and at least a dozen pages long. No one else I'd interviewed had gone to that much trouble. James's plan was professional but at least half the length, while Seth had given me what looked like a cocktail napkin with a few scribbles on it.

'You okay?' I glanced at Beth. She was fiddling with the hem of her skirt. 'We missed you at dinner last night.'

'I'm fine.' Her eyes flicked up to meet mine for a split second before she looked away again. 'I ordered room service.'

'Great.' I nodded enthusiastically, desperate to break the horribly awkward atmosphere. 'Did you have anything nice?'

'Sausage and mash with onion gravy. I fancied the pasta arrabiata, but they were all out.'

I raised my eyebrows in sympathy. 'Bummer.'

Beth looked at me from under her eyelashes and frowned. 'Are you being funny?'

Funny? Huh? Oh God. *Bummer!* My brain clicked into gear. She probably thought I was taking the piss about what had happened yesterday. Not cool, Matt, not cool at all.

'No,' I said. 'Of course not.'

'Good.' Beth smiled nervously.

'So ...' I skimmed the CV in front of me. 'It says here that you've been at the Picturebox for the last six years.'

She nodded. 'That's right.'

'And you've taken responsibility for marketing, customer accounts and a number of promotions. Could you tell me a bit about the promotions you organised and how successful they were?'

'Sure. The first one I organised was—'

'Hang on a sec.'

'Have you lost something?' Beth asked as I searched around among the bits of paper on my desk.

'Arse!'

'Sorry, what did you just say?'

'Not arse. Definitely not arse. Er ...' I grimaced apologetically. 'James must have walked off with my pen.'

'Right.' She narrowed her eyes suspiciously, then reached into her handbag and handed me a biro. 'You can borrow this.'

I took it and desperately searched for something non-offensive to say. What was wrong with me? I couldn't get rid of the image of Beth's naked bum hanging from the cliff. It was a nice bum too, really rounded and ...

Oh no. Now she was glaring at me.

'Did you just say peachy, Matt?'

Oh, shit. Had I just said that aloud?

'No. I said ... er ... it doesn't matter what I said. On with the interview, let's not backside, I mean backslide ...'

'Backside! Backside?' Beth's eyes flashed with anger as she pushed her chair away from the desk and stood up. 'What is this? Some kind of dare to make as many references to my bum as you can? Because I don't think it's very funny, Matt. I don't think it's funny at all.'

'I'm sorry.' I clasped my head in horror. 'Please sit down, Beth. Honestly, I really didn't—'

'Don't even bother!' She waved her hand dismissively. 'Because I won't believe you. You're surprised that I didn't come to dinner last night? Well I'm sorry if I didn't want to stick around to be made fun of, but I'm sick of being the butt of everyone's jokes. Butt, there you go, you can have that one on me. You can have this one too. Stick your job up your arse, Matt Jones!'

I watched mutely as she stormed out of the room and slammed the door behind her, then slumped forward on to the desk and covered my head with my hands. The right thing to do would be to go after her. Then again, I was suffering from an extreme case of foot in mouth and I'd probably just make things worse. She was absolutely fuming too, and if she was anything like Alice, there was no way she'd accept an apology until she'd cooled down.

I glanced at my watch. Raj would be in for his interview in ten minutes. There was no time to go after Beth anyway. I reached for her business plan and skimmed idly over the first page. I paused at the bottom, then reread it, more carefully this time. Wow.

I turned the page and read the next sheet, my jaw dropping as I digested each of the plans she'd detailed.

They were amazing. More than amazing; they were inspired. She had come up with ideas – wonderfully creative money-making ideas – that I couldn't have thought of in a million years. Her plan, if it worked – and I was pretty sure it could – would mean that the Picturebox would increase its net profit by two hundred per cent in the first year alone. And to think she'd been working there for six years with all of these ideas bubbling inside of her, and none of them had been implemented. Was Mrs Blackstock insane?

I gazed at the closed interview door. Beth was perfect for the manager's job, absolutely perfect, but she'd been pretty definite about where she wanted me to stick it. I couldn't imagine her changing her mind about that, even if I did apologise to her.

I reached for James's business plan. None of his ideas were ground-breaking or inspired – they weren't a patch on Beth's – but they were solid. As was James. He'd been working in the Hove branch of Apollo for a couple of years and had jumped at the idea of managing the Picturebox, because he wanted a challenge. Ballbreaker had met him – she'd liked him, too. In fact, she'd specifically ordered me to give his application my 'full attention'. He was the obvious candidate.

'Matt?' The door clicked open and Raj poked his head round it. 'Are you ready for me?'

I glanced down at Beth's business proposal, resting my hand on it as I weighed up my options, then shook my head and moved it to the bottom of the application pile. What a shame. What a damned shame.

'Yep.' I looked up at Raj and smiled. 'Come on in.'

Chapter Twenty-One

Beth

I ran from the interview room, cheeks burning, and headed straight to the bar.

'Pinot Noir,' I said, gripping the smooth mahogany counter like my life depended on it. 'Could you put it on room 102's tab?'

The barman nodded. 'Large or small?'

'A bottle.'

'Certainly, madam. We have a lovely Volnay Premier Cru that I'd recommend. It's an elegant, velvety wine with a muscular finish.'

'Great.'

The barman plucked a bottle from the row behind him, then turned back with a flourish. 'How many glasses would you like?'

'Just one.'

'Very good, madam.' He didn't so much as raise an eyebrow as he twisted the corkscrew into the bottle, yanked it out with a satisfying pop and poured a large measure into a glass so clean it sparkled.

'Thanks.' I clasped the bottle to my chest and slunk through the bar, waving the wine glass in front of me as I headed towards an armchair by the window. I slumped into it and took a huge glug of wine.

It was over. It really was over. I'd totally screwed up any chance I'd ever had of getting the manager's job. All that hard work with the business plan, the hours spent poring over Mum's book, the countless repetitions of the visualisation exercise – all for nothing.

I shook my head. I couldn't believe I'd actually told Matt to shove his job up his arse. What the hell was I thinking?

I knocked back my wine in one go and refilled the glass. Actually, I knew exactly why I'd told Matt where to shove his job.

When Aiden had dumped me, I'd taken Lizzie's advice and ignored him instead of asking for answers. Then, rather than giving Carl what-for about the party, I'd avoided him. And when my biggest humiliation had occurred – splitting my trousers during the abseiling task – I'd just run away! Matt's bum references during my interview were the last straw. I'd been biting my tongue for so long, something inside me had snapped. I was sick of being Beth the 'put up and shut up' professional doormat. Only I hadn't taken my anger out on the people who deserved it, had I? No, I'd screamed at the one person who didn't.

I sighed heavily, lifted the second glass of wine to my lips and gazed around the bar. A Christmas tree, tastefully decorated with red and gold glass baubles and small hand-painted wooden figures and topped with a delicate gold angel, glowed warmly in the corner of the room. Elegant arrangements of holly, ivy and bright red berries adorned picture frames and doorways, while a vat of mulled wine on the edge of the bar filled the air with the spicy, warm scents of orange and cinnamon. It was nearly Christmas and I was single, out of a job and out of luck. I topped up my glass and glanced out of the window. Maybe I should just run away so that I didn't have to share the minibus with everyone else. It couldn't be, what, more than ten miles to the station. Nah. I rested my head against the glass and took another sip. I should finish my wine first. It would be rude not to. And anyway, fluffy white snowflakes were drifting gently down from the sky. They were so pretty, so very …

'Hey, sleepyhead! Are you planning on spending the night in that chair?'

My eyes flew open and I looked wildly around. It was dark outside and the bar was virtually empty, all the tables apart from mine polished until the wood gleamed.

'What time is it?' I rubbed my eyes, peeled away the strands of hair that were stuck to my lip gloss and stared up at Raj. 'Is the minibus here?'

'That's just it.' He grinned down at me, his hands in his pockets. 'There is no minibus.'

'What do you mean?'

'Have you taken a look outside recently?'

I twisted round in my chair and cupped my hands to the window.

'My God,' I gasped as I peered outside. The light, fluffy snow was now several inches thick. Trees bowed low under its weight, the ornamental fountain looked like a skating rink and the driveway had all but disappeared.

Raj lowered himself into the chair opposite me and glanced at his watch. 'I hope you haven't made any plans for this evening, because the road between here and town is a total no-go.'

'So we're stuck here?'

'Looks like it.'

I looked around again. The barman who'd served me earlier was polishing glasses behind the bar, a bored expression on his face. 'Where's everyone else?'

Raj nodded towards the lobby. 'Matt's talking to reception about keeping our rooms for another night. The other guys are upstairs.'

'Wow.' I looked out of the window again. It was like I'd woken up in a winter wonderland. 'What's the plan, then, Raj?'

He laughed. 'Have dinner, then get pissed, I guess!'

As Raj wandered back towards the lobby, I drained the last gulp of wine in my glass, signalled to the barman to bring me another bottle, then reached for my mobile. Oh! I'd missed four text messages while I was asleep.

The first one was from Mum.

Hello darling! How did the interview go? I'd love you to get it but you know how keen I am for you to join me in Australia. Let me know.

Her timing was freaky – it was like she knew I was one step closer to becoming her secretary. I sighed, pressed delete, and looked at the other messages.

We need to talk about what happened at the Grand said the first one.

I dropped by your flat but your flatmate said you'd gone away. Where are you? said the second.

I opened the third. *Are you ignoring me? Please call me. It's important. Aiden x*

So important that you wait over two weeks before you get in touch with me! Yeah, right! What do you want – to remind me how much I humiliated myself at your grandad's birthday party?

I moved my thumb quickly over the keypad.

Delete.

Delete.

Delete.

By the time we sat down to dinner, I was so pissed it didn't bother me in the slightest when I overheard James telling Seth that he'd got the job in the bag. And I wasn't fussed that the only free chair was opposite Matt. I could see him glancing at me out of the corner of my eye, but I ignored him and talked to Jade instead. The wine had taken the edge off my embarrassment, but there was no way I wanted to risk him mentioning what had happened in our interview in front of everybody.

Carl was sitting at the other end of the table. He was looking at me too, but for once, he kept his mouth shut.

'What'll you do if you don't get the job?' Raj asked, leaning closer to whisper in my ear.

I shrugged. 'Probably move to Australia.'

'Seriously?' He laughed as though I'd just made a joke. 'You'll apply for something similar, right? If you don't get this job, you'll get another one no problem. You're, like, one of the biggest film geeks I've ever met.'

'Hmm.' The Picturebox was the only independent cinema in Brighton. I'd have to work in London or Hastings if I wanted a similar job, and that would mean commuting at ridiculous times of the day. It would cost a fortune, too. I'd have even less of a social life than I did now. The only place I wanted to work was the Picturebox, and that wasn't going to happen. Anyway, I'd made a promise to Mum.

I reached for my wine glass. The second the rim touched my lips, a phone rang.

'Shit, that'll be her,' I said, reaching down for my bag. Half a glass of white wine slopped down my front as I dug around under the table.

'Hello, Matt Jones speaking.'

I looked up to see that Matt had his phone pressed to his ear. He grinned as he said his name, but as the seconds ticked by, the colour seemed to drain from his face.

'Where is he?' he said, his voice tight. 'Can I speak to him?'

Everyone fell quiet as Matt pushed back his chair and hurried out of the room. James and Jade shared a confused look. Even Carl looked surprised.

Finally Raj nudged me. 'Do you know what's up with him?'

*

'Matt?' I tapped tentatively on his door. 'Are you okay?'

Dinner had ended an hour ago and no one had seen or heard from Matt since he'd left the table halfway through the starter. At first the others gossiped about the phone call he'd received – James thought he'd been made redundant by Apollo, while Raj thought maybe his house had burned down – but then the conversation had turned to films, and Carl and Seth had started arguing about whether or not M. Night Shyamalan was a shit director or if he'd just had a run of bad luck since *The Sixth Sense*. I didn't join in. I couldn't forget the expression on Matt's face just before he'd hurried out of the restaurant. He'd looked utterly devastated, like someone had just died.

I was probably the last person he wanted to talk to after my little interview outburst, but it wasn't right that no one had gone to check how he was. As the rest of the table raised their voices and waggled their fingers at each other, I slipped quietly out of my seat and headed for the lift.

'Matt?' I knocked again, then pressed my ear to his door. 'It's Beth. Are you okay? Can I come in?'

I waited for a couple of seconds, then turned to walk away. What was I thinking, going after him? I was drunk and it was a stupid idea. He'd probably just had an argument with his girlfriend or something.

'Beth?' The door opened an inch, and Matt peered at me through the gap. His eyes were red and bloodshot.

'Are you okay?'

He opened the door wider and stepped back. 'Come in.'

I followed him into the room, taking in the double bed, the heavy scarlet curtains, the bland countryside-scene artwork on the walls and the worn beige carpet. It was a carbon copy of my own room. The only difference was the pile of empty miniatures on the bedside table. I wobbled towards the chair, a leather-look effort by the desk, and concentrated hard on making sure my bum hit the seat and not the floor.

'Could you grab me a whisky from the minibar?' Matt asked. He was lying on the bed in a pair of jeans and a navy blue T-shirt. His work suit lay in a crumpled pile on the floor. I stepped over it to reach the fridge.

'And whatever you fancy,' he added.

I crouched down, grabbing on to the desk for balance, and wrenched open the minibar. The wine and beer were long gone, but there was still plenty of whisky and gin. I grabbed one of each.

'Here you go.' I staggered back towards the bed, reached out to hand him a bottle, and promptly lost my balance.

'Oops!' I cried as I fell face first on to the eiderdown.

'Thanks.' I felt Matt take one of the bottles from my outstretched hand. 'You might want to make yourself a bit more comfortable, Beth. You'll find drinking a bit tricky in that position.'

I twisted on to my side and waved my bottle in the air. 'Good point. Cheers!'

'Merry Christmas,' he said half-heartedly, as he tapped his bottle against mine.

I twisted open my gin, took a sip, then placed the bottle on the bedside table. The room was silent, apart from the faint hum of the minibar in the corner of the room. Beside me, Matt lay completely still.

I propped myself up on my elbow. 'We missed you at dinner. Is everything okay?'

He leaned forward to slug at his bottle, then slumped back on to the pillow and stared at the ceiling.

'My grandad's had a heart attack,' he said softly.

'Oh no. Is he all right?'

'Stable but heavily sedated, apparently.' He sighed heavily. 'It's killing me that I'm stuck here and he's all alone in the hospital.'

'He'll be okay,' I said, searching desperately for something reassuring to say. 'The doctors and nurses will look after him.'

'Yeah.' He nodded. 'They're doing what they can.'

The room was starting to spin, so I gave up trying to stay upright and lay down, resting my head on the pillow. It was soft and comfortable, and I felt strangely relaxed.

'Thanks, Beth.' Matt shifted on to his side and looked at me steadily. 'For checking I was okay.'

'No problem. I … we were worried about you.'

'I dunno.' He grinned. 'I imagine the boys are tucking into the booze just fine without me.'

I smiled. 'You could say that.'

Matt fell silent again and I shifted awkwardly on the bed, suddenly aware that I wasn't chilling out with a mate. 'I should … I should probably sit on the chair. You're my … could be …' I nearly said the word boss but changed my mind. 'Well, it's not very professional, is it?'

'You're fine.' He reached out a hand as though to reassure me, then seemed to think better of it.

'Sure?'

'Yes. It's nice to talk to someone.'

I slumped back on to the pillow. 'Is it?'

'Yeah.'

We lay silently for a couple of seconds, glancing shyly at each other. I couldn't tell what Matt was thinking, but his hazel eyes seemed clouded with worry. I was just about to ask which hospital his grandad was in when he spoke.

'It's only when something happens to the only person in the world that you love,' he said, flipping on to his back again and staring up at the ceiling, 'that you realise how alone you really are.'

He looked so lost, I wanted to reach out and hug him.

'You're not alone,' I said instead.

'Aren't I?' He didn't look convinced.

'No. Of course not. You've got … well, I don't know who you've got, but I'm sure lots of people care about you.'

'You know what?' He twisted back on to his side, his hand brushing mine as he propped himself up. 'My grandad said you were kind, and he was right. You're pretty special, Beth. None of the others would even have thought to check in on me.'

I looked at him in surprise. My hand was still tingling as though I'd been given a mild electric shock. My heart was beating like mad, too. We weren't just two drunken people lying on a bed having a chat any more.

Matt was looking at me intently, and the air between us had changed. It was charged with anticipation.

'Why does he think I'm kind?' The question came out of my mouth but my brain was still trying to work out what was going on. I wanted to look away, to break the strange spell that had been cast over us, but I couldn't. 'Has he been into the Picturebox?'

'Yep.' Matt smiled. 'Seems like you made a bit of an impression on him. He said you were pretty, too.'

'Oh.' I covered my face, suddenly embarrassed.

'What?' He nudged my hands. 'What's the matter?'

I could smell the warm, intoxicating scent of his aftershave and hear footsteps reverberating down the corridor outside.

'Look at me, Beth,' he said softly.

I opened my fingers an inch.

'You are pretty.' His gaze didn't flicker from my face. 'Don't you believe that?'

I shook my head mutely. My heart was beating so heavily in my chest I could hardly breathe.

'I like you, Beth,' he whispered as he gently wrapped his hands around mine and moved them away from my face.

'I …' I began, but his lips were on mine before I could say a word.

He kissed me so gently, so tenderly, that our lips barely touched, then he pulled away and looked at me, his hand still cupping the side of my face.

'I like you a lot.'

His hand slipped to my waist as he rolled towards me and pressed his lips against mine again – softly at first, brushing them with the lightest pressure, then more intensely, desperately, as though something terrible would happen if he stopped. I kissed him back, tentatively at first, then, as he twisted his hands in my hair and leaned his weight against me, something inside me dissolved. All my cares and worries vanished as we moved against each other, pulling at each other's clothes and slipping our hands beneath them. It felt so right. The smell of him, the shape of him, the way our bodies fitted together.

'Beth,' murmured Matt as he shifted so that he was on top of me. He pressed himself into me, kissing me deeply as he ran a hand from my thigh to my waist and brushed the side of my breast before entwining his fingers in my hair. I pulled at his T-shirt, sliding it up towards his shoulders, my fingers trailing up his broad, smooth back until they couldn't go any further. He sat up, yanked his T-shirt over his head, then lowered himself back on to me and kissed me again, his tongue searching out mine, his fingers unbuttoning my shirt and pushing it down over my shoulders. His mouth moved down to my neck and he flicked his tongue against my skin, so lightly, tantalisingly that I thought I might scream. Instead I wrapped my arms around him and ran my hands up and down his back as he reached behind me and unclasped my bra. Then his hands and his mouth were on my breasts, his tongue flicking over my nipples, his thighs locked around mine.

'Mmmm,' I murmured as his tongue moved from my breast to my belly, teasing, playing, tormenting me. He paused as he reached the waistband of my skirt, then I felt his hands on the zip and my skirt was gone, along with my knickers.

Oh my God! I thought as he lowered his head. Oh my God! Is he going to do what I think he's going to do? *Oh … my … God …*

'Yes,' I moaned, unable to keep quiet a second longer. 'Oh yes. Don't stop. Don't stop. Oh God. Oh God. Ooooh …'

'BIG BOY CALLING! PICK UP THE PHONE, SUGARTITS!'

My eyes flew open, and Matt's head jerked up from between my thighs so quickly I thought it was going to fly off his neck and catapult across the room.

'BIG BOY CALLING! PICK UP THE PHONE, SUGARTITS!'

I knew that voice. Oh my God, it was …

I clamped my hands over my boobs and curled up into a ball, kneeing Matt in the jaw as I pulled my legs up towards my chest. He lurched backwards, slipped off the edge of the bed and landed on the floor with a thump. A couple of seconds later his head popped up from the bottom of the bed. 'What the hell is that?'

'I …' I wrapped myself in the duvet and stared wildly around the room. That was Carl's voice. What the hell was he doing in Matt's bedroom?

'Beth. BETH!' Matt was standing by the bed, rubbing his jaw with one hand and passing me something with the other. 'I think it's for you.'

'What?' I stared in surprise at the phone in his hand. It was shouting, 'BIG BOY CALLING! PICK UP THE PHONE, SUGARTITS!' Hang on a second …

I grabbed it and turned it over.

It was *my* phone. And it was Aiden who was calling. Carl!

My brain cleared and everything fell into place.

He'd stolen my phone that afternoon in the Picturebox, snuck into the staff room and recorded a voice tag for Aiden's number. No wonder I hadn't spotted what he'd done. Aiden hadn't rung me since we'd split up. He'd texted me that afternoon, but a phone call …

'Beth.' Matt was standing by the bathroom door, a towel around his waist. 'Er … who's Big Boy?'

'BIG BOY CALLING!' my phone insisted, right on cue. 'PICK UP THE PHONE, SUGARTITS!'

I hit the 'Ignore Call' button. 'No one.'

'Really?' Matt shot me a bewildered look.

'No … honestly … It's … it's complicated.'

He studied my face. 'An ex?'

'No. I just … I …' I slipped off the bed, the duvet wrapped round me like an enormous flowery toga, and moved towards the door. 'I have to go. I really have to go!'

I could still hear Matt shouting my name as I hurried down the corridor, the eiderdown trailing behind me.

Chapter Twenty-Two

Matt

I threw up twice before I'd even left my hotel room. Getting out of bed, dressed and down to the breakfast room for eight o'clock took every ounce of determination I had, but I needed to get back to Grandad.

Carl raised an eyebrow as I approached the table. 'You're looking a bit rough, Matt? Heavy night, eh?'

I ignored him.

'Look, guys,' I said, immediately noticing that one member of the team – a short, dark-haired woman with big grey eyes – was missing. Since Beth had shot out of my bedroom like the hotel was on fire the night before, I hadn't seen or heard a word from her. 'I'm leaving. The snow's thawed a bit and a taxi's taking me to the station in five minutes. Your minibus should be here in a couple of hours.'

'What about the job?' Seth asked, waving his fork at me. It was loaded with sausage and egg and made my stomach turn. 'When do we find out who's got it?'

'I'll ring you all at some point this week. Okay? Gotta go.'

I threw up again just as the taxi pulled on to the gravel driveway outside the hotel.

Six hours after I'd stumbled out of the Royal Albert Hotel in Wales, I charged through the heavy glass doors of the Royal Sussex County. I was sweating, I smelt like a brewery, and when I finally got to the reception desk, I had to repeat Grandad's name three times before the nurse finally understood what I was saying and pointed me in the direction of the cardiovascular ward.

I hurried down the corridors, desperately trying not to inhale. The smell reminded me of a really bad asthma attack I'd had when I was eight. The whole experience – being rushed to hospital in the back of an ambulance, being jabbed in the hand with an IV drip and then having a thermometer shoved up my arse – had terrified me (not to mention given me a lifelong thermometer phobia), and the disinfectant stench brought it all rushing back. I sprinted up two flights of stairs, down two dead ends and into one cleaning cupboard before I finally found the right ward. Twelve gaunt, grey men in stripy pyjamas greeted me – six beds on the left of the ward, six opposite them on the right. I scanned the tired-looking faces, searching for Grandad, and immediately discounted six sleeping men, one moaning quietly to himself in the bed nearest me, and zoomed in on the white-haired man checking out a nurse's bum as she bent over to get something off a trolley in the corner of the room.

'Grandad!' I grinned and raised a hand.

'Matt!' His wrinkled face lit up as I strode towards

him. 'If it isn't my least favourite grandson. I thought you'd forgotten about me.'

'If only!'

The nurse, a heavyset woman in her late forties with curly brown hair streaked with grey, stopped whatever it was she'd been doing and looked me up and down as I approached Grandad's bed.

'Ah, so you're the grandson,' she said in a thick Irish accent. 'I've heard a lot about you.'

I pretended to look nervous. 'He's spilled all my secrets again, hasn't he?'

The nurse and Grandad shared a look and she laughed. It was a warm chortle.

'Oh, I don't know about that, although I have heard a few choice stories.' She winked at Grandad. 'I'll be back to do your obs in half an hour, Mr Ballard.'

'Not unless I get my hands on you first,' Grandad said, winking back.

'Promises, promises.' The nurse squeezed his foot through the sheets then turned and pushed the trolley back down the ward.

I looked across at Grandad. He was still smiling, but there were dark circles under his eyes and his skin looked so thin it was almost transparent. 'So,' I said. 'How've you been?'

His grin slipped for the first time since I'd walked into the room. 'I've been better, lad, but they're taking good care of me.'

'Are they? You don't want me to get you some food or anything?'

'No.' He shook his head. 'The food here's better than anything you've ever cooked for me, son.'

'That's not hard.'

'Aye. I never even knew a microwave could explode until you put a steak and kidney pie in it with the foil still on.'

I laughed, but I couldn't take my eyes off the thin outline of his body under the sheets. He'd only been in the hospital for just over twenty-four hours, but he looked like he'd shrunk. When I was a kid, he was a big man with bulging biceps. Now he looked small and frail.

'I'm not dead yet,' he said, heaving himself into a sitting position and flexing his arms like a 1950s body-builder, like he'd just read my mind. Their twig-like shape just about broke my heart. 'I've still got a lot of fight in me yet, our Matt.'

'Course you do. How are you feeling?'

He rested back on his pillows. 'Like I've been punched in the heart. Never felt pain like it.'

For all his bravado, he looked utterly exhausted. And very, very old.

'I'm really sorry, Grandad. I should have been there for you. If I hadn't been in Wales ... if I'd been in Brighton, then maybe ...'

'No, no.' He looked at me sternly and patted my hand. 'I won't have you blaming yourself. You've got a job to do, son. Anyway, there's nothing you could have done.'

I pulled the chair closer to the bed with my free hand

and sat down. 'Well there's no way I'm leaving you on your own any more. I'll move in and look after you.'

'Move in?' Grandad leaned away in horror. 'I think I'd rather have another heart attack.'

We both laughed, but he didn't move his hand from mine.

'I thought I had a bit of indigestion at first,' he said seriously, 'but when my left arm started to tingle, I remembered what Paul O'Grady had said about how his heart attack started, and I thought I'd better ring Mrs Harris next door. She came around right away, but everything went black and the next thing I knew I was in an ambulance.'

'What did the doctors say?'

'That I need to give up my nightly tipple. Oh, and I need to start taking some drugs.'

'Drugs?'

'Yes. I started my course of Ecstasy and LSD yesterday.'

'What!'

Grandad took one look at my expression and laughed so long and hard I thought he'd give himself another heart attack there and then. When he finally got his breath back, he reached for the glass of water on his bedside table.

'So, lad,' he said after he'd taken a sip. 'What's going on with you, then? You've got a bit of a glow in your cheeks for once. Have a roll in the hay in Wales, did you?'

'A roll in the hay? Grandad! What are we, back in the 1940s?'

'In case you hadn't noticed, it's not exactly buzzing with conversation in here.' His eyes flitted around the ward. 'So who was it? Blondie?'

'No, not Alice.'

'Who then?'

As I looked at his grinning face, the memory of the night before came flooding back. What had happened with Beth had been completely unexpected. Actually, that's not strictly true. Since the night by the pier I'd wondered, more than once, what it would be like to kiss her, but I'd pushed the thought from my mind, telling myself that:

a) it wasn't appropriate to fantasise about an employee; and

b) she was more mental than a tone-deaf *X Factor* auditionee.

Only the fantasies had come back with full force during the interview weekend, hadn't they? While I was interviewing Raj on Sunday afternoon, my mind kept flitting back to Beth, remembering the little crease between her eyebrows when she concentrated, and the way her face lit up when she laughed. When her trousers had split during the abseiling task, I'd suddenly felt insanely protective of her. All I wanted to do was cover everyone's eyes to stop them from laughing. Okay, so she'd told me where to stick my job, but who could blame her after what she'd been through the previous day? I'd mentioned more synonyms for the word 'bum' than *Roget's Thesaurus*. If it had been the other way round, I'd have lost my shit too.

When she'd turned up at my hotel room on Sunday

night, I wasn't surprised. Not because I thought she fancied me or anything like that. God, no! Just because it was exactly the sort of kind, thoughtful thing she'd do. I was so pleased to see her that I acted like a bit of a dick at first – asking her to get drinks for me and stuff – but I couldn't keep up the pretence for long. All I wanted to do was kiss her, and when she propped herself up beside me and told me she was sure people cared about me, I couldn't stop myself.

It had all felt so right – the way her body fitted against mine, the smell of her, the way her hair brushed my cheek when she kissed me, the feel of her lips. Everything. *We'd* felt right – like we were meant to be together somehow.

When her phone went off with some bloke calling himself Big Boy, I felt like I'd been thumped in the guts. The intensity, the passion, the magic – it all vanished in an instant. Beth disappeared pretty sharpish after that, and I hadn't heard from her since. Not a phone call to my room to explain, not a note left with reception, nothing.

'Well?' Grandad said. 'Don't tell me you don't know her name, lad!'

'It was Beth,' I said. 'Beth Prince.'

'That pretty lass from the cinema?' He winked. 'Good on you. You've got a keeper there.'

I was about to point out that 'keepers' didn't have men called Big Boy ringing them in the middle of the night, but Grandad's stomach grumbled angrily and interrupted me.

'I was right!' I said triumphantly. 'You *are* hungry.

Let me go to the canteen and get you something. How does a bacon and egg sandwich sound?'

He smiled. 'Add in a nice cup of tea and I think you'd be pretty close to heaven right there.'

I asked three different nurses and two orderlies where it was, but it still took me twenty minutes to find the canteen. I felt like a rat in a maze, sniffing the air to see if I was any closer to food. Finally the smell of overcooked school dinners filled my nostrils and I pushed open a pair of white double doors and walked smack-bang into a short woman carrying an enormous balloon.

'Matt!' she said, peering at me over the top. 'Hi!'

I stared at her in shock. 'Beth! What are you doing here?'

Her beaming grin slipped and she shrugged awkwardly. 'I'm not really sure.'

'Right … well … um … I'm getting some food for Grandad. He's in a ward upstairs.' I turned to queue up for sandwiches, but Beth grabbed my arm.

'Could we talk?' she said quietly. 'Please.'

Talk? About the interview, or the whole Big Boy thing? I was too curious to say no.

'Okay.' I grabbed a brown tray from the pile at the end of the queue and pointed at the sandwiches. 'I'll just grab a few of those. Do you want to get a seat and I'll join you in a sec?'

'Sure.' She looked hesitant.

'Do you want anything?'

'No, I'm fine. Thanks.'

I watched as she wandered off and drifted towards

a couple of empty tables across the canteen. She hesitated, as though trying to decide which one to choose, then plumped for one in the corner and sat down, hugging the balloon to her chest. The queue shuffled forward, so I grabbed a tired-looking bacon and egg sandwich and a smoked salmon bagel from the chiller, and two cups of tea from the urn, then paid the cashier.

'Hi,' Beth said as I sat down opposite her and put the sandwiches and the cups of tea on the table.

'Hey.' I nodded.

She looked at me hesitantly, then down at her balloon. I snapped the plastic lid off my cup of tea, took a sip and promptly scalded the roof of my mouth. I set it back on the table and tried not to wince. Beth was still staring at her balloon.

'Hmmm,' she murmured.

'Sorry?'

She looked up, surprised. 'I didn't say anything.'

'Oh. Okay.'

I reached for my tea and took another sip, scalding the roof of my mouth a second time. When I set it back on the table, Beth was looking at me.

'How are you?' we both said at the same time, then laughed.

'Who's the balloon for?' I asked, before silence had time to settle again. 'I didn't realise you had someone in hospital too.'

'I don't.' She shook her head, a nervous smile playing on her lips. 'It's for your grandad.'

'A Merry Christmas balloon?'

'I didn't realise hospitals don't sell flowers any more,

and they didn't have any Get Well Soon balloons left.'

'What? But why would you buy Grandad something in the first place? I don't get it.'

Beth lowered her chin and looked at me sheepishly. 'You're going to think I'm weird.'

'Weird*er*,' I said, and she grinned.

'Last night you told me that your grandad was in here all alone,' she said softly, the base of her neck and the top of her chest flushing red, 'and … well, I couldn't get it out of my head. I thought it was really sad. I know I don't know him, but I thought some flowers … or a balloon … might cheer him up.'

'Wow.' I stared at her.

'But when I got to reception, I realised I didn't know your grandad's name, so I asked for a Mr Jones who'd had a heart attack and—'

'Grandad's called Jack Ballard. He's my mum's dad.'

'Now you tell me!' She grinned. 'I only realised I'd got the wrong man when I asked him if his grandson Matt had been to visit and he said, "If someone's told you I've got a grandson, they're pulling your leg, darling. I haven't been near a fanny since I popped out of my mother's in 1932."'

I grinned. 'What did you say to that?'

'I didn't. I laughed so hard I snorted Diet Coke out of my nose. George didn't seem to mind. He said it was the first time someone had ejaculated on him since—'

'Whoa!' I laughed and held up a hand. 'I don't want to know.'

'Anyway, he was lovely, but he wasn't your grandad,

so I thought I'd come down here and grab a coffee before I went home.'

'Wow,' I said again.

I couldn't believe that after everything she'd been through, she'd travelled all the way back from Wales and headed straight for the hospital to give Grandad some flowers. She was either a complete saint or she had an ulterior motive. And I wasn't sure which.

I studied her face as she gazed around the canteen, the ridiculous Santa-and-his-reindeers balloon still pressed to her chest. Twelve hours earlier she'd run out of my hotel room with my duvet wrapped around her, and now she'd just breezed back into my life like nothing had happened. I couldn't make sense of it. All I did know was that I didn't want her to leave, not yet.

'Beth,' I said, sealing the lid back on to my tea and gathering the sandwiches together, 'if you're not in a hurry, you can meet Grandad if you'd like. I need to take this lot up to him.'

'Really?' She flashed me a dazzling smile. 'That would be great.'

'Matt,' Beth said as we rounded the corner before Grandad's ward. 'There's another reason I came to the hospital. I was … um … hoping I'd bump into you. We need to talk about … um … last night.'

Ah, okay. I stopped walking and looked at her. So she hadn't just come here out of the goodness of her heart. But she had come after me to clear things up. That had to be a good thing. The least I could do was hear her out.

'Okay …'

'The thing, the phone call …' She looked at her feet and blushed violently. 'I didn't know anything about it. The voice tag, I mean.' She glanced back up at me from under her lashes. 'Someone … Oh God, it's going to sound ridiculous …'

'What?'

'Someone stole my phone and added the voice tag. I guess they thought it would be … funny …' Her voice cracked on the last word and something inside me lurched. She obviously didn't find it the slightest bit amusing, and I was gripped by the sudden urge to thump whoever had done it.

'We were having such a nice time, and it … that … it was such a shock.' She fumbled with the balloon's curly ribbon. 'I shouldn't have run off. I'm sorry.'

She looked so miserable, it was all I could do not to throw my arms around her and give her a big hug. Instead I put a hand on her shoulder and smiled.

'Don't worry about it. Honestly. We'll probably laugh about it one day. On the up side, my jaw has finally stopped aching after you kneed me in the face.'

'Oh God!' Beth clamped her hands over her mouth in horror. 'I'd forgotten about that.'

I laughed. 'It's fine. Honestly. Sex-related injuries happen to the best of us. Hell, I once had to take a girl to Casualty afterwards.'

'No way!' Beth's eyebrows shot up in surprise.

'Way!' I grinned. 'We were having sex and she was screaming out my name really, really loudly – "Matt! Matt! MATT!" – and I figured, wow, she's really loving this. Apparently she wasn't. She'd got her foot caught in one of the slats at the end of the bed.'

'No!'

'Yes.'

'Did you see her again?'

'Nope. She dumped me before the plaster cast came off.'

'Oh.' Beth looked dejectedly at the floor.

'Look.' I squeezed her shoulder. 'Unlike that girl, I have a sense of humour, so don't beat yourself up. These things happen. It's no big deal.'

She looked back up. 'Really? You're sure?'

'Of course. It wasn't your fault. Though I'd like to have words with whoever put that voice tag on.'

Beth frowned. 'Me too.'

'You're not going to tell me who did it, are you?'

She shook her head.

'Okay. I won't push it.' I reached for her hand and smiled. 'Come on, there's someone I'd like you to meet.'

Chapter Twenty-Three

Beth

As far as stupid ideas go, turning up at the hospital with a balloon for Matt's grandad was probably right up there with Jordan doing a Eurovision entry dressed as a Teletubby, but it was the only idea I had. My first instinct, when I'd woken up alone in my hotel room and remembered what had happened the night before, was to pull the covers back over my head and wish for a speedy death. The second was to call Mrs Blackstock and tell her that I'd come down with an incurable disease and couldn't go back to work. That way I'd never have to see Matt, or the look of horror in his eyes, ever again.

While both of those options appealed, they were just wishful thinking. The best, and the right, thing to do was to talk to Matt and explain what had happened, but the more I thought about doing that, the sicker I felt. The only thing that made me feel more nauseous was the thought of seeing Carl's smug face across the breakfast table. He had no idea what had happened the night before, but I knew there was no way I'd be able to bite my tongue. I'd already screamed at him once, during the abseiling task; did I really want everyone, including Matt, to watch me lose my rag in public again?

It was eight o'clock when I finally finished showering, dressing and untangling my hair and padded down the corridor towards Matt's room, hoping I'd catch him before breakfast. The door was ajar, so I pushed it open.

'Matt?' I said, poking my head in. 'Matt, are you here?'

The room was empty. His jeans, his suit, even the empty miniatures by the side of the bed, were gone.

'Matt?' I said again.

'Madam?' I jumped as a maid, her arms full of towels, emerged from the bathroom. 'Can I help you?'

'Um …' I frowned. 'Matt Jones – the man who was staying in this room – has he, has he checked out?'

The maid nodded. 'Yes, madam. About twenty minutes ago, I think.'

'Oh.' I turned to go.

The minibus wasn't due to collect us until ten o'clock. Why had Matt left early? Of course! I slapped myself on the forehead as I hurried back to my room. He'd gone back to make sure his grandad was okay. I glanced at the time on my phone. Five past eight. With any luck, the rest of the guys would still be having breakfast. If I could get reception to order me a taxi, I could escape without running into Carl, *and* I might be able to catch Matt at the hospital before he left.

I felt sick with nerves all the way from Abergavenny to Brighton, but when the train finally drew up at the station, instead of pegging it back to my house as quickly as I could, I found myself jumping into a cab and saying, 'Royal Sussex County, please.'

I'd argued with myself all the way there, one side of my brain saying, *You're sworn off men, why do you care if you hurt Matt's feelings by running off last night? Go home!* and the other going, *If the boot was on the other foot, you'd want the guy to explain what happened. It's the right thing to do.* By the time the taxi had pulled up on the street outside the hospital, I was too tired to argue with myself any more, and my legs carried me out of the cab, through the double doors and into the gift shop.

In a way I was relieved when I couldn't find Matt's grandad. The adrenalin of rushing around trying to find Matt had worn off, and turning up at the hospital suddenly seemed like a really stupid, hungover idea. Any normal person would just have waited until Monday morning and then rung him at work.

Ah well, at least I tried, I told myself as I wandered into the canteen to grab a cup of coffee before I went home. I'd just pushed open the doors and was trying to decide what film to watch when I got back when I bumped into Matt! I felt like such an idiot, standing there with an enormous kid's balloon while he looked at me like I'd beamed down from another planet.

Sitting opposite him at that white Formica table was one of the most awkward moments of my life. We stared at each other like we were strangers and there was this huge, horrible silence just hanging in the air. When Matt asked me who the balloon was for and I told him it was for his grandad, he looked so touched, I immediately felt guilty. I came clean when we were walking to the ward, though. I just couldn't keep it to myself any more. I expected him to have a go at me or be really distant or something, but he was actually really cool about what had happened. He even made me laugh. Things were easy and natural between us again, just like they had been the night before. I couldn't believe I'd been torturing myself all morning about talking to him about what had happened.

His grandad was a sweetheart. He beamed at me the second I stepped into the ward with Matt, then patted the chair by his bed and said, 'Well, if it isn't the lovely lassie from the cinema,' as though me turning up to visit him was the most natural thing in the world.

Matt gave him the sandwiches and polystyrene cup of tea he'd bought in the canteen, then didn't get another word in for the next twenty minutes. His grandad asked me question after question – where I was from, what my family did, how long I had lived in Brighton – and then told me all about his late wife, only pausing to 'wet his whistle' with a sip of tea. My grandparents had all died by the time I was thirteen, and I'd forgotten how nice it was to put the world to rights with someone who didn't care about careers or fashion or Botox and could make me giggle just by raising his eyebrow at the end of a sentence. He laughed easily, tipping his head back and guffawing unselfconsciously, just like his grandson. I could see why Matt adored him so much.

I was so enchanted by him, that I barely registered the fact Matt was pulling on his coat.

'You off, then, son?' Mr Ballard asked, looking up.

'Yep.' He squeezed his grandad's foot through the sheet and nodded at me. 'I'll give you a ring, Beth.'

What? Give me a ring? My God, was he actually interested in me? After everything that had happened – my drunken waffling on the seafront, my bare arse on the abseiling cliff, kneeing him in the jaw …

'You will?' I stared at him in disbelief.

'Yeah. Tomorrow.'

Wow. No game-playing, no waiting for the phone to ring, none of this 'three days before ringing a woman' nonsense. Tomorrow.

'Brilliant,' I said, beaming at him. 'I'll *really* look forward to it.'

Matt rubbed his head. 'You will?'

'Well, yeah.'

'Okay, but don't get your hopes up, Beth. There's a lot of competition for the manager's job.'

'Manager's job?' My cheeks burned with embarrassment and I looked away, suddenly fixated by the metal urine bottle on the bedside table. 'Of course. I always … um … look forward to getting feedback from interviews.'

'Really?'

'Are you back again tomorrow, lad?' Mr Ballard interrupted, glancing at Matt and then at me. 'Or will you have forgotten all about me by then?'

Matt smiled. 'Fat chance, old man.'

I watched as he pulled his iPod out of his pocket and pressed the earphones into his ears. Our eyes met briefly before he turned away.

'Right then,' he said. 'I'm off. Bye.'

'Be happy, lad!' his grandad called after him.

Matt paused and looked back, his expression confused.

'Right,' he said, then ambled out of the ward, his hands in his pockets, his head nodding to whatever song he was listening to.

'So,' Mr Ballard said, turning to look at me, 'how long have you two been in love?'

The question went round and round my head as I stepped through the double doors at the front of the hospital and headed for the nearest bench. Visiting hours were over, and it was late. I pulled my jacket around me and sat down. An ambulance drew up outside the hospital, and I watched as a doctor and two nurses rushed out to meet it.

'How long have you two been in love?'

Matt's grandad might be ill, but he definitely had all his marbles. So why would he say something like that? Despite being cool about what had happened the night before, it was obvious that Matt wasn't the slightest bit interested in anything more than a drunken fumble. And besides, I was sworn off men.

Wasn't I?

I pulled my coat more tightly around me and tucked my hands under my armpits. It wasn't snowing in Brighton yet, but it definitely felt cold enough. Don't do this, Beth, I told myself firmly. Don't start analysing a drunken snog to see if there's more to it. There are five very good reasons why you need to forget about Matt as soon as possible:

1) he's not interested;
2) he's way out of your league;
3) you don't fancy him;
4) he might become your boss;
5) his grandad obviously has undiagnosed Alzheimer's.

Actually, scratch 3), that's a blatant lie.

I watched as the ambulance pulled away and turned down Eastern Road, its lights beaming through the gloom. Even though it was dark, the hospital was still teeming with people. A couple were kissing passionately against a wall, oblivious to the two men who stood, anxiously puffing on cigarettes, in the smoking area a couple of metres away. I looked back at the snogging couple. They'd stopped kissing and were staring into each other's eyes. I watched as the man said something, then cupped the woman's face in his hands and lowered his lips to hers. I'd melted when Matt had held my face like that and kissed me softly, pausing to look into my eyes before kissing me again. It was like a scene from a 1940s love story where the couple muddle through a series of obstacles and misunderstandings and finally fall in love and …

Stop it, Beth! I shook my head angrily. There you go again, reading too much into a situation and romanticising it. It was a one-night stand that went wrong, and that was all there was to it.

Chapter Twenty-Four

Matt

'Be happy, lad!' Grandad had called as I was leaving the ward.

Why had he said that?

The phrase went round and round in my head as I flagged down a taxi and gave the driver my address.

Everything that had happened – the Picturebox sale, the disastrous meal with Alice, meeting Beth by the seafront, Neil telling me he was leaving, Grandad's heart attack, the night in the hotel room with Beth, her getting on with Grandad so well – it was all too much to take in. That was why I'd left them chatting in the ward. Once I'd realised he was okay, I had to get out of there. My head was a wreck. All I wanted to do was go home and get my shit together. My life had become some kind of weird TV show that lurched from amazing to awful and back again. Kind of like *The Secret Millionaire* meets *Carry On Up the Craphole*.

As the taxi sped down Edward Street and back into town, I stared out of the window and watched the world flash by.

I'd been happy before. In fact there were at least four times in my life when I'd been truly happy:

1)When I received a Millennium Falcon for Christmas when I was seven. I was so happy I burst into tears and only stopped crying when Dad shoved a mince pie into my mouth and told me Father Christmas would take it back if I didn't shut up.

2)When Portsmouth won the FA Cup in 2008 – the first time they'd won it since 1939. They're not even a team I support, but the boys weren't the only ones with tears in their eyes when they lifted the cup.

3) Hmmm …

4) Er ….

I scratched my head. Were there really so few moments in my life when I'd been truly happy?

The taxi driver glanced at me in the rear-view mirror. 'Watching the match at the pub tonight?'

'Nah.' I shook my head, glad of the excuse to stop thinking about happiness. 'I've had a really knackering day. I think I'll grab a beer and watch it at home instead.'

'Sounds good.'

It did. Very good indeed.

I stood in the doorway of my living room and stared.

And stared.

And stared.

When I'd left the house on Saturday morning, the living room had been a bomb site of takeaway cartons, empty beer cans, magazines, socks, paperwork and dust. Now it looked like someone else's flat. It was all shiny and clean, like some kind of show home. My *Q* magazines had been neatly stacked beside the sofa, the cups on the coffee table had been replaced with a vase of flowers, the grubby sofa cushions were pristine and plumped. Even the vindaloo stain on the carpet had gone.

I stared wildly around the room, trying to work out what the hell had happened.

My TV was still in the corner. So was the Xbox. I hadn't been robbed by the world's neatest burglars, then.

Shit. Had my landlady paid me an impromptu visit? It had been a while since she'd last popped round for an inspection. A couple of years, at least.

I crossed the room, ran a finger along the mantelpiece and shook my head. Completely dust-free. No, it couldn't have been Mrs Aston. She would have sent me a bollocking text, not tidied the place up.

So who the hell … I spun round and sniffed the air. What was that? The scent of furniture polish and cleaning spray had been replaced by a new smell, a familiar one. Beefy and rich, like some kind of stew. I frowned in confusion. It couldn't be next door. I'd never smelt their cooking smells before. And I couldn't have left the oven on; I'd had takeaway pizza on Friday night. What the hell was going on?

'Hello?' I said as I wandered out of the living room and down the hallway towards the kitchen, the smell growing stronger with every step I took. 'Is there anyone there?'

I put a hand on the door and pushed it open an inch. 'Hello … SHIT!'

'Hi, Matt.'

Alice was standing at the sink, her blonde hair piled up on top of her head and a spotty apron tied around her waist. Her arms were plunged into a bowlful of soapy water, gleaming plates and dishes piled up on the drainer beside her.

'What …' I started as my brain struggled to catch up. 'What's going on?'

'What does it look like?' Alice craned her neck to look over her shoulder at me, a beaming smile on her face. 'I thought I'd surprise you.'

'You've certainly done that!'

'Your secretary told me you were spending the weekend in Wales doing interviews,' she continued as she rinsed a handful of cutlery and placed it in the rack, 'so I thought I'd surprise you by tidying up for when you got home. There's a lovely steak and ale stew in the oven if you're hungry.'

'You rang Sheila?'

'Well yes,' Alice said, still smiling. I was surprised her cheeks weren't aching. 'When you didn't reply to any of my texts, I thought I'd check you were okay.'

'Alice, you sent me texts telling me I was bastard scum!'

'Oh, those! I was just a bit angry after the restaurant thing. I'm fine now.'

'You said you hoped I'd rot in hell!'

The smile slipped. 'I was annoyed, Matt, okay? And with good reason if you ask me. But let's not go there,' she added, throwing back her head and laughing in a very odd, forced way. 'I found your shirt, the one I accidentally spilled red wine on, in the bottom of your washing basket. I can't believe you let it fester there for so long, really, Matt! Anyway I got the stain out. It's as good as new now.'

'Accidentally spilled ...'

'Yes. Anyway, what's done is done, and we need to wipe the slate clean if we're going to make a new start.'

'A new start? Alice ...'

'What?'

'You can't just let yourself in, tidy the place up, cook a meal and assume we're back together.'

'If you think this is good,' she said, ignoring the last part of my sentence, 'you should check your wardrobe. I've totally rearranged it. All your shirts are in colour order now.'

'What?'

'Yeah. It looks amazing. So does your bathroom. You had far too much clutter, so I had a bit of a blitz. I replaced your aftershave, too. I never could stand that Gucci stuff you used to wear.'

'You threw that away? Alice, it's my favourite!'

'There's no accounting for taste.'

I stared at her in astonishment, utterly lost for words. This was exactly the way she'd been in our relationship. Fire and brimstone one second, and sweetness and light the next.

'I ... I ...' I stuttered. 'I can't believe this is happening. Alice, this is my flat.' I spread my arms open. 'These are my things. You can't do this.'

'I think you'll find I just did,' she said, turning her back on me and yanking the plug out of the sink. 'So if you'd like to take a seat in the living room, I'll bring your dinner through.'

'Alice.'

'Yes, darling.'

'Alice, look at me.'

She turned slowly, wiping her hands on her apron.

'I'd like you to leave,' I said calmly. 'And I'd like my spare key back.'

'I haven't got it.'

'Then how did you get in?'

She shrugged. 'The door was open.'

'No, it wasn't. Alice, please,' I uncrossed my arms, 'I really don't want to fight. I've had a hell of a day. Please just give me my key back and leave.'

She shook her head. 'I'm not going anywhere.'

I looked at her steadily. I had two options. One of them involved staying and arguing. The other …

'Then I will,' I said.

'Neil,' I said into my phone as I stepped into the Pull and Pump and made my way to the bar. 'You need to meet me in the pub. Now.'

There was a pause. 'No can do, I'm afraid, mate. I'm up in Birmingham. I thought I'd fit in a quick visit to my folks before I fly off to Californ-i-ay!'

'Oh, right. Yeah. I'd forgotten about that.'

'Everything okay? You sound a bit stressed, mate.'

I sighed. 'You could say that.'

'I'd ask why,' he shouted as the sound of sirens

wailing, people shouting and horns beeping filled my ear, 'but we're out for dinner and the taxi's just pulled up at the restaurant. Can I give you a call tomorrow?'

'Sure.' I nodded. 'You have a good night.'

'Will do. Speak soon.'

With the disconnection tone still buzzing in my ear, I shoved the phone back in my pocket, suddenly feeling a bit lost. With Neil in Birmingham and Grandad in the hospital, there was no one I could talk to. I had other mates, sure, but they were the 'go out and have a laugh' sort, not the 'listen to your fucked-up life woes' type. I glanced at the barman. He was standing at the end of the bar, his expression one of brain-dead resignation, as one of the OAP regulars chewed his ear off about something or other. He didn't look like the listening type either.

'Mate.' I raised my hand. 'Pint of lager, please.'

The barman nodded, relieved to have something to do.

'And a whisky chaser,' I added.

Chapter Twenty-Five

Beth

'Lizzie?' I called as I walked through the front door and into the hallway. 'Lizzie, are you here? You wouldn't believe the weekend I've had!'

I peeked into the living room. Normally, if I'd been away for a while, the sofa would be piled high with Lizzie's discarded clothes, make-up, empty Diet Coke cans and chocolate wrappers, but it was as tidy as I'd left it.

I slumped down, pulled my mobile out of my bag and turned it on. I'd switched it off while I was in the hospital and hadn't bothered checking it since. A text message envelope flashed on to the screen and I groaned. Not Aiden again!

Nope. It was from Lizzie.

Gone on holiday with Nathan, it said. *Don't think I'll ever come home :) Hope you had a good weekend in Scotland. See you soon, Liz x*

I shook my head as I moved my thumb over the delete button – Scotland! Did she never listen? – then jumped as the phone began to ring.

'Hello?'

'Hello, darling, it's Mum.'

'Hi, Mum.' I knew what was coming and tried not to sigh. 'How are you?'

'As busy as always. I'm having the Frasiers and the Turners round for bridge tonight, so I can't talk long. How did your interview for the manager's job go?'

'It was fine,' I lied.

'So it went well?'

'Uh-huh.'

There was a pause. 'You're lying to me, Beth.'

'No, I'm not!'

'What happened?'

I don't know if it was tiredness, the fact that Lizzie wasn't around to chat to, or pure stupidity, but it all spilled out and I told her everything. Well, not quite everything – she didn't need to know exactly what had happened between me and Matt in his hotel room – but I did tell her I'd kissed my boss.

'Well?' I said when I reached the bit about Matt saying he'd ring me about the job. 'I know I messed up the interview, but what do you think?'

'Tosser!'

'That's a bit harsh. I know I was stupid, but you can't call your own daughter—'

'I wasn't talking about you. I was talking about him, your boss.'

'He's not a tosser,' I objected. 'He's a good bloke.'

'Beth! The man used you.'

'No, he didn't. It was mutual, and it was my fault that things went a bit … well, never mind how things went. Matt was lovely to me when I bumped into him earlier.'

'Lovely? Or dismissive, because you've served your purpose? Beth, the man's just cast you aside. Exactly like your dad did to me.'

'Mum, don't. That's not fair.'

'What's fair about dedicating the best years of your life to a man, only for him to discard you like an unwanted dishcloth just because he's having some kind of mid-life crisis and needs some space?' I could imagine her doing quotation marks in the air when she said that. 'Where was your dad when you hit puberty or needed some pocket money? If it wasn't for me, Beth, you'd—'

'Have starved. I know, Mum, and I really appreciate what you did for me, but Matt's not like Dad. He's different, he's—'

'I don't know why you bother with men, Beth. You don't need one. Just look at me – I built my business up from scratch after your dad left and I don't need some man to come along and screw it all up for me. I can't believe you're standing up for someone who blatantly used you for a cheap thrill. I thought I'd brought you up better than that.'

Aaaggh. It was all so confusing. I'd sworn off men, but here I was, standing up for Matt. What was wrong with me?

'I bought some vol-au-vents at Marks for bridge tonight,' Mum said, changing the subject when I didn't reply. 'You wouldn't believe the price of fresh prawns. I wouldn't have bothered, but Mary Frasier's a huge snob, and …'

I stopped listening. What was it Matt had said before he'd kissed me on the hotel bed? It was all so hazy.

'Blah … blah … blah … Australia.'

'Sorry?' I said, suddenly aware that Mum had asked me a question.

'Honestly, Beth.' She sighed heavily. 'Do you never listen to a word I say? The flight is on Christmas Eve, that's in just over two weeks. Write it down. We need to meet at Pool Valley to get the coach to Heathrow at eleven in the morning.'

'Mum …'

'We had a deal, darling. If you got the job, you'd stay, and if you didn't, you'd come with me. Those were your words, Beth.'

'But we don't know who's got the job yet. I know things didn't go as planned, but my business plan was good and there's still a chance that—'

'Things didn't go as planned?' She laughed shortly. 'Beth, you insulted your boss, stormed out of the interview and then let him kiss you! I don't remember any of those tactics being mentioned in *Visualising Success*. Face it, darling, you've got as much chance of getting this job as you have of winning *Britain's Next Top Model*.'

'Thanks, Mum.'

'I'm just being cruel to be kind, dear. Forget about this stupid film obsession and come to Australia with me. You can see it as a new start.'

'But films aren't stupid. They're my passion. They're—'

'Must go, that was the doorbell,' Mum interrupted.

'I'll see you soon, darling. Only bring one suitcase, maximum weight twenty kilos. Speak soon. Bye.'

The phone went dead in my hand and I stared at it, annoyed. Why did she have to be so bloody … I yawned deeply. I'd barely slept the night before, and it was all I could do to keep my eyes open. Oh sod it. There was over a fortnight until the flight, so there was no point worrying about it now. I dropped the phone on to the coffee table, then padded into my bedroom, pulled the duvet off my bed and wandered back into the living room, where I curled up on the sofa. There was an old black and white film on TV that I'd been meaning to watch for years. I tucked a cushion under my head, pulled the duvet up to my neck and stared blearily at the flickering image across the room. Ten minutes later, I was asleep.

Ding, dong, ding, dong, ding, dong.

I shifted on to my side and pulled the duvet over my head. What was that noise?

Ding, dong, ding, dong.

My eyes flicked open.

Ding, dong, ding, dong.

The doorbell continued to ring.

I groaned, rubbed my hands over my face and glanced at the clock on the DVD player: 11.55 p.m. Bloody Lizzie, she'd probably forgotten her keys again. I stretched lazily, then rolled off the sofa and padded out of the living room and into the hallway.

'Coming!' I said as I reached the door. 'Where'd you leave your keys this time?'

I twisted the lock, opened the door an inch and peered outside, my eyes slowly adjusting to the darkness.

'Matt!'

Unlike snowy Wales, it was tipping it down in Brighton, and Matt's dark hair was flattened to his head, his black jacket soaked through. He was staring at his sodden trainers and jumped when I said his name.

'I ...' He ran a hand through his wet hair. 'I ... I'm sorry, Beth, I shouldn't have come.'

He turned to go, but I reached out a hand and touched his shoulder. 'Matt, wait.' I had no idea what he was doing on my doorstep, but I didn't want him to go. 'Come in, you're soaking.'

There was an ominous rumble above us, and he glanced past me into the warm, dry hallway. His eyes searched mine as though he was weighing up his options.

'Okay,' he said finally, shoving his hands in his pockets. 'Just for a bit. If you don't mind?'

'Of course not.'

I opened the door wider and stepped inside, flattening myself against the wall so he could walk past me. He hesitated for a second in the doorway, then swayed down the hallway. He paused at the entrance to the living room and smiled back at me.

'It's good to see you, Beth.'

Matt was sitting on my sofa, his size 11 feet squeezed into a pair of my size 5 pink and white polka-dot socks, his wrists poking out from the only sweatshirt I had that was big enough to fit him. He was sitting so close to me I could smell his aftershave. I had to remind myself to breathe.

'So.' I handed him a large glass of really nasty Sauvignon Blanc from the corner shop, the only booze in the house apart from Lizzie's special twenty-first-birthday bottle of fancy French wine, then reached for my own glass. 'How did you know where I lived?'

'Um.' He shifted uncomfortably on the sofa and adjusted the fluffy pink cushion he was leaning against. 'I brought you back in a taxi that night we ran into each other on the seafront. Remember?'

'Oh yeah.' I took a sip of my wine. We'd chatted so comfortably at the hospital, but the mood had changed. The air between us was charged with awkwardness. I still had no idea why he had turned up at my flat. He couldn't even look me in the eye.

'So …' I started, unable to keep the question to myself for a second longer. 'Er, I'm not really sure why you're here.'

Matt looked at me for a second, then stood up, his wine slopping dangerously close to the edge of the glass as he lurched upwards. 'I should go.'

'It's okay.' I touched his wrist. 'You don't have to. It's nice to see you.'

'Really?' His brow creased into a frown.

'Yes.' I smiled. 'Who else am I going to share rank wine with at this time of night?'

The uncertainty on his face disappeared, and he

grinned. 'If you're sure? I could always go out and find you a tramp or three?'

I shook my head. 'They'd only laugh at you in those socks.'

'Ah, yes.' He glanced at his feet. 'Good point. Looks like I'll have to stay. At least until my toes dry out.'

'I am *so* going to get into trouble for this,' I said as I yanked on the corkscrew and the cork came out with a pop. 'Lizzie has been saving this for a special occasion for as long as I can remember, but,' I glanced at my watch; it was after 1 a.m., 'all the off-licences are shut, and we're having such a nice time!'

It was true. We were having a nice time. After drinking our way through the foul Sauvignon Blanc, Matt and I were now chatting and joking like old friends. With Aiden, I'd always been so careful not to disagree with him or say the wrong thing, because he'd get in a mood with me and freeze me out for hours. Matt was different. He pretended to act hurt when I said that *Jay and Silent Bob Strike Back* was the shittest Kevin Smith film I'd ever seen, then took the piss out of me when I told him how *About Last Night*, a cheesy eighties film starring Rob Lowe and Demi Moore, always made me cry.

He'd just launched into a rant about *Daredevil* when a horrible smell hit me and I wrinkled my nose. I glanced down. Oh God. Never mind Matt's undersized socks; mine positively reeked!

'Uh-huh. Yeah,' I said, nodding along to whatever Matt was saying as I subtly shifted on the sofa so I could tuck my feet under my bottom and hide the smell.

'What's up?' He stopped mid-rant and gave me a look.

'Nothing,' I said innocently. 'Just trying to get more comfortable.'

'Okay.' He raised an eyebrow.

'Yep.'

'So, um …' He sniffed the air. 'Is it just me, or can you smell Stilton too?'

'Nope.' I reached around behind me for a cushion and pressed it up against my feet. 'I can't smell anything. I think there's something wrong with your nose.'

'I don't think there is.' He sniffed the air again, big, exaggerated lungfuls, then looked at me from under his eyebrows. 'Are you cooking something?'

'Nope.' I grinned and inched away.

'I think you are, Beth. I think you're cooking up something pretty deadly.'

Before I could move, he'd lurched forward, tipped me on to my back and grabbed hold of one of my feet. To my horror, he put his nose up against it and sniffed my sock.

'Urghhhhhh!' he shouted, pushing me away from him and clutching his throat. 'You're not cooking food; you're creating deadly chemical weapons in your socks. That smell could kill small animals!'

I was so mortified, I didn't know whether to laugh or cry. Before I could defend myself, Matt had yanked off both my socks, run across the room and dangled them out of the living room window.

'Next door's cat's looking a bit ill,' he said, grinning back at me. 'Ooooh, no, he's trying to run for it. He's streaking away, trying to outrun the pong, but it's closing in on him. It's getting closer ... closer ... Oh God ... the Stilton Stink is surrounding him. Nooooooo!' He pulled a horrified face. 'He's dead. You killed the cat!'

I laughed so much my nose started to run.

'You're evil.' I grinned as I reached for a tissue 'You, Matt Jones, are the most evil man I've ever met.'

'Aaaggh!' he shouted, staring in horror at the tears of laugher that were rolling down my face. 'The sock crud is affecting you too. I need to dispose of these socks immediately before you go the same way as the cat.'

I watched, incredulously, as he threw my socks out of the window and slammed it shut.

'Oh no. I think I was too late.' He turned back to me and clutched his heart. 'I've been infected by the Stilton Stink too. Beth, help me. I'm not long for this world.'

'Come here,' I said, opening my arms wide. 'Tell me your last words and I'll put them on the tombstone you can share with the cat.'

Matt lurched across the living room, half play-acting, half pissed, and slumped on to the sofa beside me as though he was dying. He rested his head on my chest.

'Beth.' He gazed up at me. 'Beth ...'

'Oh, Matt,' I said, playing along. 'Please don't leave me. Don't go. You have been so brave. You fought the evil Stilton Stink, do not be defeated.'

'My love.' Matt reached up and cupped the side of

my face with his hand. 'My dear … dear … love …' He paused, and I waited for him to say something funny, but his grin had slipped.

Say something, I thought. Say something stupid, Beth. He's just teasing you. That look, that soul-searching, thoughtful look he's giving you doesn't mean anything. He's just pushing this joke too far.

'I really like you, Beth,' Matt said.

I held my breath, too scared to exhale. Any second now his serious expression would crack and he'd laugh and shout, 'Got you!'

'Beth?' Matt said again, his eyes not leaving mine.

'Yes?'

He ran his thumb over my cheek. 'I'm not joking.'

'You're not?'

'No.'

Every single cell in my body was screaming, *Tell him you like him too*, but I couldn't speak. I was too terrified.

Matt continued to gaze up at me, his dark eyes filled with an emotion I couldn't read. I gazed back at him, sick with indecision. There was so much tension in the room, I couldn't breathe.

When I couldn't bear it a second longer, I opened my mouth to speak. At exactly the same time, Matt pulled away from me and shifted across the sofa. He sat back heavily. 'This was a mistake. I should go.'

I reached for his hand and squeezed it. 'Don't.'

He looked at me. 'Why not?'

'Because I don't want you to. It's just …'

Could I tell him? Could I admit how much Aiden had hurt me? That I was terrified of falling for Matt

236

and having my heart broken? That I wasn't sure I believed in happy-ever-after endings any more?

'It's just ... it's just ...' I stuttered.

'What is it?'

'It's just ...' I met Matt's steady gaze. I could let my fear hold me back and watch him walk out of the door, or I could be brave, take a leap of faith and see where it took me.

'Just ... what?'

'Matt ...' I took a deep breath, and decided to jump.

Chapter Twenty-Six

Matt

I opened my eyes, then immediately shut them again, half blinded by the winter sunlight that spilled through a pair of thin cream curtains across the room.

My right eyelid flicked open a millimetre. Why was my bed facing the wrong way? The window was normally on my left, and ... Both my eyelids flew open and I stared around the room. There was a framed print of *Breakfast at Tiffany's* on the wall to my left, *Brief Encounter* on the right and a bookshelf crammed with books on film and screenwriting at the end of the bed. Next to that was a dressing table piled high with perfume bottles, make-up and hair products.

Where the hell was I?

A soft snuffling noise beside me made me turn my head.

Beth.

She was curled up beside me, her long eyelashes almost touching the tops of her cheeks, her dark hair plastered to her face and one hand balled up near her mouth. My breath caught in my throat as I gazed at her.

Beth.

I hadn't planned on turning up at her place. I'd sunk pint after pint in the pub, with the sole idea of drinking myself into a stupor, but I couldn't push the image of Beth sitting beside Grandad's bed out of my head. There was something about the way she'd answered his never-ending questions, her face lighting up as she laughed at his crap jokes, that had really touched me. The more I thought about it, the more I realised that her turning up at the hospital wasn't freaky or weird; it was pure kindness. She'd gone to all that trouble to say sorry to me when she could have just walked away and pretended it had never happened. And she genuinely seemed to care about Grandad too.

The more I thought about Beth as I propped up the bar and nursed my lukewarm pint of lager, the more I wanted to see her. I wanted to see her eyes crease when she smiled. I wanted to see her tip her head forward when she was embarrassed. I just wanted to see her. I wanted to feel the warmth, the affection and the safety I'd felt in the hotel room the night before. It took me seconds to check the address on her CV (I still had a pile of them in my bag), then my legs propelled me through the night.

'Matt?' she murmured, her fingers twitching against my leg.

'Go back to sleep,' I whispered.

I thought I'd blown it when I told her I liked her. She'd looked so shocked, I half expected her to tell me to leave, but when she'd leaned in to kiss me, it was my turn to be surprised. She kissed me so passionately it took my breath away. It was inevitable we'd end up in bed.

'Mmm.' She snuggled up closer to me and pressed her face into the crook of my neck.

Why had she kissed me? Surely she wouldn't have let me in last night or cracked open her flatmate's expensive wine if she didn't like me too. And she'd cried with laughter when I threw her socks out of the window. But what if the sex didn't mean anything to her? What if she woke up and went 'Well that was fun, see you'? I shook my head. No. There was more to it than that. Afterwards we'd curled up together and looked into each other's eyes and ...

Jesus! I mentally shook myself. Neil would take the piss out of me for ever if he knew I was analysing a shag for hidden meaning. I rubbed my head. My hangover was starting to kick in, and all I could think about was whether or not Beth would cook the fried breakfast she'd mentioned before we finally fell asleep. I folded my hands behind my head and stared up at the ceiling, trying to decide whether I fancied fried bread or toast. Fried bread was good because it was, well, fried, but toast dripping with butter was really ...

'What the fuck!'

I sat bolt upright, my neck craned towards the ceiling, and squinted at the words written in capital letters on a piece of A4 and Blu-Tacked to the ceiling above the bed.

I WILL DO WHATEVER IT TAKES TO GET THE JOB WITH APOLLO.

My jaw dropped as I reread it.

Whatever it takes?

I looked down at Beth. She was still asleep, her face the picture of innocence. What did 'whatever it takes' mean? Slipping into your boss's hotel room on the interview weekend? Pretending to take his grandad a balloon? Sleeping with him? My stomach clenched violently – not because I was angry, but because I was gutted. Totally gutted.

How had I got it so wrong? I'd really believed that Beth was sweet, kind and funny, the total opposite of Alice. She'd fooled me into thinking she was something she wasn't, just like my ex-girlfriend had. I was a mug, a total, fucking mug.

I'd done it again. I'd fallen for another psycho.

I inched my way towards the edge of the bed, freezing as Beth's hand slipped off my thigh and landed on the sheet. Her eyelids flickered, and I held my breath as she shifted position in her sleep.

Don't wake up, I prayed silently. *Please, please don't wake up.*

As she wriggled deeper under the duvet and pulled it over her head, I sighed with relief, slipped off the bed and scanned the floor for my underwear. My boxer shorts were hanging from a knob on the chest of drawers – I'd yanked them off the night before and chucked them across the room. We'd both laughed when we saw where they'd landed, and I was about to say something witty about my tossing skills when Beth had pulled me towards her and said, 'Yeah, yeah, very clever, just kiss me, you idiot.'

Hmmm, she'd got the last word right. I pulled on

my underwear, reached under the bed for my jeans, retrieved my T-shirt from the top of the laundry basket and wandered into the living room. I found my shoes and socks under the coffee table. My socks were still sopping wet so I shoved them into my pocket, slipped on my shoes and walked on tiptoe to the front door. One of the floorboards creaked under my weight, and I froze. When nothing happened, I turned the key in the door, twisted the handle and let myself out.

I didn't look back.

Chapter Twenty-Seven

Beth

'Morning,' I murmured. My eyes were closed, but I could hear seagulls squawking outside the window. I rolled on to my side and reached across the bed in search of Matt's warm body.

'Last night was so amazing ...' My fingers brushed cold cotton, and I opened my eyes. 'Matt?'

I propped myself up on one elbow and listened for footsteps in the hall or the sound of taps running in the bathroom. 'Matt, are you there?'

My eyes wandered across the bedroom to the pile of clothes by the door: a bra, some knickers, a black top and a pair of jeans.

Just one pair of jeans.

'Matt?' I threw back the duvet, grabbed my dressing gown from the back of the rocking chair in the corner of the room and wandered down the hallway and into the living room.

He's just popped out to buy the papers and some breakfast, I told myself as I looked on the coffee table for a note.

Nothing.

'Matt!' I called again as I walked back down the hall to the kitchen.

Nothing.

It's fine, I told myself as I went back to the bedroom and crawled into bed. He's just gone to the shop. He'll be back and ringing the doorbell in ten minutes. I closed my eyes and quickly fell asleep.

An hour later, I woke with a start. The other side of the bed was still empty.

'Matt?' I called as I rolled back out of bed and wandered from room to room again. 'Matt?'

The empty wine bottles and glasses were still on the coffee table but there was no sign of him. I slumped on to the sofa and hugged the pink cushion to my chest.

It didn't make sense. Why would Matt tell me he really liked me, and then leave before I woke up? He didn't seem like the kind of guy to play games. Or maybe he was. Maybe he'd only turned up because he was drunk and wanted to get me into bed again. But why be so lovely if it was all about a shag? The night before had been so impossibly romantic it hadn't felt real. There was no weirdness after we'd had sex. Instead of farting, rolling over and going to sleep (Aiden was such an expert at that move, he could have won gold in the post-coital Olympics), Matt had pulled me close to him, whispered, 'There's something very important I need to tell you, Beth' and then cracked the crappest joke I'd ever heard. When I finally did fall asleep, several hours later, my cheeks were aching from grinning.

So why did he just up and leave? Of course! I threw the cushion away from me in relief. His grandad!

There was me assuming the worst of Matt when he'd obviously just snuck off early to visit Jack and didn't want to wake me.

There's nothing to worry about, I thought as I stood up from the sofa, padded into the kitchen and switched on the kettle. Nothing at all.

I was still smiling to myself an hour later as I strolled up to the Picturebox and twisted my key in the lock. Today was going to be a good day. A very good day.

I made myself a coffee and busied myself decorating the foyer and putting up the artificial Christmas tree. I hummed to myself as I loaded its branches with gaudy baubles, chipped figurines and tired tinsel. The first thing I'll do, I thought as I tipped my head to one side and surveyed my handiwork, if I get the manager's job is chuck it all away and start again. New job, new decorations. The Picturebox deserved to look bright and sparkly, not tired and ready for the knacker's yard.

I leaned over the counter and checked the date on the computer: 9 December, and I hadn't bought a single present. I shook my head. I was normally so organised. Right – time to make a list. I sat at my desk as the Christmas tree twinkled away in the corner of the foyer.

'What should I get Lizzie?' I asked George Clooney. He was looking particularly festive with his red tinsel tie and a gold tinsel halo. 'Something from Ann Summers? Again. And what about Matt? Should I get him a present? Too soon, do you think?'

My festive mood continued even when twenty mums

with buggies filed in, and the foyer was filled with the sound of babies' grunts, babble and screams.

In fact, I was having one of the best days I'd had in a long time until, twenty minutes after the Sob Showing started, the front door opened and a gaunt, greasy man walked in. My stomach sank to my feet.

Carl.

'Hi, Beth,' he said, his lips twisting into a smarmy smile as he took in the Christmas tree and the tinsel-lined counter.

I glanced at my watch. He was three hours early for his shift and that could only mean one thing ... trouble.

I shoved my Christmas present list under a pile of programmes. There was no way I was going to let him ruin my good mood. Maybe if I just ignored him he'd bugger off.

'So ...' Every hair on my body prickled as he moved across the foyer towards me. 'Have you had the call yet?'

I looked at him. 'What call?'

'From Matt, about the job.'

My heart did a double beat when I heard Matt's name, but I shook my head. 'No.'

'Really?'

Carl's tone was incredulous. Even the open pores on his nose seemed to be smirking at me.

'What?' I said. 'Why are you looking at me like that?'

'No reason. I just thought Matt might have called you first seeing as you two seemed to be so ...' he raised a dark eyebrow, 'close last weekend. He's called Raj, Seth and Jade. None of them made the cut for the manager's position. In fact there's only you and James that haven't had a call yet.'

Ha! If everyone apart from me and James were still waiting for phone calls that meant Carl hadn't got the job!

'I'm sure Matt's been very busy,' I said breezily, even though my heart felt like it was about to beat itself out of my chest.

Despite what had happened during my interview, I was still hopeful about my chances. Matt knew me now, and I was sure he'd realise I'd only messed up because I'd been provoked. He'd seen my business plan, he'd watched me at work in the cinema, and I was pretty certain he knew I could handle the job.

'There's plenty of time for him to call,' I added, shooting Carl a defiant look.

Almost on cue, the phone beside me started to ring.

Oh no. Oh no, oh no, oh no. Please don't let that be Matt. Please don't let him ring while Carl is here. Please, please, please …

'Hello!' I said, in my best professional yet chirpy voice. 'The Picturebox. How can I help you?'

'Is that Beth Prince?' said a female voice.

'It is.'

'Hello, Beth, this is Sheila from Apollo.'

'Oh! Hello.' My heart thumped violently in my chest. 'How can I help you, Sheila?'

'I'm ringing on behalf of Matt Jones. You attended an interview for the new manager position last weekend?'

What? Why wasn't Matt ringing me to tell me how I'd done? He'd called everyone else.

'I did, yes.'

'Well the thing is, Beth,' Sheila's tone faltered, 'I'm afraid you didn't get the job.'

'Oh.' I could feel Carl staring intently at me and swivelled round in my chair so that I had my back to him.

'Was there any feedback?' I asked quietly.

'Feedback? No, Matt didn't ask me to give you any.'

'Oh. Okay. Is Matt there? Could I talk to him?'

'One second, Beth.' There was a clunk, then the low murmur of voices. I pressed my ear against the phone.

'She wants to talk to you,' Sheila's muffled voice said. 'What should I tell her?'

'That I never want to speak to her again,' said a voice. Matt's voice.

'Sorry, Beth,' said Sheila, her voice suddenly clear. 'I'm afraid Matt's in an important meeting at the moment and he can't be disturbed, but he did ask me to tell you that, as per the memorandum that was circulated last month, you'll work your notice to the end of December and will be paid your final salary on the last working day. If you require a reference, you should request one from your current employer, Mrs Blackstock ...'

Sheila continued to waffle on, but I'd stopped listening.

I never want to speak to her again.

Had I heard that right? I couldn't have. Could I? Why would Matt say that?

'Beth?' Sheila was saying into my ear. 'Beth, are you still there?'

'Yes … yes. I'm here. Thank you for letting me know. Goodbye.'

I twisted round, slammed the phone on to the cradle and glared up at Carl. 'If you say anything, I won't be responsible for my actions.'

He didn't say a word.

Chapter Twenty-Eight

Matt

The man in the next bed raised an eyebrow at me as I tipped back my head and yawned loudly. The nurse had closed the curtains around Grandad's bed so he could use the loo, and I was waiting outside.

'Cover your mouth, lad,' the man said, shaking his head. 'No one wants to see what you had for breakfast.'

I shrugged apologetically and rubbed my hands over my face. I hadn't had any breakfast. I hadn't even showered. I'd escaped from Beth's house just after 6 a.m., and headed straight to work. My clothes were crumpled and I smelt like a brewery, but I couldn't go home and risk finding Alice still there, not after what I'd seen on Beth's ceiling. My head was too much of a mess.

Sheila had wrinkled her nose at me when she came in after nine, but didn't say a word. Good job too, because my hangover was so hideous, I felt like my brain was being smashed in with a shovel if someone even breathed a bit too loudly. It took two hours and five cups of coffee before I felt ready to make the interview follow-up calls, and even then I called Jade Jane by mistake. I made all the calls though. All but one.

I glanced at my mobile as the nurse slipped through the curtains with a bedpan in her hand. It was 7 p.m. and I'd popped into the hospital to see how Grandad was doing.

'Is he okay?' I asked, lowering my voice. 'He looks a bit greyer than yesterday.'

'He's as well as can be expected.' She placed the bedpan on the metal trolley and covered it with a paper cloth. 'He's not a young man any more and it's going to take a while until he's back to his old self.'

'He is going to get out in time for Christmas, isn't he?'

She shrugged. 'Your grandad needs to have an operation. Have you spoken to his surgeon, Mr Harlow?'

'Yeah.' I nodded. 'I met him briefly yesterday. He said Grandad's booked in for some kind of heart surgery in a week's time.'

'Well then.' She gripped hold of the trolley and took a step, keen to be on her way.

'But ...' My question faded to nothing as her shoes clip-clopped across the ward.

'Matt?' Grandad called. 'Is that you, son?'

I pulled back the curtains. He was lying back on his pillow, the sheet loosely gathered around his waist, his wiry grey chest hairs poking out of the top of his pyjamas.

I placed my palm on his forehead. I wasn't sure why, but I'd seen people do it on TV when their relatives were ill. 'Are you sure you're okay? You feel a bit sweaty.'

'You'd be sweaty too if you had to do your business in front of a nurse!' He grinned, then craned his head to the left to look behind me. 'Where's that pretty young thing who came with you yesterday?'

'Beth? She's …' I didn't know what to say.

'Oh.' Grandad shook his head and shot me an exasperated look. 'Don't tell me you're not courting her any more.'

'I wasn't courting her. We were just …'

'Just what?'

'I don't know.' I really didn't.

'It's not often I'll admit I'm wrong,' he said, trying and failing to sit up, 'but I shouldn't have encouraged you to work things out with blondie. I'd never even met the girl. But I could see the way you and Beth looked at each other. And she's nice. Properly special. You know that, don't you?'

'I did. I mean, I thought I did, but …'

Grandad's thin chest rose and fell as he sighed in disappointment. 'What have you done now?'

'Nothing.' My mouth dried as I remembered the sign I'd seen above Beth's bed, and I licked my lips. 'Honestly. But you're wrong about her. Nice girls don't stick signs on their ceilings reminding them to be a … a … slut.'

I regretted my choice of words the second they came out of my mouth.

'Matt!' Grandad shot me a disapproving look. 'You need to wash your mouth out and leave the flannel in. I thought I'd brought you up better than that.'

'Sorry. I shouldn't have said that.'

'Too right you shouldn't.' He tried to reach for a cup of water on the bedside table, but it was too far away.

'So go on,' he said as I handed it to him, 'what happened?'

I shook my head. He wouldn't believe me even if I told him. 'It's too complicated.'

'There's no such thing as too complicated. You need to talk to her is what you need to do.' He clamped his hand over mine, his expression suddenly serious. 'Listen to me, son. I don't want to shuffle off this mortal coil and leave you all alone.'

'Hey! You're not shuffling anywhere. Apart from to the bathroom maybe,' I added, desperately trying to lighten the mood. I'd never been able to bear it when Grandad talked about death. Just the thought of him not being around made me feel like I was plummeting through the air at a thousand miles an hour.

'Aren't I?' He pursed his lips and looked at me intently. His cheeks were hollow, there were deep, dark circles under his eyes, and it hit me how tired he looked. 'You heard the nurse. I'm not getting any younger.'

'You'll be fine.' I squeezed his hand. 'You're just feeling a bit weak after the heart attack. Once you get your strength back, you'll feel much more—'

'Matthew. Shut up.'

I stared at him in surprise. He never, ever called me Matthew.

'I'm serious,' he continued. 'Your mum's God knows where, your dad's off with his South African flouncy and I'm the only family you've got left. I just want to see you happy, son. Before I go.'

'With Beth?' I shook my head, choosing to ignore the last bit of his sentence. 'That's not going to happen, Grandad.'

'Hmmm.' He took another sip of water, swallowed and then passed me the glass to put back on the table. 'Your grandma was a good woman, Matt, you know that, don't you?'

I nodded. 'The best.'

'The best in the world, in fact, but she broke my heart. Did I ever tell you that?'

'No.' I looked at him in surprise. He'd told me a lot about his life, but mostly about his childhood, being in the army during the war, and his time with the electric board. He never mentioned 'personal business'. 'What happened?'

'She kissed Bert, my best friend, two weeks after we got engaged.'

'No!'

'Afraid so.' He smiled tightly. 'I asked her to marry me when I was back in Morpeth on leave from the army. You should have seen her face, Matt. It lit up like a Catherine wheel and she threw her arms around my neck and told me I'd made her the happiest girl in the world. Two weeks later I left to go and fight the Boche, and Mary went to a dance in the village hall with a few of her friends. Apparently she had a few sherries, got a bit emotional about my chances of making it out alive, and when Bert went to offer her a few words of reassurance, she kissed him.'

He looked up at the ceiling, his pale blue eyes suddenly damp.

'It was a mistake,' he rasped. 'A one-off mistake because she was scared. My nose was knocked out of joint, of course it was, but it didn't stop me loving her. Not for one second.'

'But that was back then,' I objected, 'during the war. Things are different now.'

'Are they?' He looked at me. 'Because from where I'm sitting, it seems that folk today get scared just like they always have.'

'But Beth …'

'Whatever she did, I don't think she did it with any malice, lad. That's a special girl you've got there, and if you let her go, you're more of a fool than I thought. Don't run away, not like your mam did. Promise me you'll give Beth a chance to explain herself.'

I ran a hand through my hair. He didn't understand. How could he? He was from a different era.

'Promise me, lad,' he said again, squeezing my hand.

'I promise,' I said.

It was the first time I'd ever lied to him.

Chapter Twenty-Nine

Beth

Two weeks.

That was how long had passed since Matt Jones had vanished from my life. Poof! Gone. Just like that. Like he'd never existed.

Two weeks.

And he'd taken my dream job with him and given it to James.

'Yes?'

The couple in front of the booth beamed in delight as I looked up at them. They were so ridiculously intertwined, it was hard to tell where one person started and the other ended.

'Two tickets to see *It's a Wonderful Life*,' said the man, squeezing his girlfriend even closer. 'We'd like one of the sofas upstairs, if that's possible.'

'We do like a snuggle at Christmas,' she giggled, gazing up at him. 'Or any time, in fact!'

'Doesn't everyone,' I snapped, then instantly regretted it. It wasn't their fault I was feeling as festive as Scrooge. I handed them their tickets. 'Enjoy the film.'

'We will!' they chorused, skipping off towards the stairs.

Ick.

The twenty-third of December, and I had exactly one week and one day left until I was officially unemployed. I stared around the cinema, taking in the displays I'd spent ages meticulously arranging, the posters I'd carefully picked out, and the twinkling cut-out of George Clooney by the front door. It really was over. The only job I'd ever loved; the only job I'd ever had.

If that wasn't bad enough, I had a flatmate who was never at home, an ex-boyfriend who thought I was a raving lunatic, and then there was Matt ...

I glanced at the phone on the desk, willing it to ring, then shook my head. No matter how much I wanted him to call and tell me there'd been a terrible mistake, I knew he wouldn't. I'd heard it in his voice down the phone two weeks ago. He wanted nothing to do with me.

It's almost like men have an inbuilt ESP that tells them when a woman has let her defences down. At the beginning of a relationship, when you're not sure if you like them that much, they'll chase you – ringing, texting and wanting to spend lots of time with you – but as soon as they sense that your feelings have changed and you've warmed to them, they back right off. Or leave, in my case. Bye bye, Beth.

Only Matt hadn't even reached the ringing and spending-time-with-me stage, had he? He'd scarpered before we'd even got that far.

If I wanted to, I could find out Apollo's number and

ask him what the hell he thought he was playing at, refusing to talk to me on the phone the day after we slept together for the first time – too gutless to tell me himself that I hadn't got the job. It would only take seconds to tell him I wasn't going to let anyone treat me like that ever again and slam down the phone.

Only there was no way I was going to do that.

Absolutely no way.

This wasn't about playing games like Lizzie's 'don't call Aiden' stand-off, or because I was gutless. It was because I had too much pride. When I'd told Aiden how I'd felt, I'd just ended up humiliating myself, and I sure as hell wasn't going to do that again.

Sod him. Sod Matt Jones and his cute smile and his stupid jokes and his tender kisses. I was worth more than that. A lot more.

I frowned as a text message arrived on my phone. It was from Mum.

Don't forget. Meet at Pool Valley at 1100 tomorrow. You are still coming, aren't you, Beth? You did promise.

Hmmm. My thumbs flew over the keys as I typed out my reply.

'Hiya, Beth.' I jumped at the sound of a male voice and glanced up. Oh, thank God. Raj was strolling across the foyer, ready for his shift. I don't know whether the gods were finally smiling on me a bit, but I hadn't seen Carl for a while. He was 'off sick' the first week after the interviews, and we'd been on different shifts during the second.

'Only a week left!' Raj said. His hands were in his pockets and he was grinning like he didn't have a care in the world. 'Not that I'm hugely fussed. I've got a job interview with Richer Sounds lined up tomorrow. Reckon I can nail it. I've always been a bit of a tech geek at heart. You cool?'

'I'm fine,' I said, smiling tightly. 'I've decided to—' I was interrupted by my mobile bleeping. 'Hang on one sec. I think my mum's just replied.'

Hi Beth, the text said. *I understand why you're ignoring me, but we really need to talk. Please call me as soon as you get this.*

It was signed with three kisses and a name. Aiden.

Chapter Thirty

Matt

It was over a week since Grandad's heart operation and he still wasn't looking well. It was to be expected, the surgeon had said, especially at Grandad's age, but I wasn't reassured. I just felt so damned useless – standing at his side, wiping his clammy brow and talking shit to try and get him to laugh.

It was 23 December, and the chances of him getting out in time for Christmas were less than none.

'Not to worry,' I said, forcing an air of cheeriness into my voice, after the surgeon had broken the bad news about Christmas. 'I'll cook up a fantastic turkey dinner with all the trimmings and bring it in for you.'

'What are you trying to do?' Grandad rasped. 'Kill me?'

'No, feed you up, you skinny bugger. And if you make another joke about the nurses and pulling a cracker, you're watching the Queen's speech on your own!'

'Tell you what.' He slowly placed his hand over mine. It didn't feel like a big, heavy paw any more. It was like a leaf, dried out, barely touching my skin. 'You bring that lovely girl Beth with you and I'll eat whatever you stick in my gob.'

'Beth's got family of her own to spend Christmas with,' I said lightly. 'She doesn't want to spend it with an old git like you!'

'That may be so,' he raised a grey eyebrow, 'but I'll bet you a shilling she'd like to spend it with you. I told you, Matthew, and I'll tell you again. She's a special girl, that one. You'd be a fool to let her go.'

I changed the subject, quickly. To be honest, I hadn't given Beth a second thought for days. Actually, that's a lie. I hadn't been able to get her out of my mind, but every time I thought about picking up the phone to talk to her, to ask her about that wretched sign on the ceiling, something inside me shut down. I wasn't sure I wanted to know the truth.

The second I stepped out of the hospital, I yanked my mobile out of my back pocket. Three missed calls from Ballbreaker. Shit! I still hadn't put the Picturebox contract in the post. I'd tried explaining about Grandad's heart problems, but she wasn't having it. In fact the last thing she'd said to me was: 'I don't care if your entire family are up to their necks in quicksand and it's down to you and Indiana Bloody Jones to save them. I want my fucking contract!'

I swiftly deleted the notifications and scrolled through my contacts until I found Neil's number. There was just one thing for it after the day I'd had. Pub!

Answer it, answer it, answer it, I silently prayed as it rang. Neil was the master at ignoring his phone. He didn't like to be at other people's beck and call, he'd told me once. That was why he always insisted on taking women's numbers instead of giving them his. Funnily enough, it used to be the other way round – before three girlfriends in a row turned down his proposal of marriage.

'Mister Jones,' he said as my thumb hovered over the 'End Call' button. 'The Neilmeister is back in Brighton! What can I do you for?'

'Are you in the pub?'

'Not yet, but I could be.'

I sighed with relief. I really, really needed a drink. 'Excellent. Pull and Pump in half an hour's time?'

'Cool.'

The line went dead, and I shoved my phone back into my pocket and headed off along the street towards town. I walked quickly, with my head down. No matter how hard I tried, I couldn't stop replaying the conversation I'd just had with Grandad.

'She's a special girl, that one,' he'd said. 'You'd be a fool to let her go.'

That was the second time he'd told me that.

'Hello! Hellooooo! Anyone at home?' A young woman was standing in front of me, a toddler screaming in the pushchair she was gripping. 'Are you going to move, or do I have to dodge the traffic to get around you?'

I shook my head. I was standing stock-still in the middle of the pavement on Edward Street.

'Sorry!' As I stepped to one side so she could pass, the left pocket of my jeans vibrated violently.

Neil, I thought as I fished out my mobile. If he's cancelled on me, I'll bloody …

Matt, the text message said. *It's Alice. Something terrible has happened. I know you don't want to talk to me, but it's important. REALLY important. I promise I'll never bother you again if that's what you want, but just hear me out. Please, come and see me and I'll explain x*

I'm not sure how I ended up on Alice's doorstep. Or why. My first thought on reading her text was *Oh God, what now?* The second was *What if there's something wrong with her?*

I don't know if it was the tone of the message, or the fact that I'd just left the hospital, but I couldn't get the second thought out of my head. She said that something terrible had happened. What was more terrible than a life-threatening illness? There was no way I could ignore that after what I'd been through with Grandad. Only a heartless bastard would have turned his back on someone asking for help, and while the jury was most definitely still out on me being a dick, I was pretty sure I didn't qualify for bastard status.

I clenched my hand and knocked three times on Alice's front door. It opened a split second later.

'Matt!' she exclaimed, her face lighting up. 'I'm so glad you came.'

I looked at her in surprise. I'd expected to be met by a distraught, dishevelled Alice with tear-stained make-up and scraped-back hair. Instead, she seemed to be groomed to within an inch of her life. Her make-up was perfect, her hair curled around her face and she was dressed in skinny jeans, high heels and a fluffy grey jumper.

'Come in!' she said, opening the door wide and ushering me in. 'Take a seat in the living room. Would you like a cup of tea?'

I took a step forward, then paused, confused. 'I thought there was some kind of emergency?'

Alice's gleeful grin immediately disappeared, and she lowered her head.

'It's not an emergency,' she said casting a look at me as though to check my reaction, 'but it is important.'

I looked her up and down, confused. Maybe I'd got it all wrong. Maybe she just wanted to tell me that she'd got a new job or she was moving to a different town or something. But she'd used the word 'terrible' in her text, hadn't she? What was that about? Or maybe there was no news. Maybe it was just one big game to get me to come over and I'd fallen for it.

'Alice,' I said, trying hard not to let my irritation show, 'what was so important that I had to rush over here?'

'Um.' She bit down on her bottom lip then sighed. 'I think you might want to sit down.'

Sit down? What? Had someone died? Alice and I didn't really have any mutual friends. And it wasn't as though I was close to her family; she'd never even introduced me to them.

'Please, Matt.' She put a hand on my arm, guided me towards the living room and gestured at the sofa. 'Have a seat while I make tea. I'll be back in a sec.'

She turned to leave the room.

'Wait!' I grabbed her wrist. 'You can't tell me something terrible has happened and then leave me to stew while you make a couple of drinks. Just tell me.'

'Okay.' She turned back, wriggling her wrist out of my grasp and intertwining her fingers with mine. I didn't say a word as she pulled me down on to the sofa and fixed me with a serious stare.

'The thing is, Matt,' she began. My heart immediately began to beat at double speed. Why was she looking at me so intently? What the hell had happened? 'The thing is …'

She paused to lick her lips.

'The thing is …'

I stared at her mouth, trying to work out what words it was she was finding so hard to say.

'The thing is … I'm think I'm pregnant.'

If I hadn't been sitting on a sofa, and if Alice's fingers hadn't been so tightly clasped around mine, my legs would have collapsed under me. I felt like the world had just been whipped from under my feet.

'What?' I stared at her. 'Say that again.'

'I said,' her eyes flicked over my face, just like they had in the hall, searching for a reaction, 'I think I'm pregnant.'

But how could … We hadn't … It was …

All the blood rushed back to my face, and I sighed with relief. Alice wasn't pregnant by me. There was no way. We hadn't slept together for over two months, and if she'd missed a period and taken a pregnancy test while we were together, she would have told me. She wouldn't have waited until weeks after we'd split up. So that meant …

'Wow,' I said, wriggling my hand out of hers and easing myself back against the sofa cushions. 'That's quite some news. I'm so pleased you've met someone. Really pleased. How did he take it?'

'He?' She frowned, suddenly pissed off. 'You're the dad, Matt.'

'What!'

'Of course you are. I was totally faithful while we were together, and there hasn't been anyone since.'

'But it can't be mine.' I sat up straight, my heart rate instantly speeding up again. 'We haven't had sex in months.'

'I know.' She raised her eyebrows. 'I'm as surprised as you.'

'But how can you be pregnant if we haven't slept together recently? How is that even possible?'

Alice leaned back on the sofa, placed her hands on her non-existent stomach and smiled tightly. 'I haven't had it confirmed by the doctor yet, but I imagine I'm two months gone. I've always had irregular periods, and when I missed my last one, I didn't think anything of it. I just assumed it was part of my weird cycle and I'd get one this month. Only,' she fixed me with a look, 'I didn't.'

'But … but …' I wiped my palms on the knees of my jeans, my hands suddenly clammy. 'We were always so careful. I always used a condom.'

'I know.' She shrugged. 'One must have split or something. We never checked them all, did we?'

I shook my head. That was true, but surely I would have noticed. Surely.

Silence fell as Alice stared at me and I stared right back at her, the full implications of what she'd just revealed slowly sinking in. Beyond the living room, the world was still noisy – a woman shouted at her dog as it veered into the road, gangs of students chatted excitedly on their way to the pub and cars beeped angrily as they fought for parking spaces. Nothing had changed outside. Inside, everything had.

'So,' I said finally. 'What are we going to do?'

Chapter Thirty-One

Beth

I sipped my cup of tea, put my feet up on the sofa and picked up my mobile phone. Lizzie was nowhere to be seen, as usual, although she had left me a note on the coffee table asking if I'd mind putting her washing on if I was doing mine. I scrolled through my texts and reread the most recent one from Aiden.

Hi Beth. I understand why you're ignoring me, but we really need to talk. Please call me as soon as you get this. Aiden xxx

What was so important that he needed to speak to me? My thumb flew over the screen and pressed 'Call' before I had time to change my mind.

'Beth!' Aiden sounded so surprised, it made my stomach churn. What the hell was I doing calling him? He was so going to bollock me for gatecrashing his grandad's ninetieth birthday party.

'Hi, Aiden,' I said, as casually as I could.

'Beth ...' I could hear people clacking away on their keyboards in the background. Oh shit. Aiden had always told me never to call him at work. 'It's good to hear from you.'

'It is?'

'God, yes! You ignored so many of my texts, I assumed I'd never hear from you again. In fact, I thought my last memory of you would be you scrambling off the stage in a most ungainly fashion—'

'Don't,' I interrupted. 'If you're going to have a go at me, I'd rather you didn't give me a blow-by-blow account of what happened that night. I'm humiliated enough without reliving the whole thing all over again. In fact—'

'Beth, I'm not going to have a go at you.'

My mouth dropped open. 'You're not?'

'No.'

'Then why did you ask me to call?'

'It's … well …' He paused again. Normally there was no stopping Aiden when he had something to say. He was Mr Unflappable. 'Could you meet me in the Lion and Lobster later? I'd like to talk to you face to face.'

'Um … I don't know. I …' Now it was my turn to hesitate. If Aiden wasn't going to bollock me, then what did he want? I'd already been messed around by Matt, and the last thing I wanted was more mind games.

'Please, Beth.' His tone was gentle, almost pleading. 'It's really important.'

'Okay.' I made a split-second decision. 'I'll be there. Nine o'clock.'

I put the phone down, stared at it for a couple of seconds and then snatched it up again. There were a couple of very important texts I needed to send.

*

The Lion and Lobster was bursting with evening drinkers, and I breathed a sigh of relief. Whatever Aiden had to say to me, he'd have to do it in public. I squeezed through the crowded tables to the bar, ordered a large glass of wine then spotted my ex-boyfriend waving at me frantically from a table across the room.

'Beth!' he hollered across the pub. He pointed at the wine glass in his hand. 'For you.'

I raised an eyebrow. Whenever I'd gone for a drink with Aiden before, he'd always got there early, grabbed himself a gin and tonic and holed up in a corner with a book about philosophy. When I turned up, he'd kiss me on the cheek and then stick his nose back in his book while I went to get myself a drink.

He was still gesturing at me to join him, so I grabbed the glass of wine the barman had placed on the bar and angled my way through the crowd.

'Hello, darling!' Aiden said as I set my drink on the table, then threw his arms around me and squeezed me so tightly I squealed. 'I'm so pleased you came.'

When he finally let me go, he patted the wooden chair beside him.

'Sorry it's a bit of a squeeze,' he said, as someone knocked into me, 'but I was lucky to get this table. If I'd got here any later, you'd be sitting on my knee.'

I grabbed my glass and took a big gulp as Aiden threw back his head and laughed like he'd just cracked the world's funniest joke. What was wrong with him? He'd *never* been so pleased to see me before. Or so weirdly upbeat.

'So …' I set my glass down, curiosity and the warm

tingle of wine hitting my empty stomach, making me unusually brave. 'What's this all about?'

Aiden stopped laughing and looked at me. His Adam's apple bobbed up and down as he swallowed.

'The thing is, Beth ...' He looked at his drink, then back at me. 'The thing is ...'

'Yes?'

He wasn't going to tell me he had a sexually transmitted disease, was he? Oh God. I *knew* I shouldn't have gone on the pill two weeks after we started sleeping together. He'd told me he'd had all the tests after he and his ex had split up, but that might have been bullshit. Or maybe he had cheated on me while we were together and caught something.

'It's about the party,' he said.

I knew it. He *was* going to bollock me.

'I'm sorry I gatecrashed it,' I said before he could say a word, then reached for my wine. 'But there was a bit of a misunder—'

Aiden grabbed hold of my fingers before they could make contact with the glass.

'Don't.' He squeezed my hand. 'Don't you dare apologise.'

I looked at him in surprise. 'What?'

He leaned towards me, his eyes fixed on mine. 'Something strange happened when you turned up at the party and grabbed the microphone.'

'You opened your wallet?' I joked, then instantly regretted it. Aiden wasn't messing around. He was still staring at me. His eyes were so wide, all I could see was big white eyeballs and massive pupils. I was starting to worry he'd forgotten how to blink.

'I saw you completely differently that night,' he continued, stroking the back of my hand.

'You did?'

He nodded and leaned even closer. There was a yellow pimple on the side of his jaw. It looked like it needed a good squeeze. 'I saw something I'd never seen before.'

'My knickers as I crawled off the stage?'

Oh God! What was wrong with me? Why did I keep saying such stupid things?

'I had seen your knickers before, Beth,' he said, totally deadpan. He still hadn't cracked a smile. 'What I hadn't seen was the gutsy, devil-may-care side of you I didn't know existed. You were like a different woman. A vibrant, passionate woman.'

'I was?'

'Part of the reason I finished with you, Beth, was because you never really ...' Aiden finally blinked as he reached for his glass and took a sip of red wine, 'asserted yourself. Whenever I asked you what you wanted to do, or where you wanted to go and eat, you'd say, "Whatever you fancy."'

I cringed. That was true.

'When I first met you, at the cinema, you were funny, spontaneous and witty, but the longer we spent together, the less I saw of that side of you. Your personality seemed to fade away and I stopped feeling like I had a girlfriend; instead I had a shadow that agreed with everything I said.'

'Hmmm.' I took a large gulp of my own wine. Great, so he hadn't dragged me out of my flat to give me crap about gatecrashing his party. He was delivering a slow, torturous character assassination instead. Nice.

'But when you walked on to that stage,' Aiden put a finger under my chin and tilted it up so I had to look at him, 'and just let rip, something inside me clicked. I couldn't take my eyes off you. You were passionate, vibrant and alive, and you'd gatecrashed the party because of your feelings for me. No one's ever done anything like that for me before, Beth.'

I was too stunned to breathe, never mind speak.

'So the thing is…' He ran his thumb over my cheek. 'The reason I asked you to come here tonight … is because I wanted to apologise and ask you …'

He was going to do it, he was actually going to do it; admit that he'd made a mistake in dumping me. I'd lost count of the times I'd fantasised about ex-boyfriends begging me to give them another chance. I'd certainly dreamed about Aiden doing it. I wouldn't have gone to all that trouble with fake tan, glow-in-the-dark teeth and too-tight dresses if I hadn't. How many times had I checked my phone, hoping to hear from him? Hundreds! Possibly thousands. The second he'd dumped me, all I'd wanted, all I'd dreamed about, was to get him back. He was the only man I was interested in, until …

An image of Matt's smiling face flashed into my mind. I pushed it away and smiled at Aiden. It was a sick kind of universe that made men who'd dumped you want you back the second you developed feelings

273

for someone else. Only Matt didn't return my feelings, did he? He didn't want anything to do with me and I was pretty certain he hated my guts.

'So, Beth, what I wanted to ask you is … is …' Aiden stuttered, still staring at me intently, '… is if you could find it in your heart to forgive me for letting you go and give me a second chance. Please, just give me a chance.'

A second chance? He wasn't giving *me* a second chance; he was begging me to give him one! The man I'd loved was admitting he'd made a mistake and wanted to put it right.

Wow.

My ex-boyfriend was looking at me so hopefully, so adoringly, that I immediately felt guilty for thinking about Matt. Aiden wasn't a bad person. Not really.

'Well?' he asked again, as a bead of sweat escaped from his hairline and rolled down his temple. 'Will you, Beth? Will you take me back? Please?'

I took a sip of my wine, set it back on the table and looked at him steadily.

'Yes, Aiden,' I said. 'I will.'

'I can't believe it,' Aiden said, for the tenth time in about as many minutes. 'I can't believe you agreed to give me a second chance. That's wonderful news, darling.'

'Mmmm,' I said, as he reached for my fingers and pressed a wet kiss on to the back of my hand.

'Things are going to be different now I know what a tiger you are, darling. A total *tiger*.'

He let go of my fingers, raised his hands to the sides of his face and curled his fingers into claws.

Don't Aiden, I prayed, as a trendy young couple at the next table turned to stare at us. The girl was dressed like a 1940s pin-up, all curled hair, nipped-in waist and red lipstick. Her boyfriend, with his gravity-defying quiff and tailored suit, was every inch the classic Teddy boy. Please don't do what I think you're about to …

'Rarrrrrrr,' he growled on cue, curling back his top lip to expose his teeth as he raked the air with his fingers. 'Grrrrrrrr. Rarrrrr. Tigerrrrrrrr.'

The couple shared a look and then sniggered. I glanced away hurriedly and pressed my hands to my cheeks. They were burning with embarrassment.

'Beth, darling,' Aiden said, grabbing my hand and forcing me to look back at him.

'Yes.'

'Do something wild,' he urged as he leaned across the table and shot me what I think was supposed to be a saucy look. 'Cause a scene, upturn the table, throw a glass of wine at me. Go on, Tiger. Get me hot, turn me on, make me do a little mess in my pants.'

Trendy woman's head twisted back to us so sharply, her neck made a cracking sound.

'Aiden, ssshh,' I hissed.

'Sorry, darling.' He winked lasciviously. 'I just couldn't help myself. It's the effect you have on me. More wine?'

I nodded enthusiastically. 'Definitely.'

As he stood up and headed towards the bar, I sank back into my seat and rubbed my temples. Why had I agreed to give him a second chance? That wasn't why I'd said I'd meet up with him. For the first time since we'd split up, I hadn't even considered the prospect of us getting back together. I genuinely hadn't. It wasn't even on my mind. I hadn't dressed up. I hadn't spent hours blow-drying my hair or making sure my make-up was perfect. I'd just grabbed my bag and headed to the pub.

The only reason I'd agreed to meet Aiden in the first place was to tell him about the life-changing decision I'd made, and he'd thrown me with his question. Really thrown me. The second the words 'I will' had left my mouth, I instantly regretted them. It was like an impulse reaction, programmed into me – Aiden begging me for another chance and me graciously accepting – because I'd dreamed about that scenario nearly every night since we split up.

So why wasn't I jumping for joy? Why wasn't I frantically texting Lizzie to tell her we were back together, feeling all smug or happy? All I felt was confusion.

I barely said a word the rest of the evening, as Aiden wittered on about what a fantastic time we were going to have now we were back together, and what great sex we'd have now that he'd seen my animal passion. A few weeks earlier I'd have been over the moon that he'd finally come to his senses, but no matter how many times I smiled and nodded at him, I couldn't ignore the sick feeling in the pit of my stomach.

'Here we are,' he said as he walked me up the pathway towards my house. 'Gosh, the last time I was here …'

He tailed off. We both knew exactly what had happened the last time he'd showed up at my front door. He'd dumped me.

'Do you know what?' he said as he slipped a hand around my waist and pulled me towards him. 'You look beautiful tonight, Beth. Utterly radiant. And I'm hugely relieved that you're not as orange as the last time we met.' He sniggered. 'I'm not sure the Costa del Essex look particularly suits you.'

'Uh-huh,' I agreed, more concerned with where Aiden's hands were than with what he was saying. I'd always felt so relaxed in his arms when we were together before. Why did it feel so uncomfortable now?

'That said,' he continued, placing a finger under my chin and tipping my face up towards his, 'I think I'd probably still love you even if you were satsuma-coloured.'

I opened my mouth to object to the term 'satsuma-coloured', but he silenced me with a kiss. His lips brushed mine, tentatively at first, then more firmly as his tongue slipped into my mouth and slid around mine.

'Mmmmm,' he murmured as he pulled me closer, his hands slipping down to my bum. He squeezed it enthusiastically. 'Mmmm, mmmm, mmmm.'

My hands fluttered awkwardly on his shoulders, as he continued to wind his tongue around mine. This was the moment I'd dreamed of – our passionate first kiss after getting back together – so why wasn't I feeling anything? I felt as emotionally involved as a blow-up doll. A satsuma-coloured blow-up doll.

Hang on! Satsuma-coloured? It wasn't the fact that he'd used that description that was bothering me. It was something he'd said before. What was it? My mind frantically rewound our conversation as Aiden's hands slid from my bum to my boobs. Replay …

'Whoa!' I put my hands on his shoulders and pushed him away.

'Sorry!' He swallowed nervously, his fingers twitching at the pockets of his cord jacket. 'That was too much, wasn't it? Too full-on? I'm sorry, Beth, I just couldn't resist. I was thinking about how sexy you looked strutting up and down the stage with the mic in your hand and—'

'Aiden.' I held up a hand. 'Ssssh!'

'Sorry.' He lowered his head and threaded his fingers together as though he'd just been chastised by his headmistress.

'Aiden, look at me.'

His eyes met mine. Nervously.

'Aiden, you just said you'd probably still love me even if I was satsuma-coloured.'

'Er, yes.' He shifted from foot to foot. 'Sorry about the fruit reference, darling. Not my most poetic moment ever.'

'No.' I shook my head. 'Not that, the other word.'

'Probably?' He looked into the distance and repeated it silently as though weighing it up on his tongue, then looked back at me. 'Sorry, Beth. Probably is rather an uncertain word, isn't it? It suggests that one is not a hundred per cent sure, and there's no uncertainty about the way I feel about you, Beth. In fact I'm probably

... sorry,' he cuffed himself on the side of the head, 'there's that word again ... *definitely* more certain about my feelings for you than I've been about anything since I decided to take French A level instead of German. It's spoken in far more countries. Did you know that in Africa, French is spoken by—'

'Aiden, shut up!'

How odd. When we were together, I'd listen, enraptured, while he spouted off about anything and everything. Now I found his inane waffling strangely irritating. 'Aiden, you said the word love.'

'Well, yes.' He looked at me blankly. 'I specifically chose that word because it most accurately conveys my feelings. I love you, Beth.'

I looked back at him, my eyes flitting from his wide, thin mouth to his perfectly straight nose and his pale blue eyes. Aiden Dowles had just told me he loved me. Someone, for the first time in my life, had just told me that they ... loved me.

So why wasn't I jumping up and down with my heart doing somersaults in my chest? Wasn't it what I'd always wanted – someone telling me they loved me? Hadn't I dreamed about it since I was eight years old and burying my nose in 'Cinderella' and 'Sleeping Beauty' while my parents screamed at each other in the kitchen? Shouldn't I be throwing my arms around Aiden and telling him how much I loved him too?

'Beth?' He was frowning at me, his arms slack at his sides. 'Is everything okay?'

I shook my head. 'I'm not sure.'

I really wasn't.

Everything I'd expected to happen after finding out I was loved ... wasn't. I wasn't exploding with happiness. I wasn't seeing fireworks, smelling rose petals or imagining joyful woodland creatures. Instead of feeling an amazing rush of emotion, I didn't feel anything. Nothing at all.

I stared at my ex-boyfriend as he waited patiently for a reaction to his clumsy declaration of love. Why did he look so different? When we were together, I was overwhelmed by how tall, noble, good-looking and distinguished he was. Now all I could see was a thin man with thinning hair, bad skin and terrible dress sense. I'd fallen in love with an intelligent, distinguished, knowledgeable man. Now I was standing in front of a pompous, patronising bore with a strange fetish for tiger impressions. He wasn't a bad man, I'd got that much right, but why had I ever felt that he was out of my league? Why had I felt so in awe of him? So much less of a person?

'Everything all right, darling?' Aiden said, poking me in the shoulder. 'Lost your grrr?'

'Aiden ...' I reached for his hand and wrapped my own, smaller hands around it.

'What is it, my love?'

'I don't think we should get back together.'

His face dropped. 'Oh.'

I squeezed his hands. 'It wasn't fair of me to agree to give it another go. I was confused and I'm sorry. You were right to dump me when you did. I was pretending to be someone I wasn't, and the person you love, the tiger, that's not me either. Not all of me anyway.'

It had taken me twenty-four years, but I finally understood two things. First, that love isn't about someone saying three little words to you, but about being loved for who you are, who you *really* are and not who you think the other person wants you to be. Second, the words 'I love you' only mean something when you can repeat them right back.

'You're not a tiger,' Aiden repeated, his forehead wrinkled with confusion. 'You're more than that. Okay. I understand. I think.'

'Do you?'

He nodded, then gave me a searching look. 'Can I just ask one thing?'

'Of course.'

'Is there someone else?'

My heart twisted in my chest as I remembered the last time I'd seen Matt.

'I thought there was,' I said softly, 'but not any more.'

'Ah.' Aiden looked thoughtful. 'I guessed as much. But do you know what, Beth? If he lets you go, the man's obviously an idiot.'

I half smiled. Hearing him call Matt an idiot didn't make it hurt any less, even if it was true.

'So.' He shrugged, and wriggled his hand from between mine. I was surprised at how tightly I'd been squeezing it. 'I guess this is good night, then.'

I smiled, properly this time. 'I think it might be more than good night, Aiden.'

'Really?' He raised his eyebrows.

'Yep.' I nodded. 'I'm going to Australia. That's what I wanted to tell you tonight. My mum's starting a business over there and she's offered me a ticket to go with her. There's nothing here for me in Brighton any more, so I've accepted. Anyway,' I shrugged, 'how awful can it be – being a secretary in Sydney? At least I'll be warm most of the year!'

Aiden looked puzzled. 'But what about your job? I thought the plan was to stay on at the Picturebox and work your way up until you owned your own cinema?'

I'd forgotten I'd told him about that when I was drunk on our third date.

I sighed. 'Some dreams don't come true, Aiden. It's time for me to grow up and start living in the real world. I'm flying out to Sydney tomorrow morning.'

'Wow.' He looked genuinely shocked. 'So this really is goodbye, then?'

'I guess so.'

'Can I have a hug?' He held out his arms. 'Would that be weird?'

'No.' I smiled. 'It would be nice.'

I pressed my cheek against his shoulder and closed my eyes as he hugged me tightly.

But it wasn't Aiden's arms I wanted around me.

It was Matt's.

As my ex-boyfriend strolled down the street, head up, arms swinging at his sides, any guilt I might have felt about my decision disappeared in a flash. He wasn't devastated at not being given a second chance with me. Disappointed maybe, but I had the feeling he wouldn't go home and cry himself to sleep.

Knowing Aiden, he'd meet someone else within

weeks. He'd just stroll into the wine club, uncork a bottle of fancy red, slide up to the nearest good-looking woman and launch into a speech about its qualities and merits. And who knows, maybe she'd be charmed by his tiger impression!

I smiled to myself as I dug my keys out of my bag, and let myself into the house.

'Liz! You got my text!'

My flatmate was sitting on the sofa in the living room, her skinny legs pulled up to her chest, her arms wrapped around her knees, her eyes fixed on the flickering TV in the corner of the room.

'Hello gorgeous!' Her face lit up at the sound of my voice and she bounded up off the sofa and wrapped me in a big hug. 'I missed you!'

I laughed and hugged her back. 'I missed you too. How was your holiday?'

'Amazing!' She held me at arms length and looked me up and down. 'What's that face for? What's going on?'

'Did you hear what we were talking about? Outside?'

She shook her head, confused. 'What who was talking about?'

'Me and Aiden.'

'Nope. Oh God.' Her face fell. 'Please don't tell me you got back with him, Beth.'

'Nope.'

'Glad to hear it. What did pickled-onion-breath want anyway?'

'Long story.' I dropped my bag on the floor by the sofa and sat down heavily.

'I don't care if it takes all night – spill!' She plonked herself beside me. 'I got your text and I want to know what's so uber-important you couldn't tell me over the phone? It had better be good. Nathan was supposed to be taking me to dinner at Graze tonight. The holiday isn't officially over until tomorrow morning!'

'Sorry.' I grabbed a fluffy pink cushion and hugged it to my chest. 'I thought it was better to tell you face to face.'

She frowned. 'Tell me what?'

'Okay.' I tucked my feet under my bum and took a deep breaths. 'A few things have happened since the last time I saw you …'

My best friend listened intently as I told her about the leadership and interview weekend in Wales (she gasped with horror when I told her about the split trousers incident) and the night with Matt in the hotel (she laughed at the Big Boy bit, then promptly apologised). When I reached the bit about Matt staying over and leaving before I woke up, she got angry.

'That's *so* out of order. Seriously, Beth, the guy's obviously a complete cock. You went to the hospital to see how his grandad was and that's the way he thanks you? Jesus!'

'I know.' A wave of sadness washed over me, but I shook it off. I didn't want to think about that morning any more. It hurt too much. Besides, I had more pressing things to worry about. 'And that's not the worst of it. I didn't get the job.'

'What?' Lizzie's jaw fell open. 'You're fucking kidding? You were *made* for that manager's job.'

I shrugged. 'I thought so too. My plan was really good, Liz, even if I do say so, but I totally screwed up – the abseiling thing, shouting at Matt in the interview; I don't know why I'm even surprised.'

'You should complain,' Lizzie said indignantly. 'Ring up Apollo head office and tell them that Matt acted unprofessionally. I can't believe he refused to speak to you on the phone. That's shocking. God, Beth. You can't leave the Picturebox. It's part of who you are.'

'I know.' I hugged the cushion tighter to me and looked up at the ceiling to try and stop myself from crying. I couldn't quite believe I'd never work another day in the job I loved.

'Anyway,' I continued, swallowing hard, 'I can't change what's happened, so I'm going to move on.'

'Really?' Liz raised an eyebrow. 'Are you sure? Because if you want to fight this, I've got your back.'

'No.' I shook my head. 'I'm not sure if the job was right for me anyway. Apollo are going to gut the cinema and turn it into one of their identikit chains. It wouldn't be the same.' I forced a smile. 'Thanks, though, Liz. I appreciate it.'

'That's what mates are for – fighting against injustice and untying bondage knots.' She laughed. 'So what now? You gonna get a job somewhere else?'

'You could say that.'

Lizzie looked thoughtful. 'Is that what you wanted to tell me face to face? That you lost your job at the Picturebox and ... hang on a second ...' She searched my face. 'You're leaving Brighton, aren't you? You're going to Australia to be your mum's secretary. Beth you can't, I won't let you. I—'

'I promised!' I interrupted before she could say any more. 'I told Mum that if I didn't get the job with Picturebox, I'd go with her.'

'Promises schromises. This is about you, Beth, not her. It's your life. Here,' she thrust her mobile into my hands, 'ring her up and tell her you're not going.'

I shook my head. 'I can't. It's all arranged. I texted her earlier to say I was coming. The tickets have been confirmed and everything.'

'What? Fuck!'

'Besides.' I handed the mobile back. 'I can't just change my mind. She's really excited. It would be cruel.'

Lizzie stared at me in horror.

'What?' I said defensively.

'Fuck cruel, Beth. You told me you'd rather die than be your mum's secretary.'

'I know.'

'So why are you running away to Australia? I don't get it.'

'I'm not running away.' I sighed. 'Anyway, it's complicated.'

My best friend opened her mouth to say something, then seemed to think better of it. 'When are you going?' she asked instead.

'Tomorrow.'

'What! Jesus, Beth, you don't do things by halves, do you?'

'I know it's sudden and I'm supposed to work my notice at the Picturebox, but,' I shrugged, 'I don't suppose anyone will mind too much if I leave now instead of at the end of the year. Raj told me that Mrs Blackstock is popping into the cinema tomorrow, so I'll drop in on my way to the coach station and let her know I'm leaving.'

'But it's nearly Christmas! You can't leave now! I've bought you a present and everything!'

'Oh mate.' I touched her hand. 'There's nothing I can do. I'm really sorry. Mum deliberately booked the tickets so that our new life in Australia would begin on Christmas Day. She said it would be symbolic.'

'Symbollocks more like! It's not your new start, it's hers. God!' Lizzie glanced around the living room, frowned, then looked back at me. 'That's why you haven't decorated this place, isn't it? You knew you were leaving. Last year I couldn't walk into the flat without banging my head on a piece of tinsel or a flying reindeer! Shit.' She narrowed her eyes accusingly. 'How long have you known?'

'That I was leaving?' I looked away. 'I only decided for sure today, but it's been on the cards for a couple of weeks – since I found out that I didn't get the job. I kept hoping that something would happen, that Mum would change her mind about going or James would resign as the new Picturebox manager and I'd be offered the job instead, but ...' I shrugged again, 'that's not going to happen.'

'But what about your room? Your stuff?'

'Well ...' I was surprised at how much I'd already figured out. 'I've got tonight to pack a suitcase and sort the rest of my stuff into two piles – one that I'd like you to ship over to me, if you don't mind, and the rest can go to the charity shop. Mum doesn't seem to think there'll be a problem getting me a permanent visa.'

'Permanent?'

'Yeah,' I said, ignoring the look of horror on her face. 'I've already paid next month's rent and I've got enough left in the bank to transfer another month's worth in lieu of notice. You'll be able to find a flatmate in eight weeks.'

Lizzie's eyes searched mine. 'You're really going, aren't you?'

I nodded.

'Oh, Beth.' She launched herself across the sofa and threw her arms around me. 'I'm really going to miss you.'

'I'm going to miss you too,' I whispered back. I meant it too. I'd really, really miss her.

'Promise me you'll look after yourself, Lizzie,' I said as I pulled back from the hug to look at her. 'I don't want to hear on the news that a woman starved to death in Brighton when she got trapped in a pub window.'

She smiled. 'I promise.'

'Right.' I clapped my hands together. 'Are you going to help me pack my stuff or what? There's a bottle of wine in it for you.'

'Wine?' She winked. 'You definitely know the way to my heart, Beth Prince.'

Chapter Thirty-Two

Matt

As nightmares go, it was right up there with the one I had as a kid – where my mum turned up to apologise for leaving but she wasn't the mum I remembered, she was a zombie with her skin hanging off and black holes for eyes – only this wasn't a nightmare, was it? I only had to replay the conversation I'd just had with Alice to remind myself exactly how real it was.

'Matt?' She wandered back into the room with two steaming mugs of tea in her hands and crouched on the floor in front of me.

I took the cup she offered me, wrapped my hands around it and took a sip. It burned the top of my mouth. I took a second sip.

'Matt, look at me.'

I looked down at my ex-girlfriend as she rested a hand on my knee.

'Have you thought about, you know, what we do next?'

'Yeah,' I said.

'And?' She tilted her head to one side, her eyes searching mine.

'I'll support you. Whatever you decide.'

'And if I want to have the baby?'

I swallowed hard. 'I'll support that decision.'

'Good.' A slow smile spread over Alice's face as she rocked back on her heels, then stood up. 'I was hoping you'd say that.'

I stared across at the living room window. It was dark outside, but the curtains weren't drawn. All I could see was the reflection of a tense, nervous man staring back at me. Alice was going to have a baby. A real, live, screaming and kicking baby. In seven or eight months' time, I'd be a dad. Me, Matt Jones, someone's dad? I ran a hand through my hair. It was all so ... so sudden. I could barely take it in. One minute I was stressing about the Picturebox contract (I still hadn't sent it to Ballbreaker), winding myself up about the Beth situation and rushing back and forward to the hospital to check up on Grandad, and the next – WHAM – this. And to think I'd thought my life couldn't get any more complicated. Yeah, right.

'It's late,' Alice said softly. When I glanced at her, she was squinting at the small silver clock on the mantelpiece. 'I don't know about you, Matt, but I'm knackered. It's been a pretty emotionally charged evening. Maybe it's time to go to bed.'

'Yes. Good idea.' I put down my cup, grabbed my jacket and shoved an arm into one sleeve.

'You're going?' Alice placed a hand on my shoulder.

'Well, yeah.' I frowned up at her. 'You just said—'

'You're going home?' Her voice rose several octaves as she took a step back. 'Now? I just told you that I'm pregnant and you're sodding off back home to leave me to deal with it? Great. Very gallant behavior, Matt.'

'But … what … how …' I couldn't understand why she was so angry. Hadn't I just said that I'd support her decision? She'd looked really happy. 'Are you saying you want me to stay?'

'You're unbelievable, Matt.' Alice folded her arms over her chest and narrowed her eyes. 'Do you know how long it took me to work up the nerve to tell you about the baby? Do you?'

I shook my head mutely.

'Days! Days, Matt! I was scared. Really scared. I actually rehearsed what I was going to say to you because I was petrified you'd freak out, or worse. It took every ounce of courage to tell you tonight, and you just sit there looking gormless, saying you'll support me but doing fuck all.'

'But …' I held out my hands. 'I don't know what else to do. When the baby comes, I'll help out financially. I'll buy stuff for it. I'll be its dad. I've never been in this situation before, Alice, and I'm still trying to take it in. What am I missing here? What do you want me to do?'

'Actually support me!' She stamped a high heel on the wooden floorboards. 'Support me, Matt. You're not the only one freaking out about this, you know?'

'And … staying here tonight would help support you?' I ventured.

'Finally!' The grim frown on Alice's forehead disappeared and she smiled at me like I was some kind of simpleton. 'You get it.'

'Okay then.' I yanked off my jacket. 'It's cool. No problem. I'll sleep on the sofa.'

'The sofa!' Alice's eyes filled with tears and she covered her face with her fingers. 'My life is in turmoil and you support me by sleeping on my sofa? How is that support? How is that taking care of me? How, Matt? How!'

'Okay, okay,' I said desperately. 'Not the sofa! Where do you want me to sleep?'

I was pretty sure I knew the answer to that question, but that still didn't make it a good idea.

'It's not about what I want, it's about what's right.' Alice dropped her fingers from her tear-stained face to look at me. 'What do you think is the right thing to do, Matt?'

My gut instinct told me to shout 'Aagggggh! Enough with the mind games!' and run all the way to the pub, but my brain wasn't having any of it. My brain was telling me that Alice was upset and hormonal and that spending one night beside her wasn't going to kill me, not if it meant she'd stop crying and looking at me like I'd just murdered a puppy. She was pregnant and freaking out about it.

'I think the right thing to do,' I said slowly, unable to believe I was going to say what I was about to, 'is to stay here with you tonight and give you the support you need.'

I held my breath as Alice looked me up and down as though considering my response. Finally she smiled. 'Thank you, Mattie.'

'No problem.'

She held out her hand. 'Come on, then.'

I took it gingerly and let her lead me into the hallway and towards the bedroom. It was all I could do not to pull away and sprint out the front door.

I shifted on to my side, careful not to wake Alice, and reached for my mobile phone.

It was 5.15 a.m.

Hours had passed since I'd been dragged into the bedroom, and I still hadn't had a wink of sleep.

Walking into my ex-girlfriend's bedroom for the first time in three months was weird. The electronic art sketch we'd had drawn in a booth on the pier one drunken afternoon last summer was still propped up on her dressing table, along with tickets to the first gig we'd gone to together and a striped pebble I'd picked off the beach and given to her.

I didn't say anything. Instead I took off my shoes and socks and got into bed fully clothed. Alice tried to kick up a fuss, claiming I'd be too hot and uncomfortable, but there was no way I was going to strip down to my boxers, so I held my ground. It was weird enough getting into bed with my ex without getting half naked too. She had no such qualms. I had to look away when she unzipped her jeans and pulled her jumper over her head, because I was fairly certain she wasn't wearing anything underneath. When I felt her crawl into bed beside me, I was relieved to see she was wearing an oversized T-shirt.

Every muscle in my body tensed up as she lay on her side, inches away from me. Everything about the situation felt wrong – so, so wrong. I shouldn't be in bed with Alice, I should be … My head filled with images of Beth's smile, the way she blew her fringe out of her eyes and the feel of her lips on mine.

'Mattie,' Alice whispered.

I screwed my eyes tightly shut.

'Matt,' she whispered again. Her hand made contact with my arm and I held my breath as she rubbed a thumb over my skin. 'Matt, are you still awake?'

Keep your eyes shut and pretend to be asleep, I told myself. When you wake up in the morning, all this will be over. All this will be …

No it wouldn't.

Alice was going to have a baby. A real baby. And I'd have a son or a daughter.

I wasn't ready.

Hell, I was still recycling the same jokes that had made me laugh when I was thirteen. God was probably laughing his head off when Alice told me about the pregnancy. What's brown and sticky now, eh, Matt?

I must have sighed loudly, because she suddenly gripped my arm. 'Ah! So you are awake!'

I opened my eyes.

'Matt.' She wriggled towards me and propped herself up on her elbow so that she was looking down at me. 'It's nice, isn't it? This.'

'Mmmm,' I murmured.

'You and me in bed, just like the old days.'

Only you haven't screamed at me and kicked me out to sleep on the sofa yet.

'We made a good couple, didn't we, Matt?'

I grunted non-committally and tried to inch away, but Alice's other hand shot out from under the duvet and cupped the side of my jaw.

'I feel very close to you tonight,' she said, rubbing her fingers against my stubble.

I immediately tensed at her touch. *Please, God, please don't let her kiss me*, I prayed desperately. *I promise I'll never tell the stick joke again.*

'You feel close to me because of the pregnancy,' I said as Alice leaned closer and I caught a waft of her spicy perfume. 'You're feeling vulnerable and—'

I didn't get to finish my sentence. Alice's lips made contact with mine, and in a move so speedy it would have put Bruce Lee to shame, she was on top of me.

'Nnnnggggg,' I said as her tongue wormed its way into my mouth and stabbed at my fillings. 'Nnnngggghh nggggggh ngggggggh.'

'Darling.' Alice released my lips for a split second before attacking them again. 'Oh darling.'

'Nnnnggggg. Nnnnggggg. Nnnnggggg.' My hands waved uselessly in the air either side of her as I tried to work out what to do. I couldn't talk because she had her tongue down my throat, and I couldn't just shove her off me. She was pregnant!

Make it stop! my brain commanded. *Now! Make it stop!* But I couldn't do anything; I felt paralysed from the neck down. *It wasn't like this with Beth*, my brain whispered. *Remember how good that felt?*

I must have twitched or shivered or something, because Alice rolled off me as quickly as she'd rolled on.

'What's going on?' she said from her side of the bed.

'What do you mean?'

'You.'

'What do you mean, "you"?'

'You. You didn't respond to me at all. You didn't kiss me back, you didn't touch me and,' her eyes narrowed, 'you didn't get hard!'

What should have been an insult was actually a relief. If I had got hard it would have given her the impression that I wanted her, that I desired her, maybe that I wanted to get back together with her. And that wasn't going to happen. She was pregnant and I was going to support her and the child, but that didn't make us right for each. It didn't paper over the cracks of all the things that had gone wrong in our relationship and the fact that we had stopped making each other happy a long time ago.

'I'm sorry, Alice,' I said softly. 'I know I said I'd stand by you, and I will, but the truth is, I'm in lo—'

I stopped mid-sentence. Whoa! I'd nearly said 'I'm in love with someone else.' Why would I say that?

I wasn't in love with Beth. Was I?

My brain whirred furiously as I tried to make sense of the last few weeks. Seeing her for the first time in the Picturebox and being blown away by her shy smile. Making sure she got home safely after our drunken conversation on the seafront bench. Feeling protective of her during the trouser-splitting abseiling incident. Being overwhelmed by her kindness when she visited my hotel room. Laughing ourselves stupid in her flat when I stole her socks. Falling into bed with her and finding we 'fitted'.

I was in love with her.

I was in love with Beth Prince.

That explained everything. It explained why I felt like I was cheating on her just by lying beside Alice. It explained why I couldn't keep my eyes off her during the team meeting in the hotel. And it explained why I'd felt like I'd been punched in the stomach when I'd seen the note on her ceiling. Not because my pride was hurt, or because, as her boss, I thought it was a sneaky and despicable thing to do, but because I was in love with her.

I was in love with her.

How had it happened? When? And why had it taken me so long to realise?

I stared up at the shadows on the ceiling, my heart contracting and aching as I remembered the long sweep of her eyelashes and the way her bottom lip squished up against her hand when she was curled up beside me, fast asleep. That morning felt like a million years ago now.

'Matt?' Alice said curtly. 'You were saying something?'

I shook my head, the image of Beth instantly evaporating. 'Was I?'

'Fine. Be like that.' She threw an arm in my direction, and for a horrible second I thought she was going to wallop me on the side of the head. Instead she switched off the bedside light.

'We'll discuss your limp dick problem in the morning,' she hissed as she rolled on to her side. 'Good night.'

I glanced at my mobile again: 5.17.

Alice was still snoring beside me, but there was no way I was going to drop off. I picked up my mobile and the fingers of my right hand twitched. Would Beth still be up? She'd told me she often stayed up late to watch a film or let her flatmate in.

No.

It was a stupid thought.

What was I going to say anyway?

You slept with me to try and get a job, but I just thought I'd call to let you know that I love you?

No. It sounded like a twisted Jeremy Kyle episode.

I sighed and placed the phone back on the bedside table, just as it started to ring.

'Beth?' I slapped it against my ear.

Beside me, Alice stirred but didn't wake.

'Beth?' I repeated in a whisper.

'This is Sister Meadows at Royal Sussex County,' said the voice on the other end.

'Grandad!' All the hairs on my arms stood up. 'What's happened?'

There was a pause on the other end of the line, then Sister Meadows spoke again. 'You need to get here, Matt. Fast.'

My trainers squeaked on the lino as I sprinted down the hospital corridor and made a sharp turn around the corner to Grandad's ward. The door was open and I flew through it, then skidded to a halt. It was dark, but there was enough light from the corridor and the single bulb that glowed dimly above one of the beds for me to notice that the curtain had been pulled closed around Grandad's bed.

'Grandad!' I shouted as I hurried towards it, oblivious to the snoozing old men on either side of me. 'Grandad, it's Matt.'

I grabbed hold of the curtain and yanked it back.

All his things were still on the bedside table – his watch, a jug of water, the card from his next-door neighbours, a photo of Gran and the copy of *Motorcycle Monthly* I'd bought in the hospital shop. Everything was exactly the same as the last time I'd visited. Except for one thing.

Grandad was gone.

'Excuse me.' I gripped the edges of the wipe-clean white shelf around the nurses' station. It was exactly the same as every other time I'd visited, only now two small symbols of Christmas had appeared. On the left of the desk, a plastic Santa Claus nodded continuously to himself, while on the right, a blow-up snowman, his carrot-like nose wilting, stood guard.

A solitary nurse was sitting behind the desk, her head bowed as she leafed through some records, pausing every now and then to lick the tip of her index finger. I recognised her grey hair and the curve of her cheek. Sister O'Reilly – Grandad's favourite.

'Excuse me,' I said again. 'Where's my grandad?'

Sister O'Reilly looked up, a smile of recognition lighting up her face as her eyes met mine. A split second later, the smile was gone.

I'd seen that look before – that serious, sombre expression. I'd seen it on Grandad's face when he'd told me that Gran had passed in the night. It was like the shutters had dropped over Sister O'Reilly's eyes, blocking out any joy, happiness or hope she might be feeling. I could see compassion, though, lots of compassion.

I pressed a hand against my chest to stop my heart from beating its way out of my body.

'It's Matt, isn't it?' She pushed the pile of papers to one side and stood up.

'Yeah,' I said, forcing the word out. It sounded like a grunt or a moan. My voice had gone.

Please tell me he's okay, I prayed silently, my eyes fixed on the upside-down watch the nurse had pinned to her uniform. If I didn't look away, everything would be okay. As long as the hands kept ticking, as long as time kept passing, everything would be okay.

I put a hand to my mouth and cleared my throat.

'Yeah,' I said again. 'I'm Jack Ballard's grandson. Where is he? Someone rang and told me to come in urgently. I got here as fast as I could.'

'Ah, yes.' The sister smoothed down her uniform, tucked a stray strand of hair behind her ear and rounded the station until she was standing beside me. Her hand cupped my shoulder. It felt heavy, steady, and despite the fact that I was wearing a jacket, I could have sworn I felt the heat of her palm sink into my skin.

'Come with me, Matthew,' she said softly.

She pronounced the t's in my name. *Matt-ew*. Not Matthew with a soft 'th' sound. I remember that. I'll always remember that. It was like she wasn't really saying my name. It was someone else's name, someone else who followed her to the relatives' room in a daze, because it definitely wasn't me. It wasn't happening to me.

'Will you have a seat?'

A room. Beige walls, beige carpet, pine-framed wishywashy watercolours. No Christmas decorations here. Chairs. Hard, made of pine, with royal blue upholstery. Unusually bright in that beige room. No arms, though. Nothing to grip. Nothing to hold on to as Sister O'Reilly settled herself next to me and began to speak.

Cardiac arrest …

Unexpected …

Rushed …

Surgeon …

Complications …

Everything we could …

And then three words. Three in a row. Three words in a row that I couldn't block out.

'I'm so sorry.'

I didn't speak. I didn't move. But something icy spread from the top of my head to the tips of my fingers. It gripped my arms, my stomach, my lungs, and then it attacked my heart.

I couldn't breathe. The air hadn't been knocked out of me; it had just vanished. Gone. I couldn't breathe, and I didn't want to. It didn't matter any more.

I can't remember how long I sat there, icy, not breathing, until Sister O'Reilly spoke again.

'Is there anyone you'd like me to call for you, Matthew?'

I might have shaken my head. I might not. I can't remember. What I do know is that we sat in that room, side by side, for a long time. At least it felt like a long time. Sometimes she spoke – soft, consoling-sounding words; at other times she said nothing. At one point I noticed a cup of tea beside me.

Steaming.

Then not.

My brain was empty. A complete void except for one word that was floating around, knocking at the sides of my skull. Each time it made contact, my heart contracted in pain.

Grandad.

Just when I thought I couldn't bear it any more, it was replaced by the word no. No, no, no, no, no, no. It echoed round my brain like a slow, torturous howl.

At some point I started to cry.

I watched as the tears drip, drip, dripped on to my clasped hands.

I thought they'd never stop.

'Matthew?' I felt someone touch the back of my hand. 'Matthew, would you like to see him?'

I looked up in surprise. Sister O'Reilly was still sitting beside me. She was still wearing the upside-down watch on her chest. The hands were still turning.

I wanted to see Grandad more than anything in the world. I wanted to watch his wrinkled face crease with amusement when I told him a joke. I wanted to catch him eyeing up a nurse's bum. I wanted to hear him say, 'If it isn't my least favourite grandson' and feel his leathery old paw on the back of my hand. I wanted … I couldn't have what I wanted. Grandad had gone.

'No.' I shook my head. 'No thank you.'

A single tear dropped off my jaw and landed on my forearm. I pressed my palm over it. When I lifted my hand back up, it had gone, evaporated or sunk into my skin. No new tears took its place. I'd finally stopped crying.

'Okay,' I heard Sister O'Reilly say. 'I understand. Now I know it's the last thing you'll want to do, Matt, but there's a bit of paperwork that needs filling out. And if you'd like, I could gather up your grandfather's things. No hurry, though. No hurry at all.'

'I'd like that,' I said. The words sounded strange. Like someone else was speaking them. 'I'd like to have his things.'

I can't remember how long I walked, or where I went, but the sun came up. It peeped through the gloomy clouds, tentatively at first as though it didn't want to show its face, then all of a sudden, the world was lit up. I kept walking, my hand tightly curled around the bag containing Grandad's things. It was a large bag, far too large for the watch, the photo, the card and the set of clothes that curled together in one corner. There was something else in the bag too, something Sister O'Reilly had found tucked under his pillow: a photo of me and Grandad. I'd never seen it before, but I remembered it being taken. We were in his back garden on a bright summer's day; I must have been eleven or twelve. Grandad was holding an enormous fish – a pike or something – up to his chest and grinning at the camera. I was clutching his fishing gear – the rod towered over me – but instead of looking at the camera, I was smiling up at him. You could see the admiration in my eyes. I was so proud of him, the tall, strapping man at my side. He was my hero. I wanted to be like him when I grew up.

Now he was gone.

And I still hadn't grown up.

Hunger, thirst and exhaustion forced me to head back to my flat. I glanced at the time on the Clock Tower as I passed it: 9.22 a.m. How had that happened? Over four hours had passed since the hospital rang my mobile. It felt like five seconds. Or a million years.

I was so tired I struggled to get my key in the lock, then stumbled through the hallway and into the living room. If I could just get my head down on the sofa for a few hours I might be able to …

'Alice?'

My ex-girlfriend was sitting on my sofa, one leg crossed over the other. She was wearing the same jumper and jeans combination she'd been wearing the night before, only now she was make-up-less and her hair was scraped back in a ponytail.

'Where have you been, Matt?'

'I went to …' The rest of the sentence faded away and I tightened my hold on Grandad's things. I couldn't bring myself to tell her what had happened. If I said the words aloud, it would make everything real.

'Cat got your tongue?' Alice shook her head in despair. 'Fucking typical.'

'What's typical?' I said, confused.

'What's typical?' She tipped her head back and laughed like I'd just told her the funniest joke in the world. 'God, you're clueless, Matt. Absolutely bloody clueless. And not only are you clueless, you're selfish too.'

'Selfish?'

I knew I was repeating everything she was saying, but I couldn't stop myself. My head was clouded with grief and sleep deprivation and I had no idea what was going on. I'd just lost my grandad and now Alice was sitting on my sofa having a go at me. I felt like I'd stepped out of one nightmare straight into another.

'I practically had to *bully* you into staying with me last night,' Alice spat, 'and then I wake up this morning and you've gone. Gone! After everything I said about needing support. You slipped away in the night like a … like a … I don't know … a slippery twat.'

I smiled. For the first time in hours. It was stupid and childish, but … *slippery twat*. I couldn't help it. It just sounded funny.

'Oh you're laughing, are you? Well, I don't think it's funny, Matt. I don't think it's funny at all. I tried ringing you, but guess what?' She laughed tightly. 'Your phone was off. Funny, that. Anyone would think you didn't want me to know where you'd gone.'

'Alice, I was …' I slipped into the nearest armchair, my legs finally giving way under me. 'I had to …'

'What? Make a house call? Go and shag someone

else? Because there *is* someone else, isn't there, Matt? Don't you dare deny it.'

I slumped forward and buried my head in my hands.

'Alice,' I groaned. 'I've just got back from the hospital. My grandad …'

'What about him?'

I shook my head. I still couldn't say the words.

There was a pause, then a quiet, 'Oh.'

I closed my eyes. *Please just go, Alice*, I prayed. *Please leave me alone.*

'Why didn't you wake me, Matt?'

'I didn't think. I got the call and I left.'

'Oh.' She paused again. 'Who went with you, then?'

'No one.'

'But there is someone else, isn't there?'

'Oh for fuck's sake.' My hands fell from my face and I sat up, suddenly angry. I'd just lost the man who'd been more of a father to me than my own dad, and Alice had decided to interrogate me. What the hell was wrong with her?

'Yes!' I shouted. 'Yes, there is someone else. Someone I love. There! Happy now? Happy you've got it out of me?'

The colour faded from Alice's cheeks and her jaw dropped open.

'There is …' she said slowly. 'There is someone else. I didn't think there was. Not really.'

'Then why …' I shook my head. 'Oh, I give up. I totally give up.'

We sat in silence for a couple of minutes, me turning Grandad's bag of things over and over in my hands and

Alice … I don't know what she was doing. I couldn't look at her.

'I'm sorry,' I said finally. 'I shouldn't have shouted at you. I've had a hell of a night and my head's all over the place. To be honest with you, Alice, I've got no idea what's going on with Be … with the girl I'm in love with. And I need to decide what to do about that. But the fact is, whatever happens, I'll be there for you and the baby. I'll support you financially and practically, but,' I looked up and met Alice's wary gaze, 'the sleeping in your bed thing, the kissing thing, you turning up here – it has to stop. There's no future for us as a couple. I'm sorry.'

I waited for her to react, for her to cry, scream or throw something at me. Instead she twisted her hands in her lap and sighed.

'I'm the one who should say sorry,' she said, so quietly I could barely make out the words.

'What do you mean?'

'The thing is, Matt …' she said, and then stopped. She was sitting right on the edge of the sofa, her feet bouncing nervously on the carpet, her hands squeezing her knees.

'What?'

She looked at me from under her eyelashes, then looked away.

'What is it, Alice?'

'I'm not pregnant.'

For the second time in less than twelve hours my blood ran cold. I stared at her in shock. 'What did you say?'

She shook her head mutely, still staring somewhere just above my head. She'd stopped bouncing around on the sofa and was sitting bolt upright, her body rigid, her hands tightly knotted in her lap, her face expressionless. Had she really just said what I thought she'd said?

'Alice.' I willed her to look at me. 'What did you just say?'

A muscle in the side of her jaw twitched. It was the only sign that she hadn't turned to stone.

'Alice …'

'I'm not pregnant,' she barked, slumping back against the sofa. 'I made it up. Okay?'

I couldn't take it in. I just couldn't. First Grandad dying, and now this. I had to be asleep. I just had to be.

'But … why would you do that?'

She shrugged, still unable or unwilling to make eye contact with me. 'I thought you were in denial.'

'Denial! About what?'

'Us.' She twiddled with the bracelet on her wrist, flicking the beads one way and then back again. 'I know we had our problems when we were together, and that's why we split up, but I was sure you still loved me.'

'Alice, I don't love—'

'Don't.' She met my gaze, suddenly brave. 'You don't have to say it, Matt. I'm not stupid. I don't need it spelling out.'

'So why pretend you were pregnant?'

'I thought it would make you realise that you still loved me.' She shrugged. 'I thought if I told you I was

pregnant you'd see that we could overcome our problems and make a go of things.'

'But what about the baby? Not that there was one.
How long were you going to let me go on believing
you were pregnant?'

'I ...' Alice stared at her shoes. 'I thought that if we
had make-up sex, it might happen. For real.'

'Wow.' My jaw dropped. I couldn't believe what
she'd just admitted to.

'Please, Matt.' She slumped forward and covered her
face with her hands. 'Please don't have a go at me. I'm
ashamed enough already. I didn't think about what I
was doing until now. Hearing it out loud, it sounds so
... unhinged.'

'You're not kidding.' She'd done some crazy shit in
her time, but this ... it was on another level.

'I'll just go,' she said.

I watched, too dumbfounded to be angry, as she
gathered up her coat, pulled on a woolly hat and
wrapped a scarf around her neck.

'I'm sorry,' she said when she reached the doorway.
'I'm really sorry, Matt. And I won't bother you again.
I promise.'

Then she was gone.

Chapter Thirty-Three

Beth

I paused at the entrance to the cinema, the Christmas present Lizzie had given me the night before (but forbidden me to open until I was in Australia) in one hand, my suitcase in the other, and stared up at the delicate, swirling font that spelled out the word 'Picturebox' in faded, peeling letters. It was really happening – I was about to set foot in my favourite place in the world for the last time – but it didn't feel real, and not just because my head was fuzzy from lack of sleep and a hideous hangover.

Getting drunk with Lizzie the night before wasn't the best idea I'd ever had, but it was better than the alternative: stay sober and risk changing my mind.

We'd begun sorting through my possessions slowly – holding up each item, deliberating about its usefulness and then carefully folding it on to a pile – but after an hour or so Lizzie was so bored and I was so fed up we decided to crack open the first bottle of wine. After that, we went through my possessions like women possessed – hurling jumpers, trousers, dresses and jeans across the room until finally we were done.

My room was empty apart from one suitcase and two teetering piles.

It was about 2 a.m. when we slumped on to the sofa and cracked open the second bottle of wine.

'You don't have to do this, Beth,' Lizzie had said, squeezing my hand so tightly I thought my little finger was going to break. 'You don't have to leave.'

'I do.'

'But why? I'm sure Dad won't mind you staying here rent-free for a bit while you get back on your feet. Oh God,' she looked me up and down, 'this is my fault, isn't it? You've been through loads of crap recently and I haven't been there for you. I've been a total bitch, haven't I?'

'Liz! Of course you haven't. You've been amazing. Okay, maybe not amazing. You've been a bit flaky.' I grinned. 'But you're still the best friend I've ever had. Honestly, this has got nothing to do with you.'

'Then why go?'

I wasn't sure. It had seemed like such a good idea when I'd made the decision at work the day before. I was about to lose the job I loved, I'd humiliated myself in front of Aiden, and Matt hated me. Why not bugger off to Australia with Mum and make a new start? At least no one knew me there.

'Because it's the right thing to do,' I replied lamely.

Lizzie didn't look convinced. 'Then why do you look so bloody miserable? Stay here! Have Christmas with me and my family. Mum cooks a mean turkey, and she and Dad will be meeting Nathan for the first time. Imagine how much fun *that'll* be!'

'I can't.' I shook my head sadly. 'I have to go. It's all arranged now.'

There was a point, right before I passed out, when I picked up my mobile and scrolled through my address book until I found the number for Apollo. I still couldn't believe I'd got Matt so wrong. There'd been something special between us, something mutual, not like my unrequited crush on Aiden. I'd seen it in the way Matt had looked at me. Or had I?

It was 3 a.m. and the Apollo offices would be empty. The answerphone would be on, though. I could leave him a message …

My thumb hovered over the 'Call' button as I weighed up my options. Do nothing and pretend Matt Jones had never existed, or call and tell him that he owed me an explanation. Tell him I was hurt and confused and I wanted to know what had gone wrong.

I shook my head. I was drunk, but I wasn't that drunk. I wasn't going to run after a man ever again.

It only took a second to delete the number for ever.

Get over it, Beth, I told myself firmly now as I looked at my watch. It was ten past ten and I needed to meet Mum at Pool Valley coach station for eleven o'clock. *You need to do this.*

I took a step forward, my suitcase trailing behind me, and walked into the Picturebox.

I didn't know whether to laugh or cry. Of all the days to find Carl in the cinema! He was leaning back in the chair behind the counter, his feet up on the desk, his arms crossed over his chest. The phone started ringing, but he didn't so much as look at it.

'Going somewhere, Pimp?' he said, raising an eyebrow at my suitcase. 'I've heard the plastic surgeons are excellent in LA.'

'Is Mrs Blackstock in?' I said. There was no way I was going to rise to the bait, not today.

'Why do you want to see her?' He looked me up and down. 'Are you after styling tips or something? You'd suit old-lady chic. It'd go with your perfume. Eau de Pensioner Piss.'

He laughed, obviously pleased with himself.

'Where is she?' I let go of my suitcase and took a step forward. 'It's important.'

'Important, eh?' He smirked. 'Well, if you need to file an expenses form for those trousers you ripped in Wales, I could give you the money out of petty cash. There's a new shop next to Long Tall Sally on East Street that could supply a replacement pair. It's called Big Fat Arse.'

'Carl.' I rounded the counter and stood beside him. The remains of a McDonald's meal was scrunched up on the floor by his chair, and there was a Nintendo DS on the desk. He was obviously planning on doing as little as possible until he'd worked his notice. 'Just tell me whether Mrs Blackstock is here or not. I've haven't got time for your stupid games.'

'Games?' He raised an eyebrow. 'You're one to talk about playing games, Beth.'

I stared at him in surprise. 'What's that supposed to mean?'

'Do I need to spell it out?'

'You obviously do, because I haven't got the slightest clue what you're on about.'

'Okay.' He shifted his legs off the desk, swivelled his chair around so he was facing me and stood up. 'Why don't we talk about Wales, Beth?'

'Fine. Let's.' I crossed my arms. If finding out where Mrs Blackstock was meant listening to Carl wind me up for another couple of minutes, I'd grin and bear it. As soon as I set foot outside the cinema, I'd never have to see his horrible smarmy face again.

'Okay.' He dug a thumbnail into the gap between his front teeth and viewed me thoughtfully. 'Why don't we start with Sunday night?'

'What about it?'

'There were reports …' he removed his hand from his mouth and smiled smugly, 'that a young lady was spotted wandering the corridors in a duvet in the early hours of the morning.'

A shiver ran down my spine. How did he know about that?

'The reports also indicated,' he continued, obviously relishing the reaction he was getting, 'that the young lady in question had departed the bedroom of a certain Matthew Jones.'

I narrowed my eyes. I wasn't going to let him upset me. I wasn't. 'Prove it.'

'Really? Okay, I will. I'll let you speak directly to the person who saw these events unfold.'

'And who might that be?'

'Me.'

As Carl grinned triumphantly at me, the two sides of my brain had a battle. *Just go*, said one side. *You don't need to put up with this crap any more. Walk straight out of the cinema and get the first taxi to Pool Valley. You can call Mrs Blackstock from the coach.*

No, said the other side. *You're not going anywhere. You've bitten your tongue for too long. Don't you dare let Carl get one over on you again.*

'Ah, silence,' said Carl as the battle continued to rage in my head. 'The sweet sign of culpability.'

'So what,' I shot back. I'd decided. There was no way I was going to leave the cinema with my tail between my legs and let him think he'd won. 'So what if I was in Matt's room? What's it got to do with you?'

'Nothing really.' He shrugged. 'It just amuses me.'

'And why's that?' I bit back.

'Well, you know.' He spread his hands wide. 'It's just typical of you and the way you live your life, Beth.'

'Oh yeah. What would you know about my life?'

'Lots. I've been there every step of the stinky, acne-ridden, perma-tanned way. You're one of life's losers, Beth. You fucked up your exams at school, blatantly too thick to get into university, and took the first job you were offered. God knows why you got it. Mrs Blackstock must have taken pity on you.'

'Don't you dare …' I was so angry, I was shaking. 'I'm good at my job and you know it, you evil little sh—'

'And don't get me started on your love life.' Carl's cheeks were flushed, his eyes glittering with excitement. 'Fuck knows what Aiden Dowles was thinking when he asked you out. He must have been on flu medication. He saw the light pretty quickly, though. Couldn't get away fast enough.'

'I'll have you know that Aiden asked me out last night and wanted to—'

'So what do you do next?' he interrupted. 'With a failed love life and looming redundancy? You decided to try and seduce the boss so you could get the job. Only you didn't, did you? So as well as being thick, fat and ugly, you're obviously a terrible shag too.'

'Aaaggh!' The shout was Carl's, not mine.

I watched in surprise as his hand flew to his face and covered the five-fingered imprint on his cheek. I'd never slapped anyone before.

'At least I've *had* sex,' I said, my right hand tingling. 'At least I'm not so greasy, slimy and repulsive that no one could bear to touch me. Are you proud of being a twenty-four-year-old virgin, Carl?'

It was a throwaway comment, a total spur-of-the-moment guess, but from the way the blood drained from Carl's face and he stared at me in shock, I knew I was right on the money.

'So why bully me, Carl?' I continued. 'Why target me all these years? You're either jealous of me, or ...' I grinned as he looked away. 'Is it something else? Is that why you pretended that Aiden was having an engagement party? Because you wanted me to humiliate myself in front of him so there was no chance of us getting back together? Oh my God, that's it, isn't it? All the insults, all the piss-takes, all the barbed comments – it's

316

the equivalent of playground name-calling and pigtail-pulling. You fancy me, don't you, Carl?'

'Do I fuck!' he said, still refusing to meet my eyes. 'Who'd fancy an ugly cunt like you?'

'LANGUAGE!'

Standing on the other side of the booth, a woolly hat pulled low over her brow and a pair of Hunter wellies on her feet, was Mrs Blackstock.

'I heard the commotion from the ladies' room. You,' she raised her walking stick to point at Carl, 'out!'

'But,' he protested, jerking a thumb towards me, 'that's not fair. She slap—'

'OUT!' Mrs Blackstock said again. 'I've never heard such revolting language in my life and I won't have you in my cinema.'

'But …' Carl took one look at the determined set of Mrs Blackstock's face and shook his head in defeat.

'You may think I'm old and past it,' she said as he yanked his jacket off the back of his chair and shoved his Nintendo into his bag, 'but I'm on to you, Mr Coombes. I have been for a while. You said that the customers who complained about your rudeness were "bitter and disgruntled", but I believe you'll find that *you're* the bitter individual. And to think I let you talk me into giving you a second chance. What a horrible little man you are.'

I looked from her to Carl and back again. She'd obviously given him at least one verbal warning over the years, and I'd had no idea.

'And if you think I'll be writing you a reference,' she called after him as he shuffled, head down, across the foyer, 'you've got another think coming. No pay in lieu of notice, either!'

'Beth,' she said, turning to smile at me as the front door slammed, 'how lovely to see you. Fortuitous too, now that the booth appears to be unmanned. Would it be too much of an imposition to ask you to step into the breach?'

I nodded towards my suitcase and smiled. 'Actually, it would …'

Chapter Thirty-Four

Matt

No sooner had Alice slammed the front door shut than my home phone started to ring.

I snatched it up, desperately hoping it was Sister O'Reilly calling to say that there'd been a mistake and Grandad wasn't really dead. They'd confused him with one of the other men on his ward and—

'Well if it isn't my long-lost salesman!'

'Sorry?' I said, confused by the lack of Irish accent. 'Who is this?'

'Jesus!' A short, barked laugh filled my ear. 'That just goes to prove how off the ball you've been recently, Mr Jones. It's your boss. Isabel. Remember me?'

'Isabel … yeah. Sorry. Why are you ringing?'

'Helloooooo?' She laughed again. 'Just the little matter of the Picturebox contract. Where the fuck is it, Matt?'

'Sorry,' I said. 'I've got it. It's just … Well … things have been a bit stressful recently.'

'Stressful? Don't talk to me about stressful! You don't know the meaning of the word. I've had the lawyers chewing my ear off all morning. If I don't get the contract today, the deal's off. Now stop being such a lazy twat and get yourself on the train to London. I want that contract in my hands by two p.m.'

'I can't.' I ran a hand over my forehead. I was sweating heavily. 'Isabel, my grandad died this morning.'

'Did he? Shame. Still, the funeral won't be for a couple of days yet. No reason why you can't catch a train today.'

'But, Isabel—'

'Listen to me, Matt. I'm sick of your bullshit excuses. I shouldn't have to chase you to do your bloody job. So your grandad died. Boo-fucking-hoo. We all die at some point and I'm sure he had a great life while it lasted. Now are you going to get on that fucking train and give me my contract, or not?'

'Not.'

There was a sharp intake of breath, and then, 'What?'

'Not,' I repeated.

'Matt,' I could almost hear her gritting her teeth, 'I'm sorry if I was a bit … sharp … about your recent bereavement, but I need that contract. The builders are ready to start, I've got a skip company primed to go, and the Japanese factory has shipped over all the panelling and parts for the refurb. If we're going to relaunch the Picturebox in June, we need to tear it down and rip its guts out now, and I can't authorise that until the lawyers have reviewed the contract.'

Rip its guts out? Tear it down? It sounded brutal. It *was* brutal.

'Have you even been to the Picturebox, Isabel?'

She paused as though to consider my question. 'Why would I want to do that?'

'Because it's beautiful. It's old, faded and worn around the edges, but that doesn't make it ugly. It doesn't make it defunct. It makes it unique. That cinema has lived in Brighton for over a hundred years and you want to rip its heart out.'

'Lived in Brighton? Rip its heart out?' Isabel repeated. 'Jesus, Matt, I never had you down as the sentimental type. Get a grip. It's a fucking cinema. A building.'

'It's not. It's more than that. Ask any of the customers. Ask any of the people who ...' an image of Beth, smiling shyly behind the counter, jumped into my mind '... work there. They love that cinema, and for good reason. It's not a corporate identikit money-maker. It's part of our heritage.'

'Then go and work for the fucking National Trust!' Ballbreaker snapped. 'Because I don't give a shit about that crap. I care about doing my job and doing it well. Now are you going to bring me that contract, or are you going to force me to send a courier down? Either way, I will have it.'

I glanced at my briefcase, wedged between the sofa and the wall, tucked the phone against my shoulder and crouched to pull it out.

'Listen, Matt,' Ballbreaker continued, her voice softening as she changed tack, 'we both know that you need your bonus money. Don't go blaming Sheila, but she let it slip that you're having to pay two lots of rent at the moment. That can't be easy, and ...'

I flipped open the case, and flicked through the pile of papers inside until I found the contract.

'… I know you'd struggle without that bonus. Rents are high in Brighton, and—'

'I don't need to pay two lots of rent,' I said. 'Not any more.'

'Really?' She sounded surprised. 'Well … um … in that case, you could always use the money to treat yourself. Maybe go on a nice holiday somewhere. Grieve for your grandpops in the sunshine. Now if you could just be a lovely and get that contract to me, I'd be ever so … What was that?'

I grinned. 'What was what?'

'That crackling noise, like something ripping.'

'Mmm-hmm.' I nodded. 'It was the sound of several pieces of paper being torn in two. What's another word for several pieces of paper stapled together, with lots of words and a signature on them? Oh, I know … a contract.'

My boss gasped down the phone.

'Oh dear,' I said. 'It appears to have been torn into four … no, eight … is that sixteen pieces now?'

'Matt!' Ballbreaker barked. 'I have two things to tell you. One, you're fired. And two, that cinema will still be mine, even if I have to get on the bloody train and come down to Brighton myself.'

'Really?' I said steadily, glancing at another pile of papers in my briefcase. 'Not if I've got anything to do with it.'

*

I stood outside the doors to the Picturebox, fished the photo of Grandad and me out of my back pocket and ran a thumb over his smiling face.

'This is the right thing to do, isn't it, Grandad?' I whispered.

He smiled back silently and I made a decision. He'd want me to do this. I knew he would.

'Okay, Grandad,' I said, tucking him back into my pocket then yanking open the front door. 'Here we go.'

A small grey-haired woman was standing behind the counter, sifting through a pile of brochures. She had her back to me, so I coughed to get her attention.

'Excuse me,' I said.

The woman didn't react.

'Excuse me,' I said again, louder this time. 'Is Beth Prince in today?'

'Beth? No, she's …' The woman turned around slowly. 'Matthew Jones!'

'Mrs Blackstock!' I smiled broadly. 'Hello.'

'Well, well, well.' She prodded her glasses up her nose to get a better look at me. 'I didn't think I'd see you again.'

'I know,' I said. 'Me neither, but I'm glad I've run into you. I wanted to talk to Beth first, but seeing as you're here, there's something important I need to tell you. Something very important. It's about the Picturebox and what Apollo is planning to do to it and—'

'Whoa, whoa, whoa.' Mrs Blackstock held up a hand and lowered herself into the chair by the computer. 'Start again, please, dear. Slowly this time.'

'Okay.' I yanked off my coat and scarf, placed both hands on the counter and took a few deep breaths. Mrs Blackstock nodded for me to start talking.

'The truth is,' I looked her straight in the eye, 'I lied when I told you we'd look after the Picturebox. That was never the plan. We were going to destroy it.'

'What?' Edna Blackstock's jaw dropped.

'I know, and I'm sorry. I'm *really* sorry. It's been eating me up for weeks, but it's not too late to put things right. You mustn't sell the Picturebox to Apollo, Mrs Blackstock. They don't want to restore the cinema to its former glory; they want to gut it.'

'Gut it?' Edna repeated, gazing at the cream columns that stretched to the arched ceiling and the dusty chandelier. 'Why would they do that?'

'Because they don't care that the Picturebox is a hundred years old. They don't care about its history. All they care about is making it look like a replica of all the other Apollo cinemas across the world and making as much money as possible.'

She looked at me steadily. 'You knew all this and you still lied to me about it?'

'I'm sorry.' I swallowed hard. 'I really am. There's no justifying it, but I was caught between a rock and a hard place. If I didn't get you to sign the contract, then I wouldn't get the money to look after my … my …' My eyes filled with tears as I remembered the last time I'd seen Grandad in his own home, sitting across the kitchen table from me, a pot of steaming tea between us, a wry grin on his face. I swiped a hand across my eyes and forced myself to keep speaking. 'Someone very special.'

Edna Blackstock's brow wrinkled with concern. 'Are you okay, Matthew?'

'Yes. No. I don't know. I lost someone who meant the world to me today. I lied to him too and I'll always hate myself for it.' I swiped at my eyes again. 'I can't ever take that back, but I can try and make things right. I *need* to. You mustn't sell the Picturebox to Apollo.'

'But it's too late. I signed the contract.'

'It's not.' I opened my right hand and showed her the ball of paper in my palm. 'I ripped it up.'

Edna stared at the remains of the contract, her eyes wide.

'It wasn't my place to do it,' I said hurriedly. 'I know that. And if you still want to sell to Apollo, you can. My boss, my ex-boss, is on her way here right now. But I'm begging you, Mrs B. Please. Please don't.'

'But the money,' she said slowly, her eyes flicking from my hand to the tired foyer. 'They offered me such a lot of money, and you said yourself when you visited me at home that the Picturebox hasn't been making much of a profit for quite some time.'

'I've thought about that.' I dropped the handful of contract on to the counter and clicked open my brief-case. 'Which is why I want to show you this.'

Edna held out a hand and took the bound document I passed her. She looked at it thoughtfully. 'What is it?'

'A business plan. Beth Prince's business plan, for the Picturebox.'

'Beth? Little Beth Prince who works here?'

'Yes. She gave it to me during the interview weekend for the manager's position and it was the best plan of the lot. None of the others even came close. I gave the job to James because … well, that was a mistake, too. James is competent enough, but he doesn't have the drive or the enthusiasm this place deserves. I should have given it to Beth. Not only is she passionate about the Picturebox, she's got the most amazing ideas that could turn it around. Mrs B, Beth lives and breathes this place.'

'But …' Edna turned the first page. 'Some of these ideas are so modern.'

'And some of them aren't. That's why they'd work so well. What Beth has done is come up with a way of tapping into the Picturebox's heritage while applying modern marketing and promotional ideas. That document is gold dust.'

'Is it?' Edna looked at me.

'It is.' I slapped my hand against the counter. 'I know you've got no reason to trust me, not after I lied to you before, but I believe in those ideas. I believe in, Beth. Just give her six months to turn this place around, and if she hasn't made a profit, you can sell it to Apollo.'

'Oh can I?' She raised an eyebrow. 'Thanks for the permission, Mr Jones.'

'Sorry,' I said hastily. 'I don't want to sound patronising. I really don't. This is your cinema and you can do what you want with it, but if you want it restored to its former glory rather than see its soul ripped out, you need to give Beth a chance.'

'Hmmm.' She went back to the business plan and turned a page.

I waited, my breath caught in my throat, as she flipped another page, her eyes scanning the text, then flicked the next sheet over. Finally she closed the document and look up at me.

'Okay,' she said.

'You'll give Beth a chance?'

She nodded. 'Six months.'

'And if Ballbreaker … I mean Isabel Wallbaker comes down here, you won't sell to her?'

Edna's stern expression dissolved into a wide smile. 'No, I won't.'

'Oh my God!' I rounded the counter and held my arms out wide. 'Edna Blackstock, I could kiss you! Beth will be over the moon. I can't wait to tell her.'

I was just about to gather the cinema's owner small frame in a big hug when she stood up and held out a hand.

'Ah,' she said.

I froze. 'Ah?'

'I was so caught up in your enthusiastic speech, Mr Jones, that one rather vital fact escaped me. Beth popped in to give her notice earlier today.'

'That's fine. You can draw up a new contract. She'll sign it in a heartbeat.'

'If she comes back.'

'What?' I frowned. 'Comes back from where?'

'From wherever she was going with that enormous black suitcase she had with her.'

Chapter Thirty-Five

Beth

'Ready, darling?' Mum was standing beside the coach, a gigantic floral suitcase at her feet.

I watched as the driver, a fluffy Santa Claus hat jammed on to his head, scooped up the cases and huffed and puffed as he shoved them into the hold. He reached for mine, then shot me a look as it swayed in the air between us. I hadn't realised I was holding on to it so tightly.

Mum patted my hand and I reluctantly let go. 'Did you hand in your notice at work, Beth?'

I nodded, too preoccupied to answer. I was trying to drink it all in, my final glimpse of Brighton – the last-minute shoppers bundled up in hats, coats and scarves, their heads ducked against the wind as they attempted to walk the promenade; the wide-winged seagulls squawking angrily over abandoned chip wrappers; the Christmas illuminations criss-crossing over King's Road and the lights of the pier glowing warmly through the December gloom. I breathed in deeply. The air was sharp, fresh and bitterly cold. It felt like it was going to snow again.

Snow. I glanced at the beach. There was nothing more surreal than the sea lapping against a snow-covered beach. And snow or no snow, you could guarantee that tomorrow at least a dozen brave (or foolish) souls would 'ooh' and 'ouch' their way across the pebbles for an early-Christmas-morning dip in the sea. I loved that about Brighton. You could turn a corner and see something utterly bizarre or totally wonderful and you wouldn't blink an eyelid: not at the 1940s dancers swinging around outside Pizza Express on a summer's afternoon; not at the huge glowing paper lanterns in the shape of bats and suns lighting up the streets during the Burning the Clocks procession; and not at the colourful explosion of camp high glamour at the Pride parade. You wouldn't blink an eye because you'd be drinking it all in – getting drunk on Brighton's vibrant, eccentric charm.

I shivered and rubbed my arms through my coat. It wouldn't be snowing in Australia. According to Mum, it was 30 degrees Centigrade in Sydney.

Sydney.

I shook my head, unable to take it all in. In twenty-four hours I'd be in another city. A city I didn't know. Or love.

I'd done everything for the first time in Brighton. Ridden a bike. Swum in the sea. Started school. Made friends. Kissed a boy. Slept with a boy. Got a job. Fallen in love ...

I sighed.

The last two hadn't worked out too well, had they? *You're one of life's losers*, Carl had said. I'd brushed it off as another of his malicious comments, but I wasn't exactly one of life's winners, was I?

No, there was nothing left in Brighton for me. I'd miss the city and I'd really miss Lizzie, but she'd be okay. I'd already promised I'd Skype her every day (if she was in!) as soon as I got an internet connection, and she'd threatened never to speak to me again unless I regularly emailed her photos. And then there was the little silver locket I'd given her for Christmas. One picture was of us aged fourteen, crammed into a photo booth in Woolworths. The other was of us doing exactly the same thing, aged twenty-four, in a booth at Brighton station. Those ten years had passed in a heartbeat.

I tore my gaze away from the seafront and looked at Mum. She was hugging herself excitedly and humming what sounded a lot like 'Rudolph the Red-Nosed Kangaroo' under her breath. She bounced up and down on her toes when the coach driver slammed the luggage doors shut and announced that it was time to board. I'd never seen her so full of joy. Maybe a new start wasn't such a bad idea after all.

She caught my eye and smiled. 'Everything sorted back at the house? Did you say goodbye to Lizzie?'

I nodded again.

'Good, good.' Her hand reached for mine. 'Come on then, darling. Let's grab some seats. I'm ever so excited. Aren't you?'

I glanced back at the seafront. If I squinted, I could just make out the bench next to the West Pier where

Matt and I had spent a couple of drunken hours after I'd embarrassed myself at Aiden's party.

A tall, dark figure sprinted across King's Road and headed straight for the bench, and I caught my breath. My God. What if …

I watched as the man lifted a foot on to the bench and bent forward. A second later he was on his way again, jogging along the seafront, his shoelace tied.

I shook my head, bemused, and looked back at Mum. It was just a weather-beaten wooden bench. What had I been expecting to see?

'Well?' she said. 'Are you as excited as I am?'

I squeezed out a smile. 'Course I am.'

Chapter Thirty-Six

Matt

I stepped out of the taxi, sprinted down the pathway to Beth's front door, jabbed a finger at the doorbell and waited.

I wasn't sure why, but I couldn't shake the bad feeling that had gripped my guts the second Mrs Blackstock had finished telling me about Beth and her black suitcase. Edna was convinced she was off on her holidays, but I wasn't so sure. What if ... no ... I shook my head. It didn't bear thinking about. Beth couldn't leave. She wouldn't. She'd lived in Brighton nearly as long as I had, and loved it twice as much.

I stared at the shut front door. Where was she? It wasn't just the job I wanted to talk to her about.

'Promise me you'll give Beth the chance to explain herself,' Grandad had said in the hospital.

Only I hadn't, had I?

I'd given Alice a second chance, but I'd just walked away from Beth, the girl who made my heart contract in my chest whenever I thought about her.

'Beth!' I clenched a fist, ready to bang on the door

again, just as it flew open. A red-haired woman in a pink negligee glared out at me.

'Do you know what time it is?' she asked sharply, rubbing at her eyes. They were red and puffy.

I glanced at my watch. 'Eleven fifteen. Sorry, were you asleep? Is Beth in?'

'Beth?' The woman rubbed at the crease mark on the side of her face. 'No, she's gone.'

'Gone where?'

She shot me a suspicious look. 'Why should I tell you?'

'Because I've got news about the Picturebox, and because …'

'Because what?'

Screw it. I was just going to say it. 'Because I'm in love with her.'

'Oh my God.' She took a step back into the hallway, looked me up and down and tilted her head to one side as though weighing me up. 'You're Matt, aren't you?'

'Uh-huh. You must be Lizzie.'

'Wow.' She rested her weight against the door frame and shook her head. 'You're a dick. You know that, right?'

I nodded. 'Yeah.'

'You're not the only one.' Lizzie shrugged. 'You, Aiden, Carl – right bunch of twats, the lot of you. Beth wouldn't be leaving with Eddie if it wasn't for you lot.'

Who the hell was Eddie? It hadn't even occurred to me that she might be with someone. Shit.

'Is Eddie her boyfriend?' I asked nervously.

'Jesus, Matt!' Lizzie folded her arms over her chest

333

and shot me a look of pure contempt. 'Are you thick as well as stupid? Eddie's her mum – Edwina Prince. Beth hasn't got a boyfriend. Well ... her ex tried to get back with her last night, but she said no because she's in love with you. Not that she'll admit that to herself.'

'What?'

'She loves *you*, you dick.'

'But ...' My mouth dropped open. 'What about the poster?'

'What poster?'

'The sign above her bed. The one that says she'd do anything to get the job.'

'Oh, that.' Lizzie shrugged. 'Edwina wrote it.'

'What?'

'Her mum wrote it. You know ...' she looked at me like I was stupid, 'with proper handwriting and capital letters and stuff. Some bollocks she'd read in that stupid book she lugs around with her everywhere. *Visualising* ...'

'*Success*,' I finished. 'Fuck! I know that book. My mate Neil's got it. I took the piss out of him, and ...'

Oh God. What had I done? Beth hadn't slept with me to try and get the job. She'd slept with me because she liked me. And I'd crept away in the middle of the night and ... OH FUCK. FUCK. FUCK. FUCK.

'Where's she gone?' I asked desperately. 'Where's Beth?'

Lizzie looked me straight in the eye. 'Australia.'

'WHAT!'

'Australia. You know, home of Rolf Harris and

334

kangaroos?' She glanced at her watch. 'She caught the coach to Heathrow about fifteen minutes ago.'

My heart caught in my throat. I couldn't let her go without telling her how I felt about her. I *had* to find her.

'There's still time!' I said. 'I can still catch her.'

I was halfway down the path when a thought hit me and I turned back.

'Can I have it?' I asked.

Lizzie rolled her eyes. 'What?'

'The sign. The one that was on the ceiling above Beth's bed.'

She frowned. 'Why?'

'Please.'

'Okay.' She disappeared back into the house and reappeared a couple of seconds later with a sheet of A3 in her hand.

'Thanks,' I said as she handed it to me. 'Thank you. Really. Thanks.'

Lizzie rolled her eyes.

'Jesus,' she said as she closed the door. 'Handsome but mental. Story of my life!'

Chapter Thirty-Seven

Beth

All I wanted to do was rest my pounding head on the window of the coach, go back to sleep and blank out the fact that it was really happening – I was moving to Australia – but Mum wouldn't have it. She was talking nineteen to the dozen and elbowed me in the ribs whenever I closed my eyes.

'Beth? Beth, are you listening to me?'

I sighed and turned to look at her.

'Thank God you've finally seen sense and decided to be a grown-up,' she said. 'I can't believe you wasted six years of your life in that dump of a cinema.'

'That's not fair, Mum. It wasn't a dump.'

'Yes, it was. Honestly, Beth, I can't understand you sometimes. While you were sitting around dreaming about film stars, you could have been building a career as an office manager or a businesswoman.'

'But I never wanted to be a businesswoman.' I frowned. 'I still don't, if I'm honest.'

'Rubbish, of course you do. Look at me. I've got a nice house, a gorgeous car and a wardrobe full of lovely clothes. I'm successful, respected and independent. I've got everything I could ever want.'

Have you? I thought, but didn't say.

'Deciding to come with me is the best decision you've ever made. We'll make a successful career woman of you yet.'

'Hmmm.' I forced a smile, even though I felt like throwing up. We were flying past the snow-tipped curves of the South Downs, leaving Brighton further and further behind us as the coach sped towards the airport. I gripped my stomach. It wasn't excitement that was making me feel nauseous. It was dread. And the more I tried to suppress it, the stronger it grew.

'So,' Mum continued, flicking through a plastic file labelled *Australia*. It was bulging with pieces of paper, each one marked with a brightly coloured sticky tab – flights, houses, insurance, car rental, solicitors, banks. There was even one with my name on it. 'Once we get into Sydney I've arranged for us to hire a car for a couple of weeks until we buy our own. And a letting agent has found us somewhere to live until the house in Brighton sells.'

I stared at the folder, transfixed. Mum had it all planned out, every minute detail of her new life – our new life – abroad. She hadn't consulted me about any of it. I felt like a stowaway, hitching a ride on someone else's dream.

What was it Lizzie had said the night before?

Why are you running away to Australia?

I wasn't running away. I was making a fresh start. What was wrong with that? People emigrated all the

337

time. I looked down at the Christmas present in my hands and ran my fingers over the shiny, sparkly wrapping paper. Lizzie had specifically forbidden me from opening it until I was in Australia. What harm would it do if I opened it now? It wasn't as if she would ever know, and maybe it would distract me from the sick feeling in my stomach and the sound of her voice in my head.

I ran a nail under the Sellotape and ripped at the paper. It's a book, I thought as the wrapping fell away. It's some kind of ...

Oh my God.

It wasn't just a book. It was a photo album. And there was me on the front, doing a handstand on the pebbles in front of the pier, with the title 'Beth Prince: Happily Ever After' dancing in the sky above my feet. My heart raced as I flicked through the pages. There was me dressed up as a vampire for Lizzie's sixteenth birthday. And there was me laughing my head off as we held up our burnt offerings at our first ever barbecue. And ... oh my God ... there was even a photo of me attempting to skateboard (that must have been when I was dating Dom). As I flicked over the pages, images from my past appeared before me and made me smile and sigh and reminisce. My eyes filled with tears as I paused at the second-to-last page. It was an image of Lizzie, obviously taken recently, holding a piece of A4 paper to her chest. On it she'd written, *Your Happily Ever After is still out there, Beth*. Oh God. She hadn't been a crap mate at all. She'd gone to loads of trouble to make the photo album to try and cheer me up. I pressed my fingers to my lips, touched them against Lizzie's cheek, then turned to the final page. It was a photo of me and cut-out George Clooney. We were standing outside the cinema and I had my arm around him. My eyes were fixed on the looping letters that spelled out 'Picturebox' and I had the most ridiculously goofy, proud look on my face.

Why are you running away? The question whirled around my head, swiftly followed by *You told me you'd rather die than be your mum's secretary.*

I watched as Mum flicked through her folder. There was a Post-it note on my page. *Book Beth on to a secretarial course*, it said. *Typing, word-processing and shorthand. Get her a haircut, new clothes and a manicure. Terrible fingernails.*

Oh my God.

I glanced at her, but she was too absorbed in the details to register the look of horror on my face.

'Mum,' I said.

She turned over another page.

'Mum,' I said again.

She ripped off a Post-it note and crumpled it in her hand. 'Yes, dear.'

'I'm not going.'

She glanced at me. 'What was that?'

'I'm sorry.' I twisted round in my seat so that I was facing her. 'I've changed my mind. I'm not going to Australia.'

She shut the folder with a slap and stared at me. 'What?'

'I'm going to stay in Brighton,' I said steadily.

'Don't be silly.' Her frown disappeared and she snorted with laughter. 'That's ridiculous. Why stay here when you could have a new life somewhere else?'

'I wouldn't, though, would I? It wouldn't be my new start. It would be yours. I'd be living the life you want for me.'

'Yes, a nice, sensible, secure life.'

'But I don't want a life like that, Mum. I want a life that makes me happy. I always believed that would involve the Picturebox, and I can't give up on that dream. I can't just run away at the first hurdle.'

She raised an eyebrow. 'I'd say not getting the manager's job was more of a wall than a hurdle, darling.'

'But it doesn't have to be. I can't let Apollo get away with ripping the heart out of the Picturebox. It's not right and it's probably against the law. That place is over a hundred years old and full of historic fixtures and fittings. I'm sure ... I don't know ... the National Trust or those people who put up blue plaques would have something to say about them destroying the interior.'

I had no idea if what I was saying was true or not, but I couldn't stop the words from spilling out of me. It was like I'd turned a tap on in my brain and now I couldn't turn it off again.

Mum snorted. 'And you're going to take on a massive international corporation all on your own, are you?'

'Yes. No. I don't know. I'll write to all the local newspapers and regional TV. I'll get the staff and the customers behind me. I'll create a petition and stand outside the station or go door to door if I have to. I can do it. I can make a difference. I know I can.'

I believed it too. I really did. In the past few weeks I'd been braver than I'd been in my whole life. I'd confronted Aiden, stood up to Carl and let Matt go instead of chasing after him. The only person I hadn't stood up to was Mum.

'And what about me?' she said on cue. 'You promised you'd come to Australia with me if you didn't get the job.'

'I'm sorry,' I said. 'Really I am. But Australia isn't my dream, it's yours. I still want you to go, Mum. I want you to be happy. But I need to stay in Brighton. Please don't hate me.'

'Of course I don't hate you, Beth!' She narrowed her eyes suspiciously. 'This isn't about a boy, is it? That's not the real reason you've decided to stay?'

'No,' I said, and I meant it. 'This is about me, and what I want. I *need* to do this, Mum. I have to at least try.'

She shook her head. 'You haven't thought this through. I know you haven't. It's a stupid pipe dream.'

'No, it's not, not if I make it happen.'

She sighed heavily. 'You've always lived in a fantasy world. Ever since you were a little girl. If you weren't dreaming about going to visit ET, you'd be …'

The sound of a car horn, honking repeatedly, drowned out the rest of her sentence.

Mum looked at me. 'What on earth is that?'

'I don't know.'

I glanced out of the window, but there was nothing outside apart from a thick fog that had faded the countryside to a murky blur of greens and browns.

'Look back there,' Mum said, tapping me on the arm, then pointing towards the back of the coach. 'Something's going on.'

I twisted round in my seat. The people who'd been sitting in the seats at the rear of the coach were standing up and staring out of the back window. The car horn continued to honk.

'Oh my God!' someone shrieked. 'He's got a death wish. He's trying to overtake the bus!'

'He's changed his mind,' someone else shouted. 'He's staying behind us. Look! He's holding up a piece of paper. There's something written on it.'

'What does it say? What does it say?' a young child squealed as several people on the second-last row of the bus jumped out of their seats to see what was going on.

'It says "Beth"!' a man with a crew cut yelled. He turned to face the rest of the bus, who were all craning their necks towards the back. 'Is there a Beth here?'

Mum elbowed me in the ribs. 'What have you done?'

'Nothing! I haven't done anything.'

'He's pointing to the sign,' crew-cut man shouted. 'He's looking for someone called Beth. Who's Beth?'

I had my hand in the air before I knew what I was doing. 'I am!'

'Come back here!' Crew-cut man beckoned frantically. 'There's some mad bloke in a car chasing after the bus. I think he wants to talk to you.'

'Beth, don't.' Mum grabbed my elbow as I stood up and edged past her. 'Whatever it is, don't do it.'

I shook her off. 'Please, Mum. Just let me find out what's going on.'

'It's trouble,' she called after me as I swayed down the aisle towards the back of the coach. 'I can smell it a mile off.'

'Move out of the way,' crew-cut man shouted as he pushed me into the tiny gap between a middle-aged woman and a dreadlocked student. 'She's here. She's here!'

I stared out of the window, but I couldn't see anything. It was too foggy outside. I squinted into the distance, then gasped as the bus passed a street lamp and the front seat of the car behind us was illuminated. A familiar face with tousled dark brown hair and a stubbly jaw grinned back at me.

'Matt!' I was so shocked, I shouted out his name.

'Who's Matt?' asked crew-cut man, but I ignored him. I was too busy staring at the piece of paper on Matt's dashboard with my name on it.

'Matt,' I said. 'What are you doing?'

He squinted up me, then shook his head.

'What ... are ... you ... doing?' I mouthed slowly, enunciating each word carefully.

He shook his head again, still grinning, turned the piece of paper over and placed it on the dashboard. He pointed at me, then at the piece of paper.

'I ... would ... do ... anything ...' I squinted to make out the words, then clutched my chest in surprise. It was the *Visualising Success* sign that Mum had told me to stick above my bed. What the hell was Matt doing with it?

I would do anything, I read, *to get ...*

The last couple of words had been crossed out and

replaced with new ones, scribbled in black marker pen in a shaky scrawl.

... you back.

I gasped so loudly, the dreadlocked student beside me jumped.

'I would do anything to get you back,' the middle-aged woman to my right read aloud. 'Oh my God.' She gripped my arm and fanned herself with her other hand. 'I think I'm having a hot flush. That's the most romantic thing I've ever seen. Arthur, Arthur.' She nudged the grey-haired man next to her. 'Have you seen that? "I would do anything to get you back," it says. Why haven't you ever chased me down a road like that?'

The man pulled a face. 'Because you never bloody left.'

I looked back out of the rear window. Matt was still staring intently at me, but his grin had faded. He looked worried. I wriggled free of the mass of bodies I was wedged between and made my way to the front of the coach, nearly losing my balance as the driver took a sharp left turn. Mum's manicured hand shot out as I passed her, but I swerved out of the way. Finally I reached the driver.

'Get back to your seat, please, miss,' he said, not taking his eyes off the road. 'Passengers should remain seated for the duration of the journey.'

'I can't.' I crouched on the step to his left.

'Oi.' He gestured at me. 'Off the step, please. It's dangerous. Health and Safety regulations.'

'I can't.' I gazed at him imploringly. 'I need to get off.'

344

'Bogs blocked again, are they?' He handed me an empty Starbucks cup from the side of his seat. 'You can go in this, but don't spill it.'

'I don't need the loo!' I cried. 'I need to get off the bus and talk to the guy who's following us.'

'Ever heard of a mobile phone? You just press a button and you can talk to another person. It's proper real-life magic.'

'I can't, I haven't got his number. Oh God, you're not going to stop the coach, are you?'

The bus driver shook his head. 'Why would I? We're only a few miles from Heathrow.'

I followed his eyes to the blue sign about two hundred metres in front of us. *Heathrow 5 miles*, it said.

'Are you sure you don't need the cup?' the bus driver asked, but I was already halfway back down the coach.

'Sorry, sorry,' I said as I squeezed between the student and the middle-aged woman and stared out into the gloom. Matt was still following us, his hands on the steering wheel, his eyes on mine.

I held out my hand, my fingers splayed. 'Five,' I mouthed. 'Five more miles.'

The next ten minutes were the slowest of my life. I stayed at the back of the coach, wedged between my fellow passengers, my eyes fixed on Matt's face. At one point I held up my phone and mouthed, 'Call me,' but Matt shook his head.

'Can't,' he mouthed back. 'No hands-free.'

As he gestured at his empty dashboard, the car lurched to the left and I squealed.

After that he kept his eyes on the road, looking up occasionally to check that I was still there.

'Beth, we're here.' I felt a hand on my shoulder and turned to see Mum standing beside me. The coach swung to the left, then the right, then slowed to a halt.

'Mum …' I said hesitantly.

I tensed, ready for the onslaught. This was her chance to accuse me of lying about wanting to fight for the Picturebox when it was obvious that I'd only decided to stay in Brighton because of a man.

'Do what you have to do, Beth,' she said softly.

'Really?'

She nodded, and gestured for me to slip into one of the empty seats. Everyone else was slowly filing out of the coach. She tucked her skirt under her bum and sat down beside me.

'I know I've been harsh sometimes,' she said. 'But I didn't want you to make the same mistakes as me.' She reached for my hand. 'I spent years trying, and failing, to please your father and it only made me miserable. My career is the only thing, other than you, that's made me happy. All I ever wanted was the same for you – to be happy.'

I swallowed hard, tears pricking at my eyes. 'I know, Mum.'

'As for the Picturebox, well.' She smiled. 'It's not the career I'd have chosen and I still don't understand why you're so entranced with that old place, but even I can see how much it means to you. Don't you *dare* give up the fight to stop Apollo from destroying it because if

346

you do I'll be on the first flight back from Australia to smack your bum. I don't care how old you are!'

I squeezed her hand tightly.

'And this boy.' She smiled. 'This man who's followed you all the way from Brighton. I don't know who he is or what he wants but if he makes you happy, Beth, then maybe this … what's his name?'

'Matt.'

'Then maybe this Matt is one of the good guys.'

One of the good guys? Was he? My smile slipped as I remembered how angry he'd sounded when he'd told Sheila he never wanted to speak to me again. In all the excitement I'd completely forgotten about that. He may have followed me all the way from Brighton but there was no denying the fact he'd hurt me. He'd really hurt me.

Mum inched her way out of her seat and stood up. She looked down at me, her expression thoughtful, then leaned down and wrapped her arms around me.

'Whatever you decide to do,' she said as she gently released me, 'know that I love you. I probably don't say it enough, but I do.'

I was still dazed from the conversation I'd just had with Mum as I walked the length of the coach and stepped down the stairs to the road. Standing ten metres away, leaning on a concrete bollard with his hands in his pockets, was Matt. He smiled a half-smile as our eyes met, and walked towards me.

'Hi, Beth,' he said softly.

'Hi, Matt.'

We gazed at each other, neither of us saying a word, as the other passengers dragged their cases from the pile of luggage the bus driver had heaped up beside the coach and wheeled them away. After a couple of minutes we were alone.

'So.' Matt shrugged. 'Australia?'

I nodded. 'I've got a ticket.'

He dug his hands deeper into his pockets and looked away. I opened my mouth to ask what was wrong, but bit my tongue.

'I'm sorry.' He looked back at me so intensely, my stomach flipped over, but I kept my nerve. There was no way I was going to turn into a mushy mess just because of a look. 'I'm an idiot. No, I'm more than that. I'm a prize dick.'

'Yeah, you are.'

Matt smiled too, but it didn't quite reach his eyes. 'I am, Beth. I really am. You didn't deserve the way I treated you. You *really* didn't deserve it.'

'So why did you? Why sleep with me, disappear, then refuse to speak to me?'

'Because of this.' He fished something out of his back pocket and carefully unfolded it. It was the *Visualising Success* sign he'd held up in the car.

'What about it?'

'I saw it on the ceiling of your bedroom the morning after we spent the night together. I thought you'd written it, and the only reason you slept with me was to try and get the Apollo job.'

'No way!' I stared at him in horror. 'I'd never do that! Never in a million years.'

'I know. I think I always knew that deep down, but …'
He crumpled the piece of paper into a ball and tossed it
away. It bounced on the pavement and rolled into the
gutter. We both stared at it.

'I could make excuses,' Matt continued. 'I could
blame it on my ex for making me mistrust women,
but the truth is, there is no excuse. I behaved like the
kind of bloke I swore I'd never be. Even Grandad was
disappointed in me.'

We both fell silent, still staring at each other. I
wanted to say something, but I couldn't. I was trying to
take it all in. The reason Matt had told Sheila he never
wanted to talk to me again was because … I shook my
head. I couldn't believe he'd think that of me.

'Beth …' Matt said.

'Yeah.'

'I don't know what I was thinking, coming after you
in the car with my stupid sign. When I saw your face
in the back of the coach and you looked so pleased to
see me, I thought … I hoped … well, it doesn't matter
what I hoped. After the way I acted, I wouldn't blame
you if you never wanted to speak to me again. There's
something else I need to tell you, though.'

'Okay …' I said nervously. I wasn't sure I was ready
for any more big revelations.

'The job's yours if you want it.'

'What?' I looked at him in surprise. 'With Apollo?'

There was no way I'd take it, not after everything
they were planning on doing. I'd fight them tooth and
nail every step of the way.

Matt shook his head. 'No. At the Picturebox. Mrs

349

Blackstock has decided to let you manage the place and try out your business plan for six months. If you agree, of course.'

'But Mrs Blackstock has never seen my business plan.'

'She has now.'

'I don't understand. What about the contract with Apollo?'

'I ripped it up. Right after I quit.'

'You quit ...' My mouth fell open. 'Why would you do that?'

'Because I realised how important the Picturebox is.' Matt stared at the floor and kicked the toe of one trainer against the heel of the other. '*You* made me realise how important it is.'

'I did?'

He nodded, still avoiding eye contact. 'That's why I held on to the contract for so long, because I didn't want to give it to my boss. It didn't feel right and I didn't know what to do. If I handed it in, it would be curtains for the Picturebox, but if I didn't, I wouldn't be able to afford Grandad's rent. I was stuck.'

'But you said you tore up the contract. Where will your grandad live if you can't pay his rent?'

Matt said nothing, but his shoulders tensed and I could see a muscle twitching in his jaw.

'What is it?'

He shook his head. He looked like he was fighting to hold himself together.

'Matt.' I put a hand on his arm. 'Matt, what's happened?'

'Grandad.' His voice choked on the word as he looked at me, his eyes brimming with tears. 'He died.'

'Oh my God.' I swallowed hard, fighting back my own tears. 'Oh my God, Matt, I'm so sorry. Your grandad was lovely.'

'Yeah.' He looked away and said something so quietly I couldn't catch it.

I tentatively ran my hand up and down his arm. 'What was that?'

'You.' He looked at me again, tears spilling down his cheeks. 'Grandad thought you were lovely too. He could see it – how nice you are, how special, how beautiful – and he only spent an afternoon with you. He told me, Beth, he told me not to let you go, but I let my hurt pride get the better of me and I ...' He pulled away, his face crumpled with pain. 'I fucked it all up. I hurt you. I hurt the best thing that ever happened to me and I fucked it all up.'

I couldn't speak. I couldn't even breathe.

'I'm sorry,' he said as he took another step backwards. 'I'm sorry for everything, Beth. I'm so fucking sorry. I've screwed up your life enough already without trying to stop you from going to Australia. I should just leave.'

I watched, rooted to the spot, as he turned and walked towards his car. I touched my hand to my face as something cold and wet landed on my nose, then looked up at the sky. It had started to snow.

Let him go, said my brain, as Matt reached into his pocket and pulled out his car keys.

Don't! said my heart.

He hurt you. He'll do it again.

He made a mistake and he's sorry. And he's trying to make it up to you. He travelled all this way to apologise, didn't he? And he got you the job with the Picturebox. How else do you think Mrs Blackstock got to see your business plan? He really cares about you, Beth. It's written all over his face.

'Matt, wait!' I said as he pressed his key fob and the lights on his car flashed. 'I'm not going to Australia.'

Time seemed to stand still as he froze, his hand wrapped around the door handle, and turned to look at me. The snow was falling more heavily now, filling the space between us with a beautiful white mist. 'What did you say?'

'I'm not going.'

'You're not?' His keys clattered to the ground as he rushed towards me and lifted me off my feet, crushing me in his arms. 'You're staying in Brighton?'

'Yes.' I laughed as he spun me round and round and round.

'Oh thank God. I love you, Beth, and I can't believe I nearly lost you. I nearly lost you for good. I …' The spinning stopped suddenly and Matt set me back on my feet, his expression changing from delight to worry as he searched my face.

'What is it?' I said. 'What's happened?'

'Shit. I'm sorry, Beth.' He ran a hand though his hair and shook his head. 'Here's me, scooping you up and assuming you've forgiven me, when you haven't said a word. I just got so excited that you were staying that I—'

'Sssh, Matt.' I took a step towards him and weaved my fingers through his. 'You're going to have to work very hard to get my forgiveness, very hard indee—'

His lips were on mine before I could say another word.

Acknowledgements

Huge thanks to Kate and the Orion team, Maddie and Darley's fabulous angels and everyone who has supported and encouraged me through the tricky terrain that is second novel territory. I couldn't have done it without you.

Special thanks to my family – Reg, Jenny, Bec, David, Sophie, Suz and Leah – for their love and support (and Jacqui for the photos) and to my new family – Nan and Granddad Hall, Steve, Guinevere, Ana, Angela, Ad, Bex and Jay – for making me feel so welcome.

Lots of love to my friends and cheerleaders – Kellie, Becky, Dan, Laura B, Joe, Kat, Amanda, Laura Barclay, Lisa, Heidi, Scott, Claire B, Georgie D, Sally, Nat, Kimberley and Tiff & the Kickboxing Girls. Thanks for getting me through the rough and cheering during the smooth!

Big hugs to the wonderful online community of writers who are always incredibly generous with their time and advice, not least Leigh, Sally Q, Helen H, Helen K, Karen, Caroline S, Nik, Carolyn, Rowan, Kate H, all my fellow Orion authors and to everyone on Facebook and Twitter who answered my pleas for #novelresearch help!

A big thank you to the Duke of York's cinema for your 100 year anniversary tour; it hugely inspired me. Thanks also to the city of Brighton and Hove and the people who live there. I saw, experienced and felt so much in the 13 years I lived there and only a tiny proportion made it into this novel. It's a magical place and it'll always have a special place in my heart.

To Chris – there's so much I could say but I'll keep it short (phew!): thank you for making me happier than I ever thought possible. You rule!

And finally . . . to everyone who bought *Heaven Can Wait* and/or took the time to email or write to me to say how much you enjoyed it – thank you SO MUCH! Your kind words frequently transformed difficult writing days into brilliant ones! I love hearing from you.

www.callytaylor.co.uk
www.twitter.com/callytaylor